Trading with the enemy

Thunder erupted in the blackened sky, briefly illuminating the interior of the vehicle. Then Craven said, "To be honest, this whole thing is just flat weird. We weren't even told who the hell you are."

Bolan suppressed a smile. It was hardly an unusual situation for him. "What did your boss tell you?" he asked.

"That the President himself ordered us to cooperate with you and give you any assistance you may need."

"Then what else do you need to know?" Bolan demanded.

Craven sighed. "Okay," he said. "Here's where the Company stands on the deal. Levi hasn't really done anything illegal. In other words, we've got no good reason to pick him up, and if he's about to defect, by the time we get one it will be too late."

DON PENDLETON's

MACK BOLAN®

RED HEAT

A GOLD EAGLE BOOK FROM

WORLDWIDE®

TORONTO • NEW YORK • LONDON
AMSTERDAM • PARIS • SYDNEY • HAMBURG
STOCKHOLM • ATHENS • TOKYO • MILAN
MADRID • WARSAW • BUDAPEST • AUCKLAND

First edition October 1996

ISBN 0-373-61450-0

Special thanks and acknowledgment to
Jerry VanCook for his contribution to this work.

RED HEAT

No villain need be! Passions spin the plot:
We are betrayed by what is false within.
—George Meredith
1828-1909

Betrayal of one's country rarely brings reward,
and in the end, remorse is the harshest punishment.
Because the man who betrays his origins betrays
himself.
—Mack Bolan

PROLOGUE

Curtis Levi had two important decisions to make. The marble ashtray sailing across the room toward his head was both hindering and helping him in the process.

Levi ducked, and the ashtray struck the wall behind him. His second decision depended directly upon the first, and what terrified him was that he suspected he had just come to that first conclusion. He stared at the wild, bloodshot eyes of the woman in front of him.

"Betty!" Levi yelled. "Dammit, Betty, stop it!" He ducked again as a small ceramic table lamp flew toward him. The lamp hit the wall and crashed to the floor of their luxury home.

Betty's voice held the familiar drunken slur Levi had grown to expect over the past few years. "You son of a bitch!" she mumbled. "Lying, cheating son of a bitch!" She stopped, her eyes cruising the room for other potential missiles.

"Betty, I'm sorry," Levi said weakly.

The words jerked her eyes back to him. "You're *sorry,*" she said. "You're sorry you screwed my best friend."

"Betty, there's nothing I can do to change the fact that it happened."

"Spare me the clichés, Curtis," she slurred. "You may be America's top rocket scientist, but you're a failure as a husband." She turned unsteadily and shoved off on a precarious course toward the wet bar on the other side of the room.

Levi watched her weave across the floor before catching herself with both hands on the Formica top. She reached for the near-empty bottle of port.

"Betty, please . . ." Levi said. "Don't. Don't drink any more."

Betty lifted the bottle to her lips.

Levi continued to watch, his heart hardening. What had he ever seen in this woman? What had caused him to marry her so many years ago? Had he once loved her? If so, it was too long ago to remember.

Betty finished the wine, and almost as an afterthought the bottle came hurtling across the room, too far from its target to cause Levi to dodge.

"Betty, I thought we were through discussing this," Levi said. "I thought we'd decided to take a vacation—just the two of us—and try to piece this marriage back together."

"*You* decided," Betty mumbled. "You made that decision. Like you make all the decisions. Like you made the decision to screw Ingrid." She pushed herself back across the living room and collapsed on the couch. "Go ahead, you cheating bastard. Tell me it *just happened.*"

Levi drew in a long, silent breath. "It didn't just happen, Betty," he said. "My having an affair has been a long time coming." He paused, forcing a gentler tone into his voice. "Come on, Betty. We've got to get ready. The plane leaves in less than six hours, and the Fergusons are coming over to say goodbye."

Betty threw back her head and laughed again. "Yes, we wouldn't want your friends to get the wrong impression, now would we? Wouldn't want them thinking we weren't the happy little couple we work so hard to make people think we are. Wouldn't want them to know that Betty drinks too much because her husband cheats on her."

Levi felt the anger rush from his chest through his throat and out his mouth. "Your alcoholism predates my one-night affair by several years," he shouted. "You're an alcoholic, Betty. It's time you faced that fact!"

Levi turned away. "Are we going to Japan or not?" he demanded.

Betty didn't answer. She pulled another bottle of port from the cabinet, grabbed the edge of the bar and hauled herself back to her feet. Next she lunged for the corkscrew.

"Are we going to Japan?" Levi asked again.

Betty jammed the end of the corkscrew into the bottle, twisted it down the neck and popped the cork.

Levi shook his head. She couldn't walk and could barely talk, but she could always uncork a bottle like the most skillful wine steward.

Betty took a drink from the bottle, and her face grew calm again. "*You* go to Japan," she said. "Have fun.

Screw white-faced little geisha girls and don't worry about me. I'll be just fine."

Levi started to answer, then clamped his mouth shut. Everything that could possibly be said had been said already. He had no other choice.

The time had come to leave his wife, and he breathed a sigh of relief. The first of his two important decisions had been made.

And so, in turn, had the second.

CHAPTER ONE

The big man in the back seat of the dark sedan stared out the foggy window into the rain. An almost tangible fear had hung in the air over South Korea for nearly half a century. He could see that fear stamped on the faces of people hurrying down the street seeking shelter from the sudden downpour. Once in a a while the pressure abated. Other times, like now, the country seemed ready to implode.

He sat back against the seat. Since 25 June 1950, when Communist troops had descended over the Thirty-eighth Parallel to drive deep into the newly created Republic of Korea, the South Koreans had lived a life of anxiety. The armistice three years later officially ended the fighting, but it did little to remove the tension. With each breath they drew in peace, the citizens of the newly formed democracy knew that another invasion could be launched. The threat was always there, and while the rest of the world breathed a sigh of relief and turned its attention to other troubled spots around the globe, the descendants of one of the world's most ancient civilizations went about their business with only one eye on their work. The other eye was kept watching the North.

Mack Bolan continued to stare silently through the window as the sedan sloshed its way through the streets of Seoul. He had touched down in South Korea only moments earlier, flown in by Jack Grimaldi—the top pilot of a secret U.S. counterterrorist installation known as Stony Man Farm. The flight had been hurried, and there had been little time for a briefing from Hal Brognola, Stony Man's director of operations. But Brognola's few words had assured Bolan that the CIA field operatives who picked him up at the airport would fill him in on the details, and that they could be trusted.

Outside the car, lightning crackled in the dark sky. Through the rain, Bolan could see what remained of the broad wall that had enclosed the city of Seoul during its period of glory centuries before. Three of the wall's extraordinary Oriental gates still stood within the ruins, and as he watched quietly, the sedan passed through one of the gates and entered the heart of the ancient city.

Bolan turned toward the front of the car. "Okay," he said. "Let's have it."

CIA Field Operative Dick Craven twisted around on the front seat. "From what we've put together so far," he said, "Curtis Levi had a short layover scheduled here in Seoul. But he got off. And *stayed.*"

"Levi's wife wasn't with him," Bolan said. "I got that much from Brognola."

Greg Booker, the field op behind the wheel, nodded. "She didn't even board the plane in New York."

"Let me make sure I've got this straight," Bolan said. "Levi is one of NASA's top missile experts. He was required to file a travel itinerary due to his high-security clearance. That itinerary stated that he and his wife were planning two weeks at the Tokyo Hilton with a few sight-seeing tours to other parts of Japan mixed in."

Both men in the front seat nodded again.

Bolan went on. "But one of your guys spotted Levi leaving the airport here. Was he still alone?"

"That's affirmative, Pollock," Craven said, using Bolan's assigned cover name. "But we're scared he's not going to be alone very long." He paused to clear his throat. "Boris Stavropol has been spotted here in Seoul, too."

The Russian name rang bells in Bolan's mental files. Boris Stavropol. Once a top-flight KGB agent whose specialties included assassination, brutal interrogations and assisting defectors from the West to escape behind the Iron Curtain, reportedly Stavropol had been working for North Korean Intelligence since the fall of the Soviet Union.

"Anyway," Craven continued, "both of them in town at the same time is a little too much for it to be a coincidence in my book."

Booker chuckled sardonically behind the wheel. "Doesn't exactly take a rocket scientist to figure it out, does it?"

Bolan and Craven ignored the weak joke as the sedan turned a corner past the famous Myongdon Catholic Church. "Our people followed Levi's cab to a fleabag hotel here in the old city," Craven said. "They've been watching it ever since. We're on our way there now."

The rain had lightened but continued to beat tinnily against the roof of the car. Bolan leaned back against the seat as they drove on. It *did* seem a little too convenient that Levi and Stavropol were in Seoul simultaneously. But that didn't explain why the President had contacted Stony Man Farm instead of letting the CIA handle the situation—this kind of thing was the spooks' specialty.

No, Bolan realized, there had to be another reason he'd been brought in on the deal. And he wanted to know what it was before he jumped into anything. "Let's cut to the chase," he said. "Tell me what makes you suspect Levi's about to roll over, and why I'm here doing *your* job."

Thunder erupted in the blackened sky, briefly illuminating the interior of the vehicle as the two men in the front seat exchanged glances. Then Craven said, "Well, to be honest, this whole thing is just flat weird, *Pollock*." The emphasis he put on Bolan's undercover name made it evident he knew it was a cover. "We weren't even told who the hell you are."

Bolan suppressed a smile. It was hardly an unusual situation for him. "What did your boss tell you?" he asked.

"That the President himself had ordered us to cooperate with you and give you any assistance you need."

"Then what else do you need to know?" Bolan demanded.

Craven sighed. "Okay," he said, "here's where the Company stands on the deal. Levi hasn't really done anything illegal. He filed an inaccurate itinerary, but that could be covered as a simple mistake. He could say his wife decided at the last minute not to go, and he got off in Seoul, then missed his connecting flight. In other words, we've got no good reason to pick him up, and if he's about to defect like we suspect, by the time we get one it'll be too late." He cleared his throat again. "Levi's also got powerful political friends who could raise hell if we grab him but can't prove he was about to turn Red."

"That explains *me*," Bolan said. "But I've got a feeling there's more."

Craven held a fist to his mouth and coughed, then looked up into the rearview mirror. "This goes no further than this car," he said. "Understood?"

Bolan nodded. "Understood."

"Rumor has it that Levi's wife is a lush. He's been thinking about leaving her. Combine that and the rest with the fact that Curtis Levi knows more about launching nuclear weapons than any other scientist in the free world. Now add in some recent Intel that North Korea already has the nukes the world is worrying they're trying to build, but they've got no good missile system to launch them . . . Well, I think you get the picture. Curtis Levi is at the top of the list of men the North Koreans would like to get their hands on.''

What Craven was telling Bolan indirectly was that the CIA had dug up the information about Betty Levi's alcoholism illegally. Somewhere along the way, her Constitutional rights had been violated, which put the CIA in a bad position. They'd have to remain behind the scenes; otherwise, there would be too many questions to answer when it came time to justify the whole operation. Which further explained why the President had chosen Stony Man to handle Levi, and why Brognola had chosen Bolan instead of one of the counterterrorist teams who operated out of the Farm. Bolan could whisk the NASA man away from Stavropol with no questions asked. He might have an arm's-length working relationship with Stony Man Farm, but that arm had a long reach.

Mack Bolan, better known to the world as the Executioner, answered to no one.

The CIA sedan left the old section of the city, and soon they were cruising down a narrow side street past cafés and small specialty shops. The strong odor of kimchi and spicy meat drifted through the damp air into the sedan as it pulled along the curb and parked.

''That's it,'' Booker said, killing the engine as he nodded toward a neon sign down the block.

Bolan stared through the drizzle toward the lights that read Hotel Koryo. Outside the hotel, he saw a raggedly dressed Oriental trying to sell jewelry to passersby. Another man, even more disheveled, sat on the curb across the street drinking from a brown paper bag. Both had to be either full-time CIA operatives or contract agents.

"You know which room Levi's in?" Bolan asked.

"Yeah—212, second floor to the right of the elevator," Craven answered. "If you take him out through the alley, there'll be a blue Toyota waiting. Untraceable. Keys are in the glove box. You planning to grab him now?"

Bolan looked back as his hand found the door handle. "You have any idea when Stavropol's planning to grab him?"

"No."

"Then now seems like the best time to me."

Bolan exited the vehicle, reaching under his sport coat as he started down the dimly lit sidewalk toward the Koryo. His fingers traced along the shoulder holster that held his Beretta 93-R machine pistol, complete with sound suppressor. On the opposite hip, he wore his trademark Desert Eagle .44 Magnum—a weapon that made a sound that was anything *but* suppressed.

Street and store lights glimmered dully through the continuing drizzle as he passed a window where a chef was preparing a mixture of fish, meat and eggs over a brazier. His hand ran on along his belt in a final weapons check. In addition to the two automatic pistols and extra magazines, he carried a Spyderco CLIPIT folding knife. The Centofante model possessed the company's patented belt/pocket clip, and its partially serrated blade was almost three inches long. Bolan had clipped it inconspicuously inside the right front pocket of his slacks.

Even more inconspicuous, and far more unusual, was the COMTECH T-Grip Stinger dangling from his key chain. Made of high-tech, nearly indestructible plastic, the Stinger was held in the hand much like a push dagger. It centralized the force of a blow on a small, blunt nose that extended between the second joints of the middle and index fingers. Combined with a powerful right cross, it became a phenomenal punching-augmentation device.

Satisfied that his weapons were in place, Bolan let his hand fall back to his side as he neared the hotel. Snatching Levi should be easy. The CIA had run surveillance on the hotel ever since the scientist checked in and had seen no signs of enemy agents. In addition, other operatives had kept vigilant watch on Boris Stavropol. There hadn't been much activity there, either, other than a visit from an old woman in a more affluent hotel on the other side of town. The woman— they assumed she had to be an agent bringing a message of some sort—had stayed only ten minutes, then vanished in the Seoul market district.

Yeah, easy, Bolan thought sarcastically as he neared the front entrance to the hotel. Just go up the stairs to room 212 and thump Curtis Levi over the head, and the next thing the rocket man knew he'd be on his way home with Bolan and Jack Grimaldi.

A hard smile stretched his lips. There was only one problem. It had been his experience that the things that looked the easiest usually turned out to be the most complex.

That knowledge was what saved his life.

Mack Bolan dived to the pavement as the first volley of submachine-gun fire blew from the passing Volvo and shattered the plate-glass window in the front of the Hotel Koryo.

A MILD depression touched Boris Stavropol as he climbed up the back staircase of the Hotel Koryo. It came partly, he supposed, from the simple fact that stairs were no longer as easy to climb as they had once been.

Stopping at the top of the stairs to catch his breath, he spied his reflection in the glass door of a vending machine in the hallway. The sight brought a grim smile to his weathered face. When he had first begun dressing as a woman to fool the Americans, he'd been chided by fellow KGB agents. He was beautiful, they'd said, warning him in jest to never run afoul of the government and be sent to a gulag where the prisoners were starved for female companionship. Then, as the years went by and he entered middle age, he'd been told more than once that he looked like the perfect Soviet mother who'd let herself go.

The Russian turned full face to the glass. As he eyed the navy blue raincoat, the gray blue wig covered by the light blue scarf, the oversize leather purse and the thick-heeled shoes, he could say he looked like the typical babushka on her way to market.

Stavropol turned down the hall toward room 212. Yes, like all men, he was aging. But he was no less capable in his work than he'd been; he simply approached that work differently. As his body weakened, he'd developed his mind to take up the slack. Relying on a foresight honed by years of experience, he predicted and "circled" potential problems that he would have bulled his way through when he'd been younger. The result was that he got the job done even more efficiently than when he'd depended on his physical prowess.

The former KGB agent stopped outside the door marked 212. He started to knock, then dropped his hand to his side as he suddenly realized the reason for his mood. Yes, he was better at his chosen profession than he'd ever been. But the Americans had grown weak after the fall of the Soviet Union. They were no longer a challenge, and the fun had gone out of the game.

Stavropol raised his fist again and rapped lightly. A moment later he saw the peephole darken, and then a timid voice said in English, "Who is it?"

"Look closely," Stavropol said, "and you will see the whiskers beneath the makeup."

The door cracked open. "Stavropol?"

"Let me in," the Russian said.

The door opened wider, and Stavropol stepped into the dark room. "Are you ready?" he asked.

Curtis Levi turned toward him, his dark complexion barely visible in the little light that made it through the windows around the curtain edges. "Yes," he said. "Just let me gather my things."

"Leave them," Stavropol said. He opened the purse and pulled out another wig and dress. "And change into these. The hotel is being watched by the CIA."

Even in the dim light Stavropol could see the dark face pale. "They . . . know?" Levi asked.

"They suspect," the Russian corrected. "If they *knew,* you would already be in their custody."

"But how—?" Levi began.

"We have no time to discuss it now," Stavropol said. He set the dress and wig on the bed and pointed to them.

Then he took a seat in the chair across from the bed as Curtis Levi began changing. His thoughts returned to the depression he had felt so often recently; an unexplained despondency that seemed to have peaked tonight. Finally the reason behind it crystallized in his mind.

When the KGB had gone out of business, the CIA had believed the war was over. As they had done with the military itself, the Americans had cut back on their expenditures for the clandestine gathering of intelligence. Their work had grown sloppy, their agents semitrained and incompetent.

Stavropol sighed as he watched Levi don the wig. He had killed many CIA agents over the years, and many had tried to kill him. Some had come close to succeeding, but he bore them no ill will. It was part of the game, and their proficiency had provided the challenge that made it all worthwhile. But those men were gone now, dead or retired or stuck behind desks at Langley to wait out their remaining years like aging bulls in a pasture. They had been replaced by mere babies who spent too much time at computer terminals and too little in the field.

Levi began slipping into the dress, and the former KGB man sighed again. The CIA was no longer a challenge. He had spotted them following him five minutes after he'd arrived in Seoul, and he'd used the oldest ruse known to covert ops to outwit them. A simple electronic check had assured him that the telephone line in his room was not monitored, and an equally simple phone call had brought a look-alike dressed as a woman a few hours later. He had changed clothes with the body double, left the hotel and then easily slipped away from the Americans in the market district.

A strong but silent vibration suddenly pulsated through the purse in Stavropol's hand, interrupting his thoughts. He opened the bag and removed a small walkie-talkie. Jamming the earplug into his ear, he said, "Yes?"

"Three more Americans have joined the others outside," the voice in his ear said. "One is exiting their vehicle." There was a short pause. "He is walking toward the hotel."

Stavropol got to his feet. "We must go quickly," he told Levi. Into the radio he directed, "Take care of this man before he enters the hotel. Then get the others. We will meet you in the alley." He grabbed Levi by the arm and opened the door.

A moment later the two men were hurrying down the splintering back steps of the Hotel Koryo. As they reached the ground floor, a burst of gunfire sounded on the other side of the building.

"Quickly!" Stavropol whispered, pushing Levi ahead of him. He hurried on, leaning around the frightened American to push open the door to the alley.

He shoved Levi into the alley, then followed. He saw the unlighted form of a vehicle speeding toward them as he gasped for air.

On the other side of the hotel, the fighting began in earnest as his Korean backup team's Chinese Type 85 submachine guns began to chatter.

The Volvo screeched to a halt, and an unseen hand swung open the back door. Stavropol jostled Levi inside. He started to dive in after the American when a lone pistol shot reached his ear above the prattle of the Type 85s. The thunderous round sounded like a cannon above the pops of the Chinese subguns.

Stavropol stopped in his tracks. The massive explosion had been a .44 Magnum, and sounded as if it had been fired from a Desert Eagle.

A small yellow face stuck itself through the passenger window. "Boris! What are you waiting—?"

A second pistol shot blasted over the lighter sub-machine guns, and this time Stavropol was sure. Yes, it was a .44 Magnum fired from a gas-recoil-operated Desert Eagle.

Stavropol slid into the back seat of the vehicle next to Levi and slammed the door. He smiled as the escape car sped toward the end of the alley.

More of the savage .44 Magnum rounds thundered. A massive explosion—a vehicle's gas tank erupting— sounded on the other side of the hotel. Boris Stavropol felt his body energized by an adrenaline rush the likes of which he hadn't experienced in years.

In the many years during which he'd fought the Americans, only one of their agents had carried a .44 Magnum Desert Eagle. The weapon was massive, with recoil far beyond what most men could control in combat situations. But the man who had wielded the mammoth Magnum seemed to do so easily. As best the KGB had been able to determine, the man was not with the CIA, but operated as a free agent when the United States called upon him. In any case, he was of the old school. A professional like Stavropol himself.

And he was proving that professionalism right now on the other side of the building.

The driver slowed near the end of the alley. To the left, the alley dead-ended—the one snag in an otherwise perfect escape route. They would have to turn toward the action on the street if fighting broke out. That fact had bothered Stavropol during the planning phase of the snatch, but he had finally regarded it as one of those stumbling blocks that could not be avoided.

Now he was glad they would have to turn toward the gunfire. It might afford him a glimpse of the face of the man giving the North Koreans a run for their money with the Desert Eagle, give him a chance to confirm his suspicions as to that man's identity.

The driver made the turn and raced toward the street. A moment later the tires squealed around the corner.

Stavropol caught a glimpse of the big shadow running down the sidewalk. He saw the huge pistol leap twice in the man's hands. Then the man turned his broad shoulders and the giant .44 Magnum toward the Russian, and for a microsecond the flames rising high into the air from the exploded gas tank illuminated the hard lines of the man's face.

Even as the Magnum rounds struck armor plating, Stavropol couldn't suppress a smile. Soviet Intelligence files had suggested a number of names, but whatever the name, the man was truly a worthy adversary.

The former KGB man's sudden laughter caused all heads in the car to turn his way. Stavropol ignored the curious faces, still basking in the surge of excitement that had overcome him. He wondered briefly if his adversary had learned the same lessons over the years that he had, and he wondered who had learned them better. Bolan had been around a long time. Was he as good at his craft as Stavropol?

The Russian didn't know. But as they raced off into the night, he suspected that before this mission was over he would have the answer to that question.

THE DESERT EAGLE LEAPED into the Executioner's hand as his shoulder hit the wet concrete. He rolled to his belly, feeling the water soak through the material of both his slacks and jacket.

The Volvo passed alongside a Hyundai and Toyota parallel parked along the curb. Leaning out of both the front and back windows of the vehicle were two Oriental men with Chinese Type 85 submachine guns.

Bolan snapped the Desert Eagle upward as the escape vehicle passed between the parked cars, drilling a .44 Magnum through the gap. The 240-grain hollowpoint struck the front door beneath one of the men with the subguns, then ricocheted off the vehicle with a menacing whine.

More volleys of fire came from both Type 85s, their 7.62 mm rounds chipping the concrete to his right and left. Bolan rolled across the sidewalk away from the Hotel Koryo, taking refuge beneath the Hyundai. He twisted beneath the chassis, his eyebrows lowering in consternation at the memory of his first shot.

He had seen the spark as the round squarely struck the Volvo. Normally the penetrating .44 Magnum round would have drilled through the door and into the passenger in the front seat. Instead, it had ricocheted away, which meant the sides of the vehicle were reinforced with armor plating.

Bolan heard the Volvo's tires scream at the end of the block as the vehicle screeched into a U-turn for a return pass.

Rolling to his back, Bolan looked from beneath the car to see the Volvo roaring toward him. The gunner in the back had slid across the seat and aimed his weapon out of the opposite window. The man in the front seat next to the driver had extended his Type 85 over the roof of the car.

More of the subgun rounds streamed toward Bolan's cover. Extending the Desert Eagle, he sighted down the barrel.

The sides of the Volvo had been bulletproofed. It was time to find out about the windshield.

He squeezed the trigger, the blast of the heavy Magnum deafening in the narrow confines beneath the vehicle. The recoil lifted the Desert Eagle's barrel up to slam against the underside of the car.

A small pocklike indentation appeared on the Volvo's windshield directly in front of the driver. But again the big hollowpoint deflected harmlessly off into the drizzling night.

As the assault vehicle raced closer and a hail of 7.62 mm lead continued to thud into the Hyundai over Bolan's head, he dropped the sights to the grille and pulled the trigger once more.

This time the .44 Magnum round glanced off the left headlight cover, barely leaving a scratch. The men continued to fire as they raced past.

Bolan jerked his arm back to cover beneath the vehicle, his jaw locking tight. The car was armored. The only way to stop it was to take out the gunners hanging out the window.

He rolled back to the edge of the Hyundai as tires squealed into another U-turn. He heard the Chinese subguns chatter at the other end of the block. A low, guttural moan of pain drifted down the street.

Craven or Booker. Or both.

Bolan had no time to mourn the CIA agents as the Volvo raced toward him from the opposite direction. Both Type 85s poked from the windows once more, but instead of targeting his cover, the men now watched the ground just below it.

They had spotted his position. It was time to move.

Bolan quickly shifted his body away from the street. He would wait until the attackers passed before rolling back to the sidewalk and finding new cover. But as he slammed up against the curb, a drop of fluid hit the back of his neck. Another drop hit him on the side of the neck as an unmistakable odor filled his nostrils. Then the drip grew to a steady stream. Gasoline.

The time for waiting was over.

Bolan rolled out from under the car as the first few rounds buffeted the Hyundai. Bounding to his feet, he dived toward the shattered window of the hotel. The second burst of fire found the ruptured gas tank, and the car erupted, red, yellow and orange flames dancing toward the sky.

Heat seared through his wet sport coat to scorch his back as the force of the explosion blew him through the broken glass and into the hotel lobby. He landed face-down on a couch, rolled to the side and bounded back to his feet as the Volvo raced on. Diving behind the couch, he looked over the back to see the rising flames and smoke at the curb.

Did the attackers think he was burning beneath the vehicle, or had they seen him fly through the air with the explosion? He couldn't be sure. And while he could hear the assault vehicle turning back toward the hotel once more, the wall of smoke and fire just past the sidewalk blocked his view of the street.

After he leapt over the couch, Bolan moved swiftly to the side of the window. Through the dancing flames he could barely make out the cars parked along the other side of the street. As the acrid odors of burning upholstery and red-hot steel met his nose, he heard the wail of a siren in the distance.

That would be the police, called by some frightened citizen after the first round of autofire.

The sound of the racing Volvo grew louder. Then, suddenly the tires screeched, and the engine quieted to an idle. Bolan heard two doors open then shut, and a moment later he saw the two men with the subguns dart around the fire onto the sidewalk.

A hard grin curled Bolan's lips. His earlier question got an answer as the two gunners appeared amid the smoke between the Hyundai and the hotel. He watched as one of them, a short, muscular man with flat-top black hair, squatted and tried to look beneath the burning vehicle.

They believed he was even now burning to a crisp at the bottom of the fire.

They were about to find out different.

Bolan stepped around the side of the window and leveled the Desert Eagle on the squatting man's temple. A squeeze of the trigger sent a massive .44 Magnum death messenger scorching from the barrel.

The Volvo was armor plated. The side of the man's head was not. The blast of blood, bone and brains that blew out the other side of his face proved it.

Bolan swung the heavy automatic to the side as the other gunner, taller and more wiry than his partner, turned his Chinese submachine gun toward him. A double tap of the trigger sent two more rounds to crush the man's chest and drop him to the pavement.

Bolan leaped through the shattered window and sprinted away from the hotel past the bodies. The light rain fell onto the fiery wreck, sending noisy hisses up and down the street as water met fire. He circled the burning vehicle, dropping the near-empty magazine from the Desert Eagle and inserting a fresh load of hollowpoints into the grip of the hand cannon.

Down the block he saw Greg Booker hanging out of the sedan. One side of the CIA agent's head was missing. The part of the torso visible was drenched in blood. Dick Craven lay to the side of the car, flat on his back, blood pumping from his chest.

In the middle of the street was the Volvo, the driver motionless. Bolan saw the back of his head as he approached the open passenger window. He needed the man alive, if possible, needed to question him in case Stavropol got away with Levi.

"Don't move!" Bolan shouted as he aimed the Desert Eagle inside the Volvo, the front sights on the back of the driver's head.

The sudden squeal of more tires down the block caused Bolan to glance that way. He saw a car, identical to the one next to which he stood, turn out of the alley just beyond the Koryo. As it turned, two faces pressed against the back windshield. Both wore scarves and had long feminine hair. At first glance they appeared to be women.

In that brief second he recognized the masculine lines of the faces beneath the wigs.

Stavropol and Levi.

What had happened suddenly became clear to Bolan. Stavropol had used the same strategy he himself had planned on employing—whisk Levi away quietly unless obstacles were encountered, and use the backup team as a diversion if there were. But the former KGB officer had been slightly ahead of Bolan's schedule, and the subgunners in the first armored Volvo had pinned him down while Stavropol hurried the American rocket scientist out the back.

There had been only a split second to wonder why the escape car had turned out of the alley toward the fighting rather than away from it as Bolan jerked the

Desert Eagle in the direction of the rear windshield. Dropping the sights on the left rear tire, he squeezed the trigger, then cursed silently as the round bounced off the reinforced rubber.

Lifting the barrel slightly, Bolan pulled the trigger twice more, knowing even as he did that the hollow-points would have no effect. As his third .44 round ricocheted off the rear windshield, a flicker of movement in the corner of his eye caught his attention. He turned back to see the Oriental man in the driver's seat of the first Volvo draw a small Tokarev automatic from beneath his jacket.

Having no choice, Bolan turned and pulled the trigger. If the driver had valuable information as to where Stavropol was headed with Levi, that information died with him.

When he turned back down the street, it was just in time to see the escape car disappear into the night. Behind him he heard approaching sirens a block distant. Holstering the Desert Eagle, he sprinted away. The rain had lightened to a sprinkle, but continued to fall steadily over the streets of Seoul as Bolan ran for the alley out of which the second Volvo had turned.

He had no idea where he was headed. He only knew he had to get away before the police arrived at the scene. He had killed more men than he cared to remember during the endless years of his personal war on crime and injustice, but none of the dead had ever been dressed in blue. It went against his code to kill cops doing their job. But if he didn't make tracks quick, he knew he'd feel some cop's bullet between his shoulder blades before he heard the roar of the gun in the officer's hand.

Bolan glanced down the street to Craven and Booker again as his feet hit the sidewalk. They were dead, and even if the keys to the sedan still dangled from the ignition, there was no time to get to the car before the Seoul cops arrived and began asking questions.

Bolan entered the alley, planning to run to the other side of the block and keep to the back streets until the heat died down. The street behind him was alive with the sound of crackling flames and shouting voices.

In the darkness he saw the wall a split second before he ran headfirst into the bricks. He threw his hands up just in time to catch himself, then turned back in the direction he'd come.

He now had the answer to why Stavropol had directed the second Volvo toward the gunfire. He'd had no choice—the alley dead-ended at the rear of a building.

Bolan took off down the side alley that ran along the rear of the hotel. At the other end of the block, he could see the open street. As he hurried that way, two more police cars raced by.

The big American slowed to a walk. Just as he hadn't known if the subgunners had seen him escape just before the explosion, he couldn't be sure now whether or not the first approaching police car had spotted his sprint into the alley. Either way it made little difference. By now, backup units would be racing to the scene, and if the block wasn't already circled with cops, it would be in the next few seconds.

Bolan arrived at the back door of the Koryo, hesitated, then reached for the knob. The door swung open with a creak, and he stepped inside, closing it behind him. Puddles on the dirty linoleum floor told him someone had entered the rear of the hotel earlier, when the rain had been heavier. A single set of tracks led both to and from the stairs not far away. That made sense. Stavropol had come in out of the rain, collected Levi, then returned with him. Levi's feet would have been dry as he descended and crossed to the back door.

Bolan studied the tracks more closely. He could see the distinctive imprints of women's high heels. Big shoes for a woman. Because the woman who made the tracks hadn't been a woman at all.

He turned back toward the alley when he heard voices. He cracked the door slightly, stopping when he heard the telltale creak begin, and peered out.

Six police officers, their badges reflecting what little light entered the alley, moved toward him from the other end of the passageway. Five of the men carried semiautomatic pistols. The sixth toted what appeared to be a 12-gauge pump gun. They whispered softly in Korean as they walked.

Their voices were too low to distinguish, but it would have made little difference had the Executioner been able to discern their words. He didn't speak Korean. But he needed no understanding of the language to know what had happened.

Either the first car at the scene had spotted him as he raced to the alley, or some witness had given him up to the cops. In any case, he had been seen going down the alley, but had not emerged again on the street. That meant he was either still between the rows of buildings or had entered one of them through a rear entrance.

Bolan hurried away from the door, following the wet tracks on the tile to the stairs, then upward to the second floor. As he'd suspected, they led directly to room 212. He paused at the door, drawing the sound-suppressed Beretta 93-R with his right hand as his left tried the knob. Locked.

On the ground floor Bolan heard the alley door creak open. He pulled a Mini Maglite flashlight from his pocket, activated the beam and held the instrument between his teeth. The same excited whispers he had heard from the alley now drifted up the stairs. With no time to pick the lock, he grasped the doorknob again with one hand, pulling it toward him as his shoulder struck the door itself.

The rotting wood around the door splintered, and the lock broke free with a minimum of noise. Pushing the door open, Bolan scanned the dark room with the flashlight in his teeth. Finding it empty, he holstered the Beretta, replaced the wood of the frame as best he could, ducked inside and closed the door behind him.

Bolan knew he had only a few minutes. He had seen six cops at the rear of the hotel, and others might well have entered the hotel from the front. They would be going door to door, probably with a passkey from the manager. Even if they passed by rooms that didn't answer their knock, anything more than a cursory glance at the door to 212 would tell them someone had just forced his way inside.

Reaching in his pocket for the flashlight again, he cast the beam across the room. In the open closet area just to the side of the door, he saw three business suits and a tuxedo hanging from the clothes bar. The labels of the first two suits read Freeman-Hickey. The third identified it as a Hart, Shaftner and Marx. When he opened the lapel of the tuxedo, Bolan learned it was a Golden Trumpeter tailored especially for one Curtis Bernard Levi.

Bolan played the light across the room to the bed, where a suitcase lay open. Polo shirts, slacks, several pairs of designer jeans and other casual wear lay carefully folded inside. He rummaged quickly through them, looking for a wallet or other ID, but the tux had confirmed what he already knew.

Curtis Levi had occupied the room. Now the American scientist was on his way to North Korea with Boris Stavropol.

He crossed over to the door and pressed his ear to the splintered wood. Down the hall he heard a voice again, but the voice no longer whispered—it shouted in command. A loud, pounding knock sounded down the hall. A door opened. Now the voice practically screamed.

Bolan waited, listening.

A few moments later there was another loud knock farther along the wall, another loud voice, then a pause. When the door failed to open, Bolan heard the familiar sound of a boot hitting wood.

They were coming. They were checking every room, kicking in the doors to the ones that didn't open willingly.

And it appeared that the Executioner had nowhere to go.

CHAPTER TWO

Bolan hurried to the window on the other side of the room. There was no way he'd get out the way he'd entered—not without injuring honest police officers. He drew the curtain aside and looked down, careful to stay out of sight.

Below him on the street, two fire engines stood just past the Hyundai. Black, billowy smoke still rose from the wreckage, but the danger was over.

Men in blue uniforms lined the street. At least a dozen covered the intersection to his left. Down the block he could see more officers at the other corner, while twenty to thirty patrolled the area in between. A trio of plainclothesmen knelt around the bodies of Booker and Craven. One was examining the corpses, another took notes and the third took photograph of the dead American agents.

Bolan turned his attention to the outside wall of the hotel. A foot to the side of the window, a drainpipe ran down from the roof above the fourth floor. He studied the pipe, his eyebrows lowering. It would be an easy climb—if his weight didn't rip the thin metal from the steel supports that held it to the brick. But there was no way to test the bolts except to go for it, and even if it held, there was a good chance he'd be spotted from below as he scrambled up the two stories between where he stood and the roof.

An escape plan began to formulate in his brain, and he took a deep breath. He needed a diversion—something to ensure that the eyes patrolling the streets below *stayed* below. Something that would keep them too busy for the chance glance upward that would end in his back filled with 7.62 mm lead or shotgun pellets.

His eyes moved back to the ground. Toward the end of the block, one of the blue-and-white police cars had parked directly under a streetlight. From where he stood at the window, he could see the small hinged flap that covered the gas-tank filler cap.

A close scanning of the area around the vehicle revealed that no one was close. Drawing the Beretta, he lined the luminous sights up with the tiny square.

The first 9 mm slug coughed from the barrel, cutting a spiderweb hole through the glass of the hotel window before zipping quietly down the block and into the police car's fuel system. A steady stream of fuel began to drip from the blue-and-white. His second near-silent round sent the police car up in flames just like the Hyundai.

As all heads turned toward the explosion, Bolan stuck the Beretta back into shoulder leather and lifted the window with both hands. A moment later, he balanced precariously on the window ledge. With a final glance down below, he grasped the drainpipe and swung out away from the window.

The thin, ribbed metal screeched ominously as he shinnied upward. He could see the shadows from the distant fire as he climbed, hand over hand, toward the roof. When he reached the third floor, he hooked a foot out to the window to the side, resting on the sill for a moment to catch his breath. But he knew he dared not wait long. Every second he delayed raised the odds that one of the cops below would recover from the shock of the second explosion, or that the drainpipe would work itself free from the wall.

With a deep breath Bolan resumed his climb, pulling himself toward the top. Three feet from the roof, he heard the squeal of metal against brick. The drainpipe groaned, bending out away from the wall.

Bolan froze. If his makeshift ladder gave way now, it wouldn't matter whether or not the Korean cops shot him. He might survive the four-story fall to the concrete, but he'd be in no shape to escape.

The drainpipe wavered back and forth, then settled. With painstaking slowness, he reached up and grasped the metal higher. Hand over hand, inch by inch, he moved closer to the top.

Below he could hear the excitement dying down. The hiss of hoses down the block told him the fire fighters had moved that way. The new fire was being brought under control. Soon the curious cops would focus their attention back on their primary mission.

Catching *him*.

His right hand was two inches from the edge of the roof when the drainpipe finally broke.

A final, agonizing screech echoed forth from the wall as the piping began to rip from the bolts in the brick. Bolan grasped the falling drain with both hands and shoved himself upward, the tips of the fingers on his left hand hooking over the concrete lip of the roof as the top section of pipe came free in his right hand. He hung in midair, his feet swinging slowly back and forth.

Sweat poured from his eyebrows as he glanced down at the street, the ten-foot section of pipe clutched to his chest. Activity was picking up just below him again, but so far no one had looked upward. He pulled with his fingers, getting the rest of his hand over the edge of the roof, then tried to pull himself up to safety.

His massive deltoids strained, but it was to no avail. His grip on the edge of the roof was shaky. And his other hand was occupied with the drainpipe.

Bolan relaxed a moment, considering his options. He had only one. Dropping the pipe meant he would then be able to swing his right arm up to assist his left. He'd then get over the edge with no trouble. But the drainpipe clanking to the pavement below would alert the cops to his escape. He harbored no illusions that he'd be able to pull himself over the edge of the roof to concealment before they looked up and saw him. That was a physical impossibility. The question was, could he scramble to temporary safety before he had more holes in him than a voodoo doll?

He didn't know, but because he had no choice, he was about to find out.

With a final deep breath, Bolan released his grip on the drainpipe. His body swung down to the left, then he pulled hard with his left arm and lunged upward with his right. The fingers of his right hand found purchase on the concrete lip just as the drainpipe hit the ground.

The noise brought a temporary lull in the voices chattering on the ground. Bolan pulled upward, hooking his left elbow over the concrete, then struggled his right elbow over the edge of the roof. He swung his right leg up, hooking the heel of his shoe over the concrete lip, pulling now with both arms and his right leg.

The lone pistol shot sailed over his head as he collapsed atop the roof. A burst of full-auto fire followed it as he leaped to his feet. He sprinted to the other side of the hotel roof, then broad-jumped the ten-foot gap over the alley and landed on the roof of the building on the other side.

A cloud drifted away from the moon, and moonlight illuminated the rooftop. Bolan ran, his eyes searching the horizon. Seeing another four-story building to the side, he vaulted through the air again.

Keeping low beneath the retaining walls, he continued to leapfrog across the buildings of Seoul, South Korea, until he had become only a ghost to the confused policemen outside the Hotel Koryo.

THE FIRST RAYS of morning light had begun to peek over the horizon by the time Bolan risked exposure. He had followed the rooftops of Seoul in a zigzag pattern for half a mile before descending back to ground level. Even then he had kept to the alleys until he'd stumbled across a man loading bound stacks of one of Seoul's local newspapers into the back of a van.

The newspaper deliveryman would wake up with a headache in a few hours. Then he'd have to figure out a way to release his hands from his own necktie and free his ankles from his belt. Otherwise, he'd be no worse for wear.

The van had taken Bolan to the dock area along the Han River, where he'd spotted the phone booth. He glanced at his watch, then punched in the numbers that would link him to Hal Brognola's private residence after routing the call through half a dozen other numbers across the world to elude any traces. It was the middle of the night for Brognola on the other side of the world, but being awakened by one of the Stony Man Farm operatives would hardly be a novel experience for him.

As the call connected, Bolan looked out over the rugged mountain wall that formed a backdrop for the sprawling city. Twisting slightly, he looked back in the direction from which he'd come.

Seoul was one of the world's most picturesque cities. But like many other stunning locales around the world, it had seen more than its share of war. Though the Koreans could boast of having one of the oldest civilizations on the planet, much of the splendor of the past had been devastated by tanks, artillery shells and violence. Still, here and there, as he'd made his night flight through the winding streets, he had encountered statues, architecture, and other monuments of the venerable Yi Dynasty, which had ruled the peninsula for a remarkable 518 years between 1392 and 1910.

Hal Brognola's sleepy but familiar voice cut into his thoughts. "Hello, Striker," the director mumbled, using Bolan's Stony Man code name.

Bolan half smiled. Brognola had known it had to be him. "Good morning," he said.

There was a pause during which Bolan knew that Brognola was glancing at the clock next to his bed. "Not quite, but close," Brognola said. "Let me grab a cup of coffee and change phones."

"Okay. But first, your scrambler on?"

"Always," Brognola said. "How about you?"

"This line isn't secure." Bolan glanced around him at the dock area. "But I'd say the chances of it being monitored are roughly the same as the success of what I'm about to propose. Say, ten million to one."

The Executioner waited silently until he heard an extension picked up. There was the distinctive sound of someone sipping from a cup, then Brognola was back on the line. "I take it something's gone wrong." His voice was clearer now, but Bolan could tell he'd clamped an unlit cigar between his teeth.

"Boris Stavropol was behind the snatch. He had a head start and a good ploy. The bottom line is Levi's gone, and two CIA men are down for the count."

"You okay?" Brognola asked quickly.

Bolan felt the minor burns on his back. "Just a little hot under the collar, Hal," he said.

"When did it happen?"

"A few hours ago. I've been tied up evading the local boys in blue ever since."

Brognola cleared his throat, then spoke around the cigar again. "By now they've made it across the border."

Bolan gripped the receiver in his hand more tightly. "No doubt about it. Which means I've got to go in after them."

Brognola was quick to answer. "Negative, big guy," he said. "Your trip to Korea was rushed. There was no time to set up a cover. We could pull that off in a friendly country like the South. But you go into North Korea, you won't come back."

Bolan and Brognola had been friends for more years than he could remember, and the director had sent him on more suicide missions than either one of them cared to recall. But doing so had always left Brognola with a semiguilty conscience, and during his weaker moments—like being awakened from a sound sleep—Brognola's "mother hen" instincts sometimes surfaced.

"Hal, take another drink of coffee and open your eyes," Bolan said.

"They're open, big guy. We didn't have time—"

"Will we have time to set up the Patriot missiles before the nukes come sailing into the D.C. area?"

Brognola paused again. Then, with a resigned voice, he said, "What have you got in mind?"

Bolan turned back toward the mountains as the sun rose higher in the sky to signal the new day. Birds began a morning concert in the trees along the river, and behind him he could hear the heavy machinery sounds of garbage trucks. "I don't know anything beyond the fact that I've got to go in, snatch Levi back and then get out again," he said. "Any suggestions?"

"The CIA can—"

"Negative, Hal. I've had enough of the Company for a while. They botched this deal, and I don't want them hanging around my neck next time it hits the fan."

"Hang on a second."

Bolan heard the sound of a computer warming up, which told him Brognola was at the PC·in his den. Clicks and buzzes sounded over the line as the big Fed linked into the main terminal at Stony Man Farm. Which in turn meant that, with the help of computer wizard Aaron "the Bear" Kurtzman of the Farm, he would soon have the files of all American and Allied Intelligence agencies at his fingertips.

A few moments later he said, "Still there?"

"Go ahead."

"The spooks have a mole planted in the North Korean State Department. Guy by the name of Rhee Yuk. I can't tell how high up the ladder he is by this."

Bolan frowned. "Can you contact him without going through the Company?"

"Yeah, but not right away. It'll take a little maneuvering."

"That's fine," Bolan said. "They aren't going to advertise where they are keeping Levi, and eventually I'll need somebody with connections who can find out. But what I need right now is somebody who looks Korean and speaks the language."

"CIA should have—"

"No," Bolan said simply.

"Okay," Brognola said with a sigh. "Can't say I blame you. Give me a second, I've got another idea." More electronic hums and clicks sounded over the line as Brognola scrolled through information. "Yeah . . . right . . ." he said to himself.

"What do you have?" Bolan asked.

"One Hwang Su. He's SKSF—South Korean Special Forces." He paused. "His English is as good as yours or mine, and he's a *worker*."

Bolan felt himself break into a grin. SKSFers were the cream of the fighting men of South Korea. They deployed both in recon/counterterrorist mode like U.S. Special Forces but could also be used as assault commandos like Army Rangers. What it boiled down to was they were as tough as they came, and if Brognola said this Hwang Su was a "worker" that was enough for Bolan.

Like U.S. elite fighting men, SKSF soldiers specialized in one aspect of warfare, then were vigorously cross-trained. "What's his specialty?" Bolan asked.

"Role camouflage," Brognola said around the cigar. "He's an undercover specialist."

Bolan's smile grew even wider. "Hal, this gets better all the time," he said.

"Well, here's the icing on the cake," Brognola said. "I'm not tapped into Korean files right now." He paused to let it sink in. "This is direct Stony Man Farm Intel on the screen."

It was Bolan's turn to pause. "I hope that means what I think it does," he said.

"It does," Brognola said. "We trained him a little over a year ago. That's why I remembered him."

In addition to fielding its own crack counterterrorist teams, Stony Man Farm provided advanced training to select police and military personnel throughout the free world. Known as "blacksuits" during their stay at the Farm, they arrived and left blindfolded, in ignorance of both the exact location and the Farm's other functions. This established a bond between trainer and trainee that often proved useful after the blacksuits returned to their respective agencies. These graduates of the Farm might not know where they'd been, but they knew they'd received training of a quality that far exceeded anything they'd ever experienced before, and that anyone willing to share such knowledge had to be on their side.

"Hal," Bolan said, "don't ever let anybody tell you there isn't a God."

"I won't, big guy. I'm going to try to circle the normal channels—no sense chancing a leak if we don't have to." Brognola quit talking, and Bolan heard him calling up another computer file. A moment later he continued. "If Hwang's following his usual schedule, he's working out at the base gym right now. I'll call him there and scramble the line both ways. But first hang on a second."

The quiet clicks of Brognola moving the cursor down the screen filled the line. A moment later he said, "Here's what I was looking for. According to the background investigation we conducted before he was accepted for training, there's a little hole-in-the-wall café where he eats on a regular basis."

"Does it have a name?"

"Yeah. Hole in the Wall."

"Which must mean it's near the Yi Wall. By one of the gates?"

"That's a roger. The palace district."

Bolan unconsciously nodded his understanding. "I'll head that way," he said. "Let this Rhee Yuk up north know that Hwang and I are on our way."

"You've got it. Striker..." Brognola's voice trailed off. "There's one other thing."

"Shoot."

"It's not only imperative that Curtis Levi doesn't give up what he knows to the Communists, but we need him back home. Levi is *it* when it comes to rockets—the Wernher von Braun of the next century."

"So what are you telling me, Hal?" Bolan asked. He already knew the answer.

"Your primary mission is to keep Levi from talking to the North Koreans," the Stony Man director said. "Goal number two is to get him back so he can keep helping us."

"And if both of those goals can't be accomplished?"

"Make sure he doesn't talk. By any means necessary."

Bolan hung up, opened the door of the telephone booth and stepped out into the new day. He had told Brognola that the chances of snatching Levi back from North Korea had to be ten million to one. That had been before he'd learned about Hwang Su and Rhee Yuk, the mole in the NK State Department. Now, he realized, he had narrowed those odds to the type of chances he was more accustomed to taking, to odds he had faced before—and overcome.

He whistled softly as he walked back to the newspaper van.

With both the mole and Hwang, the odds against success couldn't be any more than one million to one.

NOTHING HAD EVER COME easily to Hwang Su. From the moment of birth it had seemed that he was fated to encounter obstacles most children never had to face. He had been forced to became inventive and creative in overcoming those obstacles.

And because of that, Hwang Su had learned the secret of success. Hard work.

As he walked along the ancient crumbling wall that had once encircled the city, Hwang's mind drifted back to his childhood. He'd been sickly as an infant, which seemed to have imprinted a memory of helpless pain in his mind.

Hwang saw the Hole in the Wall ahead as he passed one of the standing gates. His thoughts moved from infancy to his childhood. The first few grades of school had been a living nightmare. He was smaller than his classmates, and physically weaker. He suffered from asthma and seemed unable to learn to read. Each day he suffered the taunts of the other children until they became unendurable, then got his butt beaten to a pulp by a succession of playground bullies. In the meantime his teachers began to treat him more as a beloved pet dog than a student, and more than once he heard the term "mildly retarded" when they thought he was out of earshot.

But Hwang Su didn't like being a "pet." He didn't like being laughed at by his classmates or going home every night with black eyes and a bloody nose. So he never gave up—never gave in to the tiny voice in the back of his brain that urged him to take advantage of the excuses available to him and hide his failures behind them.

When he finally arrived home every night after his daily thrashing, young Hwang went to the small shack behind his home where his grandfather lived. There, between bouts of asthma, he studied the arts of tae kwon do and *hapkido,* and learned that Hwang Han, the white-haired old man with the thin beard and even thinner body, had once been a *sulsa*—one of the Korean warrior elite.

A smile broke out on Hwang's face as he neared the Hole in the Wall. He remembered the old man who had taught him martial arts but insisted he spend even more time on his reading. When each day's fighting lesson ended, Hwang Han sat with his grandson and helped him to read.

When Hwang Su cried in frustration, the old man cried with him. But when the boy threw the book down one day and announced he would no longer try, Hwang Su slapped him soundly across the mouth.

"Never speak of this again," the ancient, white-haired *sulsa* said. "You are a Hwang. You are a member of a family that predates recorded history. This family does not understand failure, and it has *never* accepted defeat."

And so the fate that Hwang Su would be a success had been sealed.

Hwang Su opened the door of the Hole in the Wall and went inside, taking a seat at his usual table against the wall, where he could face the door. His eyes scanned the small café for an American but saw none. He wasn't surprised. Brognola had reached him only a half hour earlier, and he guessed that the man he was to call Rance Pollock would not have arrived by the time he did.

The waitress arrived, and Hwang ordered tea and a milder breakfast version of the spicy national food, *kimchi*. He let his mind wander again as he waited.

Hwang Su's asthma cleared up, and by the beginning of the eighth grade he found that while he was still forced to look upward to meet the eyes of his classmates, the distance between them was not as great as it had been. In the mirror he saw that his shoulders were broadening, and a hard jawline had driven away the baby fat that had once rounded out his face. During the martial-arts sessions with his grandfather, he suddenly realized that he didn't need the rest periods anymore, and that he could now practice with one hundred percent effort for as long as Hwang Han demanded.

But the big discovery didn't come until the end of his ninth year of school, when he was tested for, and then diagnosed as suffering from, dyslexia.

The waitress brought Hwang Su's breakfast and set it down before him. He poured hot tea into the small cup, then lifted it to his lips. How well he remembered that day so long ago when he had learned for certain that he was *not* retarded, that this thing called dyslexia could be corrected and that he would soon read as well as the other students. Of course, he rushed home to tell his grandfather.

"I have a disease!" he cried. "A reading disease that can be corrected!"

"Yes," Hwang Han said calmly. "It is called dyslexia."

Hwang Su stopped in his tracks. "You knew of it?" he said, astounded.

"Of course. It was most obvious."

Anger flooded Hwang's adolescent limbs. "Then why did you not tell me?"

By Hwang Su's fifteenth year, his grandfather had reached his eighty-fifth. Old injuries kept him in bed most days, and the inactivity had begun to affect his general health. Pain usually kept him from smiling anymore, but as he spoke then, his eyes twinkled like those of a child. "And rob you of the gift God gave you?" the old warrior told his grandson. "You have learned to work, Hwang Su. To work harder than those who did not have the gift of dyslexia. And now that you have sharpened the false edge of that double-edged sword, the edge you have honed is far sharper than it would have been otherwise."

Smiling at the memory, Hwang Su lifted his chopsticks to begin his breakfast when he saw the big American enter the café. He saw first the American sport coat and slacks, the white shirt and tie, all stained with both last night's rain and the grime of activity. Then he looked beyond the clothing, into the eyes that met his, and saw a man very much like himself. A man who was not only a *sulsa,* but a man who had chosen never to retreat in the face of adversity and never to listen to that tiny voice that tempted all men to hide their failures behind convenient excuses.

Hwang Su nodded silently to himself, for he saw even more. Before him he saw not just a warrior from whom he would happily take orders during this mission. He saw also a man much like his grandfather—a leader he would follow though the gates of hell itself if Rance Pollock asked it of him.

TEN MILES SOUTH of the North Korean border, Hwang Su pulled the Oldsmobile Firenza off the highway and onto a hard-packed dirt road. Coming to a halt behind a grove of trees, he exited the vehicle.

Bolan followed the smaller man to the trunk of the car. Hwang flipped the lid and pulled out a North Korean license plate and a screwdriver, then squatted behind the vehicle and began removing the tag presently on the bumper. As the first screw came out, he nodded toward the hodgepodge of weapons and other equipment in the open trunk. "I understand you have your own pistols and ammunition," he said, looking up at Bolan. "But perhaps you could use a rifle."

Bolan smiled. "They do come in handy sometimes." He watched Hwang as the undercover specialist continued to remove the screws. He had liked the little man ever since meeting him a few hours earlier at the Hole in the Wall—liked his friendly attitude, obvious professionalism and willingness to get down to business with a no-nonsense approach. "But tell me this," he asked as Hwang pulled the South Korean tag from the bumper and began screwing on the one from the North. "How do you plan to explain guns of any kind to the border guards?"

Hwang chuckled. "I don't," he said as he returned to his feet. "But then, we aren't going to see any border guards because we aren't going over the border. We're going *under* it."

Bolan waited. He already knew the man well enough to have learned that Hwang loved to speak cryptically, then explain what he'd actually meant.

He returned to the passenger seat as Hwang slid back behind the wheel and started the engine. A few seconds later they were bumping on across the rugged road away from the highway, but still angling toward the border. Hwang guided the Firenza through a bean field, then took a fork in the road that led down into a valley surrounded by hills.

At the bottom of the valley, Bolan saw a dilapidated and apparently deserted barn. A light bulb flickered on in his brain. "You've got a tunnel into the North?" he asked.

Hwang turned toward him and smiled. "I learned an American expression when I was training at your facility," he said. "A man in a wheelchair we called Bear. You know him?"

Bolan smiled back. "I do," he said.

"The Bear instructed us in intelligence gathering through computers. He had an expression he liked to use when someone understood what he had said."

Bolan waited, knowing what he'd hear.

"Give the man a cigar," Hwang said. "We will surface in another barn on the other side. Even though it will still be light, we can get on the road immediately. I have already checked with our intelligence officers, and there is strong cloud cover over the area, which will prevent the North from detecting us with satellite surveillance." He guided the car down into the valley.

Bolan studied the dilapidated barn as they neared. He changed his mind about the deserted part when two dozen men dressed in camouflage combat suits, web gear and black berets bearing silver South Korean special-forces badges suddenly appeared out of nowhere to surround the vehicle with M-16 A-1s. His eyes zeroed in on the pocket patches each of the men wore. They bore the emblem of a lion, which meant the men represented the special-warfare branch. "Friends of yours, I hope," he said as Hwang rolled the Firenza to a halt.

"And I hope not," Hwang said. "If any of them know me personally, we are both in trouble."

A muscular man who could have passed as an Occidental appeared at the driver's-side window. Bolan was reminded that the people of Korea were a race apart, distinct from the Chinese and Japanese in that they had descended from both the ancient Mongolians and Caucasians of western Asia. Most Koreans exhibited features of both strains, but this man's genes had come primarily from the tribes of the West.

Hwang rolled down the window and spoke to him.

The man shook his head.

A short argument ensued, then Hwang turned to Bolan. "He wants to see my papers authorizing us to cross over."

"Show them to him," Bolan said.

Hwang shrugged. "I don't have any."

Bolan's eyebrows lowered. "Excuse me?" he said.

Hwang shrugged. "Brognola said this should be kept quiet," he said. "I have taken vacation days to accompany you. My superiors believe I've gone fishing on the coast."

Bolan sat back in his seat. The worst that could happen would be that the tunnel guards would refuse to let them cross and take them into custody. That could be worked out, but it would take time. And the more time passed before he found Curtis Levi, the more time the North Koreans had to pump the American scientist for information.

Hwang turned back to the window and spoke again. The muscular man shook his head again. Hwang's voice suddenly rose three octaves, and he screamed at the man just beyond the window. With a lightning-fast move, he reached into his pocket and produced a leather ID holder. Flipping it open like a detective in a cop movie, he shoved it out the window and under the guard's nose.

The guard nodded excitedly, stepped back and began mumbling what even someone who spoke no Korean could identify as an apology. He waved the car forward, and Hwang drove toward the door of the barn.

Other spec-war troops had hurried to slide it open. As they entered the barn, Bolan said, "Okay, what was the magical piece of paper you just showed him?"

Hwang grinned as he stuck the leather case back in his pocket. "Just a normal military ID," he said.

"It didn't get what I'd call a *normal* reaction."

"Well," Hwang said, grinning slyly, "it *did* have one thing on it that was exceptional."

"And what would that be?"

"The name. Colonel Bong Kim. He happens to be the officer in charge of all South Korean special forces. He also happened to be playing racquetball this morning at the gym when Brognola called. Those lockers aren't hard to jimmy." The undercover man handed Bolan the ID card.

Bolan looked at the picture. Before he could ask how the special-warfare guard could have mistaken Hwang for this colonel, who was obviously fifteen years older, Hwang looked at him wryly.

"Hey," the Korean said. "You know what they say—we all look alike."

Bolan couldn't suppress a chuckle.

"Actually," Hwang went on as Bolan handed back the card, "you may have noticed I kept talking the whole time he examined the ID. Took part of his attention away." He smiled proudly as the Firenza entered the barn. "It's a common trick of undercover men—same principle as the sleight-of-hand tricks magicians use."

Bolan nodded as the Firenza came to a halt. He'd worked with many undercover specialists over the years, and found one thing common to the best ones: to accomplish their goals, they had to run almost as many con jobs on their administrators as they did on the bad guys. Well, Hwang had proved he could do that. He was a professional, and a professional was exactly what the Executioner would need once they surfaced again on the other side of the border.

Hwang killed the ignition, and both men exited the vehicle, not far from the narrow concrete ramp in the middle of the barn floor. It led down into the earth roughly twenty feet, then angled off out of sight toward the border. Bolan turned to the rear of the automobile, where Hwang had opened the trunk again. Slowly and methodically, his eyes scanning the floor of the trunk as he worked, the Korean removed the weapons and other equipment from the trunk and set them on the ground behind the car.

The same guard who had checked his ID card entered the barn and spoke in Korean. Hwang shook his head and waved him out again. Looking up at Bolan, he said, "He asked if I needed any help."

Bolan nodded. "He's impressed with you right now, *Colonel,* but in a few minutes he's going to start questioning why the top dog of South Korean special forces and a 'round-eyes' are sneaking under the border into the North. It doesn't make sense."

By now Hwang had picked the equipment he wanted from the stack and returned it to the trunk. "Right," he said as he closed the lid again. "Which is exactly why we've got to be gone when that happens." He reached behind the bumper, and an unseen latch clicked. The bumper fell down on hinges, revealing a long, hollow storage panel.

Hwang removed the magazines from two Chinese Type 85s and slid the weapons into the hidden storage area. The magazines, and extras, went in around the rifles. Flipping the bumper back up in place, he nodded toward the interior of the car again. "Ready?"

Bolan got back into the passenger seat. "What about our pistols?" he said.

"Not to worry," Hwang said as he slid behind the wheel again. He started the ignition, then reached inside his jacket and produced two straight pins. After handing one to Bolan, he leaned forward and inserted the other into a tiny hole in the dash just to the side of the steering column.

Bolan felt something fall against his arm, and looked to his side to see that the panel above the armrest in the door had fallen open. Another hidden compartment was revealed.

"I've got one on my side, too," Hwang said. "They're on hinges with trunk latches. Wired for electrical release when a simple straight pin makes contact with a metal switch in the dash. If you have to do it without me around, remember that the ignition has to be on."

Bolan nodded. He fastened the other pin to the inner side of his jacket, then shrugged out of his shoulder rig. Unthreading his belt holster, he stowed the Desert Eagle, Beretta and both holsters inside the door. The Spyderco Centofante and COMTECH Stinger followed, then he flipped the side panel back up in place. Turning to Hwang, he said, "You've gone over the rest of the car for any telltale giveaways already?"

Hwang nodded. "As you Americans sometimes say, with a fine-tooth comb. So. We are ready?"

Bolan nodded. "We are ready," he said.

Hwang threw the Firenza into gear, and they started forward toward the ramp.

Just as they reached the concrete, the barn door slid open and a half dozen of the special-warfare men hurried excitedly inside.

Hwang floored the accelerator, and the Firenza shot down the ramp. As the tires left the concrete and began bumping down the packed dirt floor of the tunnel, he turned to Bolan. "I'd say they just figured out I wasn't Colonel Bong," he said. "What would you say?"

"I'd say the same. How do you plan to explain all this when we come back?"

Hwang shrugged. "I doubt that I'll have to," he said. "You and I are about to illegally enter Communist North Korea, Pollock. The odds are against us ever getting back at all."

CHAPTER THREE

Less than a foot of clearance stood between the Firenza and the side tunnel walls as Hwang drove slowly down the dark passageway. The quiet hum of the engine was the only sound, but it was enough to cause an occasional bat to flutter its wings across the headlights. The odor of damp soil penetrated the windows of the vehicle, and somewhere along the way, during the four-mile drive, they passed under the border and entered North Korea, one of the last bastions of communism on the face of the Earth.

Bolan used the quiet time to review the role he would have to slip into should they be stopped by NK troops. Hwang had papers left over from a previous mission. They IDed him as a North Korean diplomat who had been south of the border negotiating a trade agreement. No such trade agreement was actually in the works, but the common soldier wouldn't know that. Such diplomatic trips from North to South, and vice versa, were common enough.

The Korean had provided Bolan with documentation that identified him as a former Soviet economic expert. "Vladimir Neptukov" had been hired by the North Korean equivalent of the Department of Commerce, and had accompanied Hwang as an adviser on the trip to Seoul.

The Firenza puttered on, the headlights the only illumination in the tunnel. Finally Bolan saw a glimmer of light beyond the beams. As they drove on, the light grew brighter, and then Hwang said, "I have entered the North this way several times. It always reminds me of the near-death experiences people talk about." He paused, turning toward his passenger. "You know, where they see the light at the end of the tunnel on their way to Heaven."

"There's a big difference, though," Bolan remarked.

"What's that?"

"For us, it's closer to entering hell."

The comment verbalized the somber nature of their mission, and both men lapsed into silence as the light continued to grow. Neither spoke again until Hwang slowed the Firenza to a halt on a concrete platform. The undercover man turned to Bolan. "Things are a little different on this side of the tunnel," he whispered.

Hwang got out of the car. A single light bulb mounted on the wall provided the light they had seen. Hwang moved to a lone red button on the concrete wall just below it. An electrical wire ran from the button through a hole in the steel trapdoor directly above them. Hwang pushed the button, then hurried back to his seat and closed the door.

A moment later they heard the grinding gears of machinery as the double overhead doors separated in the center and rolled back away from each other. The platform on which they were parked began to rise.

The concrete platform rose through the opening, finally creaking to a halt inside another barn. Several scraggly, underfed horses whinnied in stalls directly ahead of the Firenza, and overhead a hayloft had been piled high with bales. Loose hay lay in piles on both sides of the hole from which they had emerged, obviously displaced by the opening steel doors.

The guards on this side of the border wore no uniforms. Instead, they masqueraded as bean farmers in the typical khaki work clothes and floppy straw hats that symbolized the profession. A dozen of them stood waiting as the platform came to rest, anxious to cover the hole again as soon as the car drove out of the way. Hwang obliged, driving down a short ramp. There was the grinding of machinery again as the doors folded back against the ground, and the men got to work with their pitchforks.

Hwang rolled down the window as a man dressed in oil-stained khakis walked forward. They conversed for a second in Korean, then the undercover expert drove forward to the closed barn door. Several other men slid the door open, and Hwang guided the car forward.

They were suddenly in Communist Korea.

Hwang took another bumpy dirt road to the highway and turned north toward Pyongyang. Bolan watched the special-forces man's eyes scan the road.

Hwang's usually pleasant expression had changed to one of deep concern as he studied the highway.

"The papers looked good enough to me," Bolan said. "And my Russian's good. Relax, Hwang. If we get stopped, we'll pass."

The Korean's head jerked toward him in surprise. Then a look of realization came over his face. "Oh, you thought I was concerned about government troops," he said. "No. I am worried about something else."

"What?" Bolan asked.

Hwang fell silent for a second, thinking. Then he said, "Basically, bandits."

"Bandits?"

"Yes. Several years ago I read an American book. The first book I had ever read in English, which perhaps explains why I remember it so well now. It was called *Lines and Shadows,* and was written by an American police officer who had become a writer. I cannot recall his name."

"Joseph Wambaugh," Bolan said. "Los Angeles PD. I have a friend who knows him well." His mind traveled briefly to Carl Lyons, the former LAPD detective who now headed Stony Man Farm's Able Team.

Hwang's somber face brightened. "Yes, that was him. Do you know the book?"

Bolan nodded. "It concerns a task force of police officers who patrolled the Mexican-American border south of San Diego," he said. "They were trying to stop the *bandidos* who preyed on illegal immigrants trying to cross into the U.S."

"Yes," Hwang said as he guided the car through another sweeping curve. "The immigrants, of course, were carrying everything of value they owned. Fertile ground for thieves." He cleared his throat. "We have a similar situation here along the border."

Bolan didn't have to ask further. It made sense. Mexicans illegally entered the U.S. for economic reasons. Political oppression caused people to flee North Korea. The reason Mexicans and North Koreans left their native countries might be different, but the results would be the same. The NKs trying to sneak across the border to the South would have everything they owned on their backs, and while that might not be much, it would be enough to lure road bandits from both countries.

Bolan turned sideways to face Hwang. "But bandits would be looking for people going the other way," he said.

Hwang shook his head. "Not always. It is not uncommon for a would-be escapee to become frightened and turn back around. The bandits know this."

"We'll just have to take our chances. How big are the bands they run in?"

Hwang shrugged. "It varies. Anywhere from two to twenty, usually."

"Well armed?"

Before Hwang could answer, the Firenza sped around another of the seemingly endless curves in the road. Hwang was forced to slow as two cars ahead blocked the roadway. It appeared to be the aftermath of a collision, as if the Toyota had smashed into the Hyundai when it came off a small side road. Two men stood next to the vehicles, talking.

Bolan frowned. Something was out of place. It took him a second, then he saw it.

Neither car was dented.

"What did you ask me?" Hwang said.

Bolan stared ahead at the cars as they drew nearer. "I asked you if the bandits were well armed," he said. "But don't waste time answering—we're about to find out firsthand."

Hwang Su turned to look at him quizzically.

"Stick the pin in the dashboard, Hwang," Bolan ordered.

As the Korean reached into his jacket, the first rounds from the surrounding hills struck the hood of the Oldsmobile Firenza.

HAL BROGNOLA WORE two hats.

In his position as a high-ranking officer in the U.S. Department of Justice, he went about his duties little differently from the hundreds of other men and women at Justice who fought crime through conventional means.

It was the other hat, however, that Brognola wore as he marched up the wheelchair ramp in Stony Man Farm's computer room. And in this role he departed from the standard, the conservative norm. Because when Hal Brognola left the halls of Justice for the hidden fortress of Stony Man Farm, convention was thrown right out the window. Creativity became the order of the day.

Aaron Kurtzman glanced up from his wheelchair, but his fingers continued to blur across the computer keyboard. "Hal," he said simply by way of greeting.

Brognola nodded his own hello. "How close are we?" he asked.

"A few more minutes," Kurtzman grunted, his eyebrows lowered in concentration. "Sorry it took so long."

Brognola chuckled under his breath. What Kurtzman thought of as a long delay in obtaining the ordered Intel would have been considered lightning speed for any other computer man. Brognola had called the Farm right after hanging up with Bolan, wanting to obtain a name and a method of contacting the South Korean mole planted in the North Korean government. Kurtzman had attempted to tap into SK Intelligence files as the big Fed waited, only to learn that the access codes had been changed within the past few days. And breaking a new access code without getting picked up by a computer trace from the South Koreans took time, even for Kurtzman.

As Kurtzman continued to work away, Brognola let his mind drift to Bolan. As always, the man he called Striker was out on a thin limb. But thin limbs had never bothered the man whom Brognola regarded as the world's premier warrior. Indeed, the "one man against all odds" challenge seemed to take Bolan to new heights. He had accomplished some impossible tasks, and even the other warriors of Stony Man Farm were sometimes still in awe of him.

"They changed everything, which meant I had to start from scratch," Kurtzman said, sitting back in his chair, his right index finger poised over the Enter key. "Hit and miss. Trial and error. But I think I've finally got it. Hold your breath and let's see." The finger came down on the button, and the computer offered a series of clicks, buzzes and flashing lights on-screen.

Brognola watched, suddenly aware that he *was* holding his breath. As he stared at the screen, the lights and noises suddenly stopped, and the round, full-cheeked face of an Oriental man in his midthirties appeared on the screen. Below the face was the name Rhee Yuk.

"Bingo," Kurtzman said. "Give the man a cigar."

The next paragraph contained a brief biography of the mole known as Rhee Yuk. Born in Seoul, Rhee had been trained by South Korean Intelligence, then shipped to the North, where a phony past was entered into the North Korean files by another mole. Since he had never worked overtly, Rhee went by his real name.

Brognola leaned past Kurtzman, tapping the cursor himself to work his way down the file. The next several paragraphs listed the occasional bits of Intel passed on by Rhee. They could hardly be called earth-shattering. As he read on, it became evident to the Stony Man director that Rhee had indeed been planted as a true mole. His job was to fit in, lie low, take no chances and wait for the day when he was needed for something big—something that merited blowing his cover in one final climax to the many years it took to get him into a position where he could be of service.

At the end of the file, Brognola came to what he'd been looking for. There were telephone numbers listed for both Rhee's home and office at the North Korean State Department, but both were flagged with cautions. As of two years ago, Rhee had worked his way up in the state department to a level where North Korean Intelligence routinely monitored his lines on a spot-check basis. They weren't always listening in, but there was no way to know exactly when they would be.

Brognola let out a deep breath, a bitten-off curse sneaking out with it. He had hoped that a simple phone call to the mole, scrambled from Stony Man on both ends, of course, would do to alert the man that he was about to be called upon. But deep in his heart, the director had known things rarely worked out that easily in covert operations. If he called now, and the bad guys happened to be listening, the words would not be detected but the scrambler would. And the scrambler itself would point a giant accusatory finger at Rhee Yuk that cried "Spy!"

Brognola turned to the wheelchair-bound man. "Any other files that might give us a clue as to how to get hold of him?" he asked.

Kurtzman shrugged. "Don't know. But I can try to get into the NK state department."

Hal Brognola nodded, knowing that would prove even tougher than the files in Seoul. "Go for it, then," he said. "Striker's going to need him. We need to get him ready and waiting."

The determination already in Kurtzman's eyes intensified. "I'll figure something out," he said. His fingers were flying across the computer again as Brognola walked down the ramp.

Stony Man's director of Sensitive Operations passed through the communications room and waved to Barbara Price, who sat at the console microphone talking to Phoenix Force over the satellite relay. Price nodded back but continued to speak into the mike.

Brognola hurried through the first-floor den to the entryway, then tapped the access code into the digital lock on the front door. A moment later he was jogging toward the landing strip, where Jack Grimaldi waited in the chopper that would take him from the Blue Ridge Mountains back to Washington.

MORE ROUNDS POUNDED into the hood and windshield of the Firenza as Hwang jabbed the straight pin into the dash.

Bolan turned to his side, ready to snatch the Desert Eagle, Beretta and his other weapons from the hidden compartment just as soon as the panel opened.

But it didn't.

He turned back to Hwang as the South Korean jerked the pin from the dash, then rammed it home again. Again nothing happened.

"The electrical circuit's been hit!" Hwang shouted above the continuing gunfire. "It's out!"

Ahead, Bolan saw the parked Toyota and Hyundai. The two men who had stood near the vehicles turned toward them now, their bearded faces scowling as they pumped out bullets from their Daewoo K1A1 carbines. More rounds assaulted the Firenza from atop the hills just off the road, and Bolan recognized the distinctive chatter of a Daewoo K3 light machine gun.

The Executioner turned back to the car door, his hand traveling to the top of the flap that covered his weapons. He worked his index finger along the groove, desperately trying to gain enough purchase to pry the barrier down by hand. Next to him Hwang was trying to do the same thing with his left hand while he guided the Firenza through the continuing onslaught of bullets that peppered the car.

The trapdoor refused to give, and Bolan twisted in his seat. Drawing back his left hand, he punched the door. The first two knuckles of his fist drove into the hard plastic. A small hole appeared.

He had drawn his fist back to punch again when bullets hit the front tires. Both tires blew simultaneously, dropping the front of the vehicle to the pavement in a burst of sparks. The force of the drop slowed them, slamming both Bolan and Hwang against the windshield as more rounds struck the car. Metal screeched against pavement as the wheels skidded toward the waiting cars. The automatic fire from the parked vehicles halted abruptly as the men dived away from the approaching Firenza, but the belt-fed rounds from the hill continued.

Sharp shards of glass and metal rained down as the Firenza slowed, then fishtailed on toward the stationary vehicles in its path.

Thrown back in his seat, Bolan immediately punched the door again. The hole opened wider, and inside he saw the dull gray metal handle of the Spyderco Centofante. Jamming two fingers into the opening, he worked them around the knife and yanked it out from the hidden compartment. Transferring the knife to his left hand, his fingers moved into the hole again. This time his index finger caught inside the key ring attached to the COMTECH Stinger.

As he pulled the Stinger free, they struck the Toyota broadside.

The impact sent the Firenza spinning off toward the ditch at the side of the road. Bolan's right fist tightened around the Stinger as he spun, the G-force pulling him hard against the door. Then suddenly the car was tumbling, first side over side, then end over end. Bolan was slammed up against the roof of the car, then back down against the floorboard. He heard Hwang grunt through the noise, and a second later they came to a halt upside down.

Bolan shook his head, trying to get his bearings as the gunfire died down. The cobwebs in his brain stabilized, then disappeared as he heard footsteps crunching across the gravel toward where he lay.

Then from beyond the footsteps, harsh male voices chattered in Korean.

In his right hand he palmed the Stinger, making sure the blunt nose was aligned with his arm and extended between his fingers. Slowly, careful that the blade gave off no telltale click, he thumbed open the Centofante with his left hand.

A short knife and a plastic punching device. They didn't seem like much against assault rifles and a light machine gun, but they would have to do.

They were all he had at the moment.

At rest on his chest against the smashed roof of the car, he saw a pair of scuffed brown army boots cautiously approach the wrecked Firenza. The tail of a long coat fell over the top of the boots, and just above that the still-smoking barrel of a Daewoo was visible.

Bolan waited. The boots stopped just outside the window. Then the tail of the coat lowered to brush the ground as a bearded face dropped down to peer into the carnage.

The Executioner drove the sharp tip of the Centofante into the right eye of the Korean road bandit. Blood shot from the punctured orb as the bandit jerked instinctively away from the pain and screamed at the top of his lungs.

Bolan shot forward, trying to wriggle through the crushed opening that had once been a car window. He reached out, catching the ankle of the one-eyed bandit and pulled.

The man fell to his back, still shrieking.

Bolan used the fallen man's body weight to tug himself free, then clambered over the prostrate body. Both of the bandit's hands were clamped over his eye, and his forearms covered his throat. The warrior brought the blunt nose of the Stinger down hard against the frail bones on the back of one hand and heard a crunching sound. The bandit's hands jerked away from his eye. His wrists moved with them, exposing his throat.

Bolan plunged the sharp point of the Centofante straight down into the man's jugular. Deep red, almost black blood geysered forth. As the bandit shivered his last breaths, Bolan twisted to the side, snatching the K1A1 from the ditch where it had fallen.

Rising to one knee, he brought the stock of the weapon to his shoulder. Automatic fire slammed into the ground near him as the other bandit who had posed by the "wreck" saw what had happened and opened up from the other side of the Firenza.

Bolan answered the fire with his own, letting a steady stream of 5.56 X 45 mm NATO rounds unleash a dance of death. Behind him the light machine gun prattled again, the rounds sailing past and striking the Toyota and Hyundai.

Both vehicles suddenly burst into flames.

Bolan turned, fired a quick burst at the machine gunner, then rolled forward behind a boulder at the foot of the hill. Behind cover now, he paused to catch his breath and drop the magazine from his captured carbine. The bandit had fired the 30-shot detachable box low, and only four rounds remained. Bolan flipped the selector to semiauto and turned back to the Firenza.

Hwang was still inside it. The undercover specialist hadn't moved or uttered a word since the crash, and Bolan had to assume he was unconscious. He also had hopes that the bandit at the trigger of the machine gun didn't know there had been anyone else in the car with him. It wouldn't take too many rounds to turn the Firenza into Hwang's funeral pyre.

Bolan turned back to the hill. He could try to work his way around it, but that would take time, time during which several things might happen. The bandit on the trigger of the gas-operated K3 could well decide to send the Firenza up in flames just in case there were other occupants. Or North Korean border troops could chance along to discover what had happened.

The warrior's decision was made quickly. No, there were too many things that could go wrong if he took the time to circle the hill. He would have to tackle the machine gun from the front. Face the lion head-on, and stick his head into the animal's mouth.

If the decision was made quickly, Bolan acted even more quickly.

Rolling out from behind the boulder, he sprinted up the side of the hill. At the top he saw the startled look on the face of the bandit on the K3. The man wore a torn and tattered O.D. green fatigue blouse and ragged khaki pants. The long, stringy mustache, combined with the bandanna tied over his head, made him look like a Chinese pirate.

The man's mouth dropped open, but only for a second. Recovering from the shock of seeing what most men would consider suicide, he leaned forward to assist in that suicide.

The first rounds came before the bandit had aligned the sight. The rounds flew wide. Bolan answered with a semiauto round of his own which struck the machine gunner in the chest.

One of the pirate's hands clamped the wound in his chest. The other froze on the trigger, and the K3 continued to sputter.

Bolan hit the grass, lying low until the gun had run dry.

He looked up to see the pirate's corpse draped over the Daewoo. Then an explosion from back down the hill swiveled his head back around. Below he saw flames dancing alongside the Firenza and realized one of the wild rounds must have ignited spilled gasoline around the vehicle.

He had only seconds.

Racing back down the hill, he saw the flames streak nearer to the Firenza. Any second now, fire could shoot to the gas tank and turn the vehicle, and Hwang Su, into an inferno.

Reaching the smashed body of the overturned car, Bolan leaped over the roof, then pivoted back toward the driver's-side window. Lying with his cheek against the ground, his eyes closed, he saw Hwang Su's unconscious face. A trickle of blood dripped down from the Korean's forehead over his lips.

Bolan wasted no time. Reaching inside the vehicle, he grasped Hwang's hair with one hand and worked the other under the South Korean's arm. The roof had caved in even lower on the driver's side of the vehicle, narrowing the opening to a crevice even smaller than the one through which he had squirmed. But Hwang Su was a smaller man, and though he lost some skin in the process, a few strong yanks got him pulled free.

Bolan threw Hwang Su over his shoulder and rose to his feet, stumbling away from the car as a hissing pierced the air. He sprinted back toward the hill, with each step marveling that the explosion hadn't yet erupted to cremate them both. Then it came, and for the second time on the mission Bolan felt himself hurled forward as heat scorched his back.

Bolan and his burden toppled to the side of the road as the flames shot toward the sky. Bolan watched briefly, then turned to the still form at his side. A little direct pressure would take care of the gaping gash in his forehead and unless there were internal injuries Bolan couldn't see, the undercover man would be almost as good as new when he woke up.

Bolan breathed a sigh of relief as he reached down, ripped the sleeve from Hwang Su's shirt and pressed it against his forehead. The cloth saturated quickly, but the bleeding slowed.

Hwang stirred slightly, opened his eyes, then closed them again.

Bolan was tearing the other sleeve away when he heard the engine on the far side of the hill. He looked hurriedly around, but there was no place to hide—no place, at least, that he could get to with Hwang before whoever it was rounded the curve and saw them.

Bolan pressed the dry cloth against Hwang's head.

Then the first vehicle of the North Korean army convoy rounded the curve and braked to a screeching halt.

Bolan looked up as two soldiers jumped out of the cab and aimed their rifles at his head.

THINGS HADN'T WORKED OUT quite as Curtis Levi had expected, and the American rocket scientist was beginning to have serious doubts about what he'd done. Ahead of him Boris Stavropol led the way up the aged stone steps. Levi followed, with the three Korean Intelligence officers who had been assigned to the Russian in Seoul bringing up the rear. Levi studied the rock walls of the corridor as he walked, thinking they looked like the hallway of an ancient castle. Which indeed, he assumed, this building must be. He had caught a glimpse of the exterior as they had hurried him out of the car and into the building. Renovations were under way to both exterior and interior, and he knew the structure had to be many hundreds of years old.

Levi slowed as they reached a landing, pausing to try to catch a flash of whatever lay on the other side of the window. He had no idea where he was, and that bothered him. He suspected that he was in Pyongyang, but he couldn't be certain. Crossing the border had taken time; there had been unexplained waits and delays before they'd finally started along the deserted winding road. Levi had guessed it was an ancient farm-to-market pathway that had fallen into disuse when Korea had been divided. But it had to be guarded—all possible routes from North to South had at least a roving patrol, and he assumed that the delays had come while men were paid off, killed or both.

The thought caused him to shudder. Were men being *killed* because of what he had done? His brain told him yes—men were killed frequently in the world of clandestine operations, a world of which he knew so little. But his heart told him no, that was not happening.

It could not be happening. Men could not be killed because of anything *he* had done.

"Come." Stavropol suddenly tugged on Levi's arm, and he realized that even though he had been looking out the window, his mind had been elsewhere and he had seen nothing. He moved on up the steps, remembering the rest of the night. They had finally crossed the border, and after that, Stavropol and the North Korean agents with him had visibly relaxed. Levi, too, had relaxed, and before he knew it, had collapsed into an exhausted sleep. It had been daylight when he'd awakened, and they had already been in the city.

The Russian now quickly tugged him past the next landing window before he could look out. The pull angered the American. He wasn't being treated the way

he'd been promised. Stavropol had assured him that he
would receive a hero's welcome, not publicly perhaps,
but certainly within the confines of the clandestine
community. The Russian had said that the director of
the NK Intelligence service himself wanted to meet him,
and there had been talk of dinner parties with North
Korean leaders and dignitaries.

In short, Curtis Levi had been promised that he
would live a life of luxury impossible in the declining
economy of the United States. But so far, he'd seen
none of that, and it was beginning to make him angry.

Levi's toe caught on the edge of a step, and he tum-
bled forward, a gasp of pain escaping his lips. Stavropol reached out, catching him, and suddenly it dawned
on the American just how childishly he was thinking.

They had just performed a clandestine operation,
and while this was hardly his field of expertise, he knew
there were aspects of covert functions far more important than polite formalities. Time, speed, expertise—
these were the crucial elements of spy work, and proper
respect and reward had to take a back seat when one's
very life was on the line.

Curtis Levi began to feel better. Already one posi-
tive thing had happened. He had now taken part in a
real spy operation, had been the core of that operation, in fact. He had never been a risk taker, and at
times had secretly wondered if he might even be a
coward when it came to physical danger. Though his
intellect told him such thoughts were beneath him—
that the physical side of life was for brutes who lacked

the brains to perform intellectually—such occasional doubts had nagged at him.

Levi climbed the steps with pride as he realized he had now proved that he wasn't a coward. The smile on his face widened. A slight swagger entered his step.

He realized that Stavropol had noted the subtle physical changes that marked the surge in his confidence. He heard the Russian chuckle softly under his breath. Yes, Stavropol could see that he had thought things through and understood why he was being treated the way he was. Stavropol could see that he knew this treatment was only temporary. The man might not be the intellectual equal of a Curtis Levi, but he was no dummy, either.

In fact, Stavropol was smart. He knew Curtis Levi was smart, and the two men had bonded in mutual respect.

Levi turned his smile to the Russian and returned the chuckle. A quizzical look passed briefly across Stavropol's face.

A moment later they were walking down a dimly lit hallway. One of the Koreans hurried past them, fished a key from his pocket and inserted it into a thick wooden door. A moment later Levi found himself in a sparsely furnished room. A bed stood against one of the stone walls. The lone chair in the middle of the floor was the only other furniture.

Levi whirled toward the Russian, who had entered the room behind him, his mood suddenly sour again. Enough was enough. If they expected him to stay in this...this *cell* of a room, they were all sadly mistaken.

"Boris," Levi said, letting a good measure of sarcasm enter his voice, "I hope you don't think I'm staying here."

Stavropol smiled. "It is only temporary," he said.

Levi shook his head. "I'm sorry," he said, "but this is quite unacceptable. Even temporarily."

Stavropol shrugged. "It is I who am sorry, but it cannot be avoided. There are certain processing procedures that must be accomplished. Then you will be moved."

"No," Levi said simply. "I will not wait here. This is not what I was promised."

Stravropol's smile returned, but this time Levi thought it looked different. "I will return when we need you," he said.

Before Levi could speak again, the door closed behind the Russian. Levi heard the sound of tumblers turning.

Locked? Stavropol had locked the door! Locked him in! Why?

The American rocket scientist turned a full 360 degrees in shock, his eyes on the bare walls. His blood grew cold, his limbs heavy, as the reality of his situation began to sink in. Suddenly Curtis Levi realized that he was totally helpless, and the magnitude of his mistake hit him between the eyes like a ball-peen hammer.

Tears began to well in the American's eyes. He stared through them to the straight-backed chair in the center of the room. He started toward it, but his legs suddenly collapsed beneath him and he fell to a sitting position on the cold stone floor.

Levi's thoughts turned to his wife. Suddenly, putting up with a drunk who threw ashtrays at him didn't seem quite so bad. Suddenly his million-dollar home, his and Betty's matching BMWs and the sixty-foot yacht he had bought the month before seemed like more than any man deserved.

Certainly more than a traitor should have.

Curtis Levi fell face forward onto the cold stone floor. Wrapping his hands over the back of his head, he let the tears that had gathered in his eyes burst forth as if driven by the force of a waterfall.

CHAPTER FOUR

Two more slat-sided transport trucks rounded the curve and braked to a halt. Through the open ports around the beds of all three vehicles, Bolan saw men sitting crowded against the walls. Here and there the glistening silver chains that bound them together flashed in the fading sun.

Bolan nodded to himself. A prison transport. The men in the trucks were either criminals or political prisoners, or a mixture of both.

Soldiers in the khaki uniforms of the North Korean special-purpose forces—the Communist counterpart to Hwang's own outfit—jumped down from the cab of each vehicle. The barrels of their Type 58 assault rifles—Pyongyang's version of the Soviet AK-47—pointed at Hwang and Bolan.

Slowly and methodically a burly Korean climbed down from the passenger seat of the middle truck. The badges of rank atop his epaulets identified him as a lieutenant. His massive shoulders strained the fabric of the heavy wool blouse as he walked forward.

As he neared, Bolan saw the massive trapezius muscles that seemed to run straight to his ears, erasing his neck. The lieutenant was clean shaven, and appeared to be bald beneath the campaign cap that sat above his head. A cruel, lopsided smile covered his face.

The lieutenant shot his crooked grin down the road to the fiery vehicles, then turned and barked orders at two of his men. They took off at a trot to investigate.

Then he turned his attention back to the prisoners before him. Walking forward with the same slow confidence he had shown climbing down from the truck, the burly officer came to a halt in front of Bolan. In the same coarse voice that had ordered his troops down the road, he now asked a question in Korean.

Bolan looked up at him from where he was kneeling beside Hwang. The man was closer now, and the big American could see his eyes. Cold, hard, piggish eyes, they were set deep in his face and were surrounded by folds of skin. But what little Bolan could see gave him confidence.

The lieutenant's build, swagger and general bearing exuded confidence, but through the windows to his soul Bolan saw a coward, a man who would cringe or turn and run if he didn't have the advantage.

The lieutenant barked again in Korean. Bolan shook his head.

The lieutenant's fist shot out with the quickness of a snake to smash against his cheek. Well over two hundred pounds of muscle was behind the blow, and Bolan found himself lying on the ground next to Hwang. Blood filled his mouth, and as he rose to a sitting position, his vision blurred.

The lieutenant repeated whatever words he had just said.

Hwang Su suddenly opened his eyes and sat up, looking upward at the husky man. He spoke to Bolan in Russian. "He wants to know who we are."

Bolan nodded his understanding, then answered in the same language, careful how he phrased his words. For all he knew, the lieutenant spoke Russian as well as he did. "Tell him," he said. "Explain that we were in the South negotiating the trade agreement, and that we were attacked by bandits on our way back."

As Bolan had suspected, a translation was unnecessary. The lieutenant looked down and said, "You are Russian?"

Bolan nodded.

The cruel grin intensified. "Then *you* explain."

"I've been employed by your government as an adviser. To assist Mr. Hwang." Bolan nodded at his companion.

The lieutenant shook his head. "I know nothing of any trade agreement," he said.

Bolan kept his voice pleasant. "So what is unusual about that?" he asked. "My government does not tell me everything it does. Does yours?"

The lieutenant ignored the question, instead addressing the statement that had preceded it. "*Your* government is no longer in existence, which is why you have come to mine begging employment." When Bolan didn't answer, the lieutenant said, "Do you have any proof of what you say?"

Bolan nodded toward the burning Firenza. The fire was a mixed blessing. It would keep the North Koreans from discovering their weapons, but it was also destroying the documentation of their undercover stories.

The two men who had hurried to investigate the fires came running back. They spoke in Korean, but Bolan caught their officer's name. Lieutenant Han. Han listened, then turned back to Hwang and Bolan. "They say there are bodies of what appear to be bandits. Perhaps your story is true."

Bolan and Hwang waited.

"And perhaps it is not. Tell me how two unarmed diplomats defeated a well-planned trap led by well-armed and experienced bandits."

Bolan looked up at him. "I have not always been a diplomat," he said. "I served proudly with Spetsnaz. And Mr. Hwang was once a member of your own forces."

Han chuckled. "Perhaps. Nevertheless, I think you should accompany us." He turned to walk away.

Hwang stood up suddenly, speaking in Russian. "Lieutenant," he said haughtily. "It is obvious you simply do not know who I *am*."

Bolan held his breath as Han turned back to face them. Hwang had decided to pull a rank bluff and attempt to intimidate Han by his position. Maybe it would work, maybe it wouldn't. In any case, they had nothing to lose.

Hwang's voice grew even more self-important. "Lieutenant, we have no desire to accompany you. I order you to immediately provide us with one of your trucks. Otherwise, I will be forced to file a formal complaint upon our return to Pyongyang."

Han's smile grew harder. Bolan watched his eyes, seeing the brain behind them consider the possibilities that their story might be true, and that it could spell trouble for him. Then a light seemed to flash in those small, brutal irises, and it was clear that the lieutenant had made a decision.

Han walked forward with the same deliberate pace as before, stopping directly in front of Hwang Su. "Then perhaps you should not return to Pyongyang," he said simply. Drawing the Type 68 7.62 mm pistol from the flap holster at his side, he swung it around in a slow arc that ended against the side of Hwang's head. Hwang's eyes closed, and he slumped to the ground, but the lieutenant didn't stop there. His expression changed to that of a rabid dog as he struck the unconscious man again, then again.

Bolan reached up, blocking the next blow. He received a blow against the temple for his effort.

Fuzzy clouds started to descend over his eyes. His head felt as if it were filled with helium, and suddenly his stomach seemed to be rolling.

Then all was black.

THE STENCH of unwashed bodies filled the air as the truck bounced over the potholes in the road. Bolan glanced toward the open portal that led to the cab. The same pair of Oriental eyes that had watched him since he had regained consciousness looked back.

Bolan glanced away. He felt the sticky drying blood on the side of his face as he surveyed the other men jammed into the vehicle's cargo area. An even twenty pairs of eyes stared down at the floor. The faces around those eyes were gray with pain, and many showed the signs of recent torture—black eyes, scarred faces, burn marks and cuts were the rule rather than the exception. Each man's hands were handcuffed in front of his body, with a thick steel chain running through loops in the center of the cuffs' smaller chain.

Bolan's gaze fell on Hwang Su. The South Korean undercover specialist had been trussed in place directly across from him, against the door. Next to him sat a tall, angular Oriental. Hwang hadn't yet regained consciousness following the pistol whipping.

Bolan glanced back to the window.

The eyes still watched.

He took a deep breath, then closed his eyes and let his head fall forward. He knew what he had to do— knew the only chance he and Hwang Su had—and knew it couldn't be done while the eyes on the other side of the window observed him.

Five minutes went by, then ten, as the convoy bumped down the untended road. Bolan waited, listening and bouncing each time the tires dropped down into another deep hole in the road. He had been to North Korea before and knew that highway maintenance and other programs designed to help the average citizen had never been a high priority.

But the highway to Pyongyang seemed even worse now than he remembered. Just another indication that North Korean funds were being used elsewhere. And Bolan knew where. Building a nuclear-weapons program that could hold the world hostage didn't come cheap.

From the front of the cargo area came the sound of the window sliding shut. Bolan waited an additional ten seconds, then opened one eye to a slit. Convinced the hole would remain shut—at least for a while—he opened the other eye.

He raised his hands to the end of the chain, trying vainly to reach the straight pin inside his lapel that Hwang had given to him to open the hidden weapons compartments in the Firenza. It was no longer needed in that role, but if he could reach it, perhaps it would serve another purpose.

His reach stopped six inches short of his goal. But when he moved his hands forward in front of his body, he found the chain had far more slack.

He glanced across the truck to the row of men facing him. Hwang Su's head still bobbed with the rhythm of the truck. His eyes were closed.

"Hwang?" Bolan called softly.

The man next to the South Korean looked up briefly, then dropped his eyes again. Hwang didn't respond.

Bolan took a deep breath. They had to escape if they expected to live and continue with the mission of retrieving Curtis Levi. And they had the *means* to escape—he had already designed a plan. But he would need help, and with Hwang still out for the count, that meant enlisting the aid of at least one of the prisoners.

Bolan studied the men again. They still stared listlessly at the floor. Who were they—criminals or political opponents of the Communist government? He had to know in order to decide how to deal with them.

With another deep breath, Bolan whispered in Russian. "Tell me who you are."

The tall, rawboned man to Hwang's side recognized the language. "You are Russian?" he said clearly in the language.

Bolan nodded. "Who are you?"

The man glanced toward the window. "My name is Sang Rhee," he whispered.

Bolan leaned closer to him. "Why are you held prisoner?"

Sang studied the American carefully, and Bolan could see he was trying to decide how frank he should be. The prisoners had doubtless heard the conversation between him, Hwang and Han, and probably wondered as much as the lieutenant himself if their story about being diplomats was on the level.

Finally Sang Rhee shrugged his shoulders. Bolan took the movement to mean the Korean realized he had nothing to lose by being honest. "We are members of the Hwarang Warriors for a New Korea," he answered.

Bolan sat back. He had heard of the resistance movement named after the sixth-century warriors of Silla, the southernmost of the three kingdoms that preceded a united Korea. Similar to Japan's samurai, they had followed a code of ethics known as the *hwarang-do*. The Hwarang had been the enemies of the northern kingdom in the sixth century, and now their descendants continued to fight the North in the twentieth century.

Bolan started to speak but stopped when he heard the portal at the back of the cab sliding open. Letting his head fall forward again, he closed his eyes.

He could almost feel the gaze of the man who checked the back of the truck. A moment later the door slid shut again.

Stretching as far forward against the chain as he could, Bolan whispered even more softly this time. "Where are we headed?"

Sang Rhee gave another listless shrug Bolan had seen earlier. "I do not know," he said. "But it does not matter. The ride will end in our deaths."

Bolan shook his head. "Not necessarily." He stretched again. "Lean forward," he commanded.

A quizzical look passed over Sang's eyes, but he obeyed.

"Just under my left lapel," the warrior whispered, "you will find a straight pin. I can't reach it. See if you can."

Sang glanced nervously toward the front of the truck, then strained forward. His cuffed hands hit the end of his chain and stopped.

Bolan strained to lean closer, suppressing a groan as the hard steel bit into his wrists. He was still an inch away from Sang's outstretched fingers. Shaking his head, he sat back.

He let his wrists relax a moment, then shrugged his shoulders, at the same time twisting his body violently to the right. The tail of his sport coat shot out from behind his back to the side, and the lapel in front of him dropped slightly.

Sang had watched the movement and leaned forward again. Bolan stretched to meet him. "Careful," Bolan warned as the Hwarang Warrior's bony fingers found his lapel. "Drop it and we're dead."

The Korean resistance man nodded. Sweat broke out on his forehead as he continued to strain, moving his fingers slowly up the lapel in search of the pin. A second later he winced as the point pricked his skin. A second after that, the wince turned to a smile.

The smile disappeared quickly as the trapdoor slid open again. Both men jerked back to their sides of the truck.

When the spot-check was over and the door again closed, Bolan and Sang leaned forward to repeat the painful and painstaking procedure. Bolan saw the pin come free of his coat to shine in the light inside the truck. "Give it to me," he whispered.

Sang tried to hand him the pin, but the angle was wrong. No matter how hard he strained, Bolan could not twist his wrist toward the extended pin. His jaw tightened. He had two choices.

He could spread his fingers and have Sang stick the pin between them, then clamp his fingers shut to hold it in place. But the movement would be clumsy, and the chance of dropping the pin to the floor more than likely.

There was another way.

He shook his head to tell Sang to stop his movements. Then, looking into the Hwarang Warrior's eyes, he whispered, "Jab it into the back of my hand."

Sang's eyebrows lowered in momentary dislike, then rose again in understanding. He knew there was no other safe way to make the transfer.

Taking a deep breath, Sang jabbed the pin into the back of the hand.

Bolan ignored the pain as he felt the point penetrate his skin between the bones that led to his index and middle fingers. "Push harder," he said. "Make sure it won't fall out."

Sang looked up. His eyes hardened. Then he jabbed the pin halfway into the back of the outstretched hand.

Bolan felt the pin lodge securely. He nodded to Sang, and both men set back. Bringing his hands close to his body, where the chain had more slack, and lifting the fingers of his right hand over the left, he jerked the straight pin from his hand.

Sang Rhee shook his head and let out a silent whistle. "As the sage of legend said," he whispered, "in the truly enlightened, pain does not exist unless the mind allows it."

Bolan ignored him, immediately working the pin down into the keyhole of his cuffs. A second later the steel restraints clicked open, and he pulled his wrists free, letting the handcuffs dangle from the loop through which they had passed.

Looking up, he saw that the activity had drawn the eyes of the other men from the floor. Something—noise or the shifting weight of his and Sang's bodies—had also alerted the men in the cab.

The trapdoor began sliding open again.

Bolan grasped the handcuffs and jammed them between his legs, closing his knees around them and his hands. He closed his eyes, wondering if the man who stared through the opening would be able to see that the restraints were off. He didn't think so, but there was no way to be sure from the angle at which he sat.

A voice barked through the hole in Korean, then the door closed again.

Bolan opened his eyes and saw that Hwang was conscious once more.

"He ordered us to remain still," the undercover man said. "I suggest we violate that order."

Even under the circumstances, the Executioner couldn't keep the ghost of a smile from his face.

Free of both cuffs and chain now, Bolan leaned across the truck and worked the pin into the cuffs around Hwang's wrists. When the undercover man's hands were free, he moved to Sang. The Hwarang Warrior rubbed his wrists as soon as the steel came off. Bolan had started to release the next man in the row when the trucks began to slow. He barely got back into his seat, his hands and the loose cuffs hidden between his legs, when the door opened again.

Bolan opened his eyes as soon as it became obvious the convoy was stopping. Through the windows he saw that they were in a valley. Beyond the truck, green trees were visible, but a foul odor permeated the air in seeming defiance of the beauty of the area.

To most, the odor would have been a mystery. But Bolan had experienced it too many times in the past to not identify it now.

The odor came from decaying human bodies.

The eyes at the portal suddenly moved away, and Bolan heard the truck doors opening. He looked toward the men he had freed, then whispered in Russian, "As soon as the door is opened." Hwang and Sang, he knew, would understand him. The others might not, but they'd realize what was happening soon enough.

At least Bolan hoped it would be soon enough.

The sound of scraping steel echoed as the bolt outside the rear door was drawn free of the lock. Bolan jammed his right hand into his pants pocket, his fingers curling around the T-grip of the COMTECH Stinger.

A second later the door started to swing backward.

Bolan and Hwang helped it.

Sang was right behind them as the big American and Hwang dived from the truck into the two surprised guards at the rear. Bolan landed on top of a soldier with a stringy mustache. Raising his fist high over his head, he hooked down with the Stinger.

The hard plastic nose of the weapon made contact with the bridge of the guard's nose. Bone and cartilage crunched as blood spurted from the man's nostrils. His face turned to the side.

Bolan looped a right hook into the man's temple, feeling the nose of the Stinger punch through the skin. The guard beneath him froze in death.

Pocketing the Stinger, the Executioner wrenched the Type 58 assault rifle from the man's hands as they went limp. Hwang had also appropriated the rifle of another North Korean guard.

Bolan did a quick recon of their position. Their vehicle had been the last of the three-truck convoy, and the other two transport vehicles had parked in line just ahead of them. Even now, guards from those vehicles were about to open the rear doors. For the moment the men in front of them had not noticed what was happening around the last truck.

The break didn't last long.

Bolan turned his rifle toward the truck ahead of them as a special-forces guard suddenly looked up. As the man went for his holstered pistol, a quick 3-round burst was discharged by Bolan's rifle. The guard took all three rounds inside a circle in the center of his chest the size of a half dollar.

The rest of the North Koreans turned toward the explosions, and suddenly a full-scale conflict erupted.

Lieutenant Han dived between the wheels of the first transport vehicle as Bolan cut loose with a steady stream of autofire. Bolan's rounds moved from a thin man wearing sergeant's stripes to a stockier special-forces guard. The 7.62 mm slugs cut through their midsections, sending them spinning up against the sides of the trucks before they fell for good.

Close to Bolan, Hwang opened up with the other guard's Type 58, and the driver of the lead transport fell, a red, pulpy mass where his head had once been. Then Hwang turned and scurried to the other side of the vehicle to cover their flank. Sang suddenly dashed up to scoop up the NK assault rifle from the hands of the downed sergeant.

Bolan waved the Hwarang Warrior around to the other side to help Hwang, then moved cautiously forward. The firing from the front of the convoy had died down as quickly as it had begun. They had taken out all the guards, but Han was waiting, hidden somewhere beneath the first vehicle.

A moment later a volley of fire came from the other side of the line. A low moan followed as the explosions died down. Judging by the sound, it was a Type 58, but the Executioner still didn't know who had been on the receiving end of the rounds. All the prisoners who remained on their feet now had access to the Korean-style Kalashnikov rifles.

Bolan stopped his advance next to the front fender of the middle truck. Proceeding farther would expose his feet to Han's fire from beneath the lead vehicle. *If* Han was still beneath the lead vehicle. It could have been the burly lieutenant who had fired the last volley. He could have rolled back out on the other side of the truck, taken out both Hwang and Sang and even now be making his way rearward.

A sudden flash of color in his peripheral vision prompted Bolan to swing his rifle over the hood of the truck. His finger took up the slack in the trigger, stopping just short of firing when he saw both Hwang Su and Sang.

"Han?" Bolan silently mouthed at the men.

Sang shook his head. Hwang pointed toward the bottom of the first truck, then whispered something to Sang in Korean. The Hwarang Warrior nodded, training his rifle barrel toward the ground just behind the lead vehicle. Not wishing to expose himself to Han's fire from below, Hwang Su leaped up onto the hood of the truck and crawled over to Bolan.

"Han is beneath that truck," he said.

Bolan nodded. "I saw him duck under, but if we go after him, one of us will die."

Hwang looked up at the taller man incredulously. "You plan to let him go free?"

"No. I plan to let him surrender."

A sudden realization came over Hwang's face. "Give him the chance, then," he said. "He will take it—his *ki* is weak."

Bolan nodded. *Ki* was the word for "life force" in both Korean and Japanese. And he had seen that same weakness of spirit in Han himself.

Bolan moved out to the side of the truck, careful to keep out of range of whatever weapon Han might have. He spoke in Russian. "Han, this is your one and only chance. Throw out any weapons you have and come out."

After a brief pause a frightened voice answered, "You will kill me!"

"No," Bolan said. "You have my word."

"Your friend—Hwang—he will kill me," the voice whimpered.

Hwang answered in Russian, as well. "Not if you come out voluntarily. You have my word."

After another long pause, Han said, "There was a third man. I saw him. One of the other prisoners."

Bolan turned to Sang. The Hwarang Warrior's face hardened, and he shook his head. "I cannot promise," he said. "Not after what this man has done to both me and my men. Would you like to see the scars beneath my clothing? Would you like to see the evidence of what this man has done—?"

Bolan cut him off before he could finish. "Promise him," he said.

The same enlightenment Bolan had seen on Hwang's face suddenly fell across Sang's. He turned to the truck ahead, leaning over to make sure his voice carried beneath the bumper. "Han," he growled, "I hate you for what you have done—for what you represent. And I will not promise not to kill you if we meet again. But for today—" he drew a deep breath "—I will not harm you."

The Type 68 pistol came skidding out first. Next came a combat knife, and finally a gaudy Chinese switchblade.

"That is his favorite," Sang growled, leaning over and scooping up the knife. He pressed the latch, and the blade sprang into view.

There were dried bloodstains on the cold steel.

Sang held the switchblade in front of him. "Han is very talented with this weapon," he said. "Especially if his victim is tied to a chair."

Bolan turned back to face the truck. Stooping slightly, he called out beneath the bumper, "Your turn, Han."

Slowly, his features twisted by anxiety, the muscular lieutenant crawled out from beneath the vehicle. "You have lied," he said, tears filling his eyes. "You will kill me." His massive shoulders shook uncontrollably.

Bolan shook his head, almost embarrassed at the man's cowardice. Muscles, physical strength—they were a vital part of the warrior's arsenal. But without the courage to use a weapon, that weapon became useless.

Bolan turned to Hwang. "Gather up weapons, spare ammo and anything else that looks like it might be of use. We'll split everything with the Hwarang men. Then go get the first truck started."

Hwang nodded and hurried out of sight.

Bolan kept his rifle trained on Han. "Sang," he said, "don't you have something you need to do?"

Sang nodded, then disappeared behind the big American.

A new terror invaded the lieutenant's eyes. "*You* may keep your word," he blurted out to Bolan. "But *he*—" he pointed toward Sang "—will not. He will come back and kill me."

"No, he won't," Bolan said. "You've got my word on that, too."

Sang reappeared in time to hear the comment. "He will not have to prevent me from killing you," he said to Han. "I gave my word. I am a Hwarang warrior. My word is my bond, and I will not violate it."

Ahead the lead truck's engine kicked over. Hwang's arm shot through the driver's-side window, waving him forward. Bolan looked back to Sang. "I'd like you to come with us," he said. "We could use a man who knows his way around the country."

Sang smiled. "Why not? I have business to attend to in Pyongyang, and since I am not going to kill this man—"

Han broke in. "Then…I am free to go?" he asked, looking back and forth between the two men anxiously.

Bolan shrugged as he walked past the man. "Okay by me," he said.

Behind him Sang said, "I will not stop you."

The Executioner paused as he started to cut between the trucks toward the passenger side of the truck Hwang had started. The rear door opened, and a man he recognized from the truck he'd been in stepped out. The other prisoners—now freed of their restraints—followed.

Looking back, Bolan saw the rest of the Hwarang Warriors pouring from the backs of the other two trucks. They gathered just behind Sang, then began spreading out to encircle Lieutenant Han.

Sang turned and handed the switchblade to the closest man, a limping warrior with fresh knife slashes covering his face and arms.

"You gave me your word!" Han whined, falling to his knees. "The word of a Hwarang Warrior. The code! The code!"

"And I will abide by the code and keep my word," Sang said, stepping back. "I will not harm you." He paused, then added, "But I cannot speak for these men who you forgot to ask." He pushed past Han and joined Bolan.

Bolan and Sang circled the truck and jumped up into the cab. As Hwang Su threw the vehicle into gear, the first of what Bolan guessed would be many screams echoed through the valley.

HAL BROGNOLA WAS NOT a man prone to frequent bouts of heavy laughter. He enjoyed a good joke as much as the next guy, but the evidence of his amusement rarely made it to his battle-hardened face.

Now, however, as he sat behind his desk in the U.S. Department of Justice and pressed the telephone against his ear, he felt his chest heave and threaten to send howls from his lips. "Bear, you want to run that by me again?" he said into the phone.

On the other end of the line, at Stony Man Farm, Aaron Kurtzman was fighting hard to contain his own mirth. "You heard me right, Hal," he said. "Rhee Yuk's got a post-office box under another name. It all comes there, and according to North Korean Intel, he checks the box every day."

Brognola's smile turned to a frown of concentration. Somehow the computer wizard of Stony Man Farm had hacked his way into the North Korean State Department personnel files, in the process learning far more than he'd ever expected to learn about Rhee Yuk. Well, that was okay. You couldn't know *too* much about a man in a situation like this, and the new knowledge might help. "Any other details?" the Justice man asked.

Kurtzman coughed on the other end. "Just that the North Koreans seem to know all about the box. The kicker is, Rhee doesn't know they know. Who knows how they got the info, but my guess is they decided to keep it to themselves in case they needed to threaten him someday...twist his arm on something." He paused to clear his throat. "Not an unusual Communist procedure."

"Right," Brognola agreed. "But you're sure they don't suspect him of being a South Korean mole?" Brognola asked.

"Of course, there's no way to be certain," Kurtzman replied. "But there's no indication of that here. And that's *not* the kind of thing they'd sit on. In any case, I think if they had any misgivings about him, there'd at least be a hint here."

The big Fed lifted the half-chewed cigar from the ashtray next to his arm and stuck it between his teeth. The new Intel about Rhee's secret post-office box not only provided a way to contact the man, but it took care of another problem Brognola had been kicking around in his head. How was he going to convince a South Korean mole in North Korea to work for an American agent when he hadn't gone through South Korean channels? Well, the same arm-twisting that the North Koreans could do was also available to the U.S. when it came to Rhee's clandestine mailing address.

"Okay," the Justice man finally said. "But the mail's too slow and too risky. We'll have to send someone." He quit talking, considering the problem. Suddenly a light bulb flashed in his brain. "Where's Phoenix Force right now?" he asked.

"Just wrapped up that job outside Manila," Kurtzman said. "I don't know their exact status."

"Punch me through to Barb."

A moment later Brognola heard a buzz. Barbara Price, the Farm's mission controller, came on and said, "Yes, Hal?"

"Give me an update on Phoenix Force," the Stony Man director said.

"Everything went like clockwork," Price said. "They're catching a few hours' sleep in Manila. Grimaldi's about to take off to pick them up."

"Tell Grimaldi to cut the engines as soon as he crosses the California state line," Brognola said. "I want him to touch down at Beale AFB."

"Ninth Strategic Reconnaissance Wing?"

"Affirmative, Barb. He'll be picking up a U-2R. I'll clear it with the Ninth while he's in the air."

"Anything else?" Price asked.

"Not for Grimaldi," Brognola said. "But when you talk to Phoenix Force again, tell them the straws have been drawn."

"Excuse me?" Price said.

"Straws, Barb," Hal Brognola said, chomping down harder on his cigar. "Katz didn't want to quit the battlefield cold turkey, so he included himself in the draw. He drew the short one, and he's about to jump out of the U-2R and land in Communist North Korea."

BOLAN DIDN'T LIKE the situation, but it had been the only answer.

The uniforms of two of the special-forces men had fit Hwang and Sang well enough, and the blood had even come off with cold water from a stream they'd encountered. Both men would pass—at least visually—as North Korean soldiers. But Bolan's height, light skin and round eyes weren't going to convince anyone he was Oriental no matter what he wore. It would take a total facial reconstruction to pull that off, and Bolan doubted that they'd encounter a cosmetic surgeon on his way to a house call on the road to Pyongyang.

Through the open trap of the window, Bolan could see both Hwang and Sang. Earlier they had spoken Russian for his benefit, but now, as they began to ascend the bluffs above the Taedong River, the two Koreans had grown silent.

Bolan glanced down at his manacled wrists. Disguising himself as their prisoner had been the only way to go. But again he didn't like it. Even if he had one of the dead NK officers' handcuff keys taped under the cuff at his wrist, and a Type 68 pistol hidden under his jacket. But in reality, if anything went wrong, he knew he'd never be able to free himself and get into action in time to help.

Hwang's voice rose slightly as he slowed the truck. "First test coming up," he said. "Roadblock just ahead. Right before we enter the city."

Bolan forced himself to relax. Helplessness went against his nature, and while he might not be completely helpless, he was a lot closer than he liked to get. As the truck continued to grind down through its gears, he forced his mind on the city ahead.

Pyongyang, the capital of North Korea. *Communist* Korea. Already a thousand years old when Christ was born, Pyongyang had once been the capital of the whole peninsula. Now, as in so many ancient cities, the remains of stone walls, gateways and crumbling buildings still stood amid skyscrapers and other modern structures.

The strong odor of smelting steel wafted into the truck as they came to a complete halt, reminding him that the steel for modern construction was manufactured right there in the city. The mills of the city lay close to iron, coal, gold and copper mines. In conjunction with consumer-goods manufacturers and the agricultural-commodities-processing industry, the mines made Pyongyang North Korea's industrial, as well as political, capital.

Through the portal he caught a glimpse of the guard who stopped outside the window. A moment later Hwang rolled the window down and spoke in Korean. The two men conversed good-naturedly for a moment, then gradually both voices grew more hostile.

The guard kept glancing at the portal as he spoke. Bolan caught none of the words of the strange language.

The sound of both cab doors opening caused Bolan's hand to move closer to the handcuff key. A moment later the rear door opened, and Hwang and Sang flanked a man wearing the uniform of a North Korean regular. On his sleeves were the NK equivalent of corporal's stripes.

The corporal turned to Hwang, shook his head and spoke again.

Hwang let his breath out slowly through clenched teeth. This time when he spoke, his voice rose several octaves in anger, and Bolan picked up one word he recognized. *Han.*

At the sound of the name, the corporal visibly shrank back. He nodded vigorously, then spoke again, but softer.

A moment later, Hwang and Sang were back in the truck and being waved on into the capital of North Korea.

Hwang waited until they were out of earshot, then leaned back to the window. "Close call, Pollock," he advised. "The man wanted to see your transport papers." He paused. "I told him we picked you up alongside the road near the border and there weren't any. So he demanded to see *you.*"

"What changed his mind?" Bolan asked.

"I threatened him with my commanding officer." Hwang chuckled. "For the coward he is, Han certainly had his bluff in with these guys."

The sounds of traffic intensified as they entered the city. Bolan was unlocking his handcuffs when Sang turned around and stuck his hand through the window. "I wish to extend my thanks for what you have done," he said. "Not only for me, but for my men."

Bolan shook the hand. "Sang, there's a man in Pyongyang we have to find," he said. "A man named Rhee Yuk."

Sang nodded. "Hwang told me. I do not know Rhee, but I have heard the name. He is high in the State Department?"

"Yes," Bolan said.

Sang handed a scrap of paper through the open hole. "This hotel is operated by warriors of the Hwarang," he said, glancing down at the paper as Bolan took it. "Perhaps they can help you contact Rhee. Ask for Wonkwang. The code of trust is simple. Make a sentence using the words 'bird,' 'Vikings' and 'talisman' in that order. They will want to know who told you. Use my name, and tell them what happened."

Bolan frowned. "You aren't coming with us?"

Sang shook his head. "I must arrange for my men to be evacuated from the area where Han and the convoy were destroyed," he said. "Word of what has happened will spread, and then a massive manhunt will be launched. Anyone found in the area and suspected of taking part will be killed."

The Executioner looked down at the paper in his hand. He couldn't blame Sang for putting his own men's well-being ahead of him and Hwang. He might not have a formal commission, but Sang was a general. The safety of his own troops had to be his primary concern.

Sang's eyes flicked away from the window to the streets, then back to the window. "You must get rid of this vehicle at the first opportunity," he said. "Military trucks are not common so deep in the city. It will draw attention.''

The leader of the Hwarang Warriors turned back to Hwang. ''The next corner,'' he said. ''Please let me out there.''

A moment later the convoy truck stopped. The door opened, and Sang Rhee was gone.

CHAPTER FIVE

Through the slats along the walls of the truck bed, Bolan watched Pyongyang's downtown workers on their way home after another day of labor. They seemed dispirited and weary, and too drained or apathetic to share in any exuberant camaraderie. They looked cowed and subdued.

He shook his head as a combination of anger and sorrow filled his heart. The difference in the attitude he saw here, compared to the one in Seoul, was distinct to the keen observer. The South Koreans lived in fear—fear that the monster of the North might invade again someday to snatch away their freedom. They kept one eye on their work, the other glued toward the border, but they were alert, uncowed and energetic.

But the monster was already in Pyongyang, and had been since 1948. The people of North Korea had lost their freedom shortly after World War II, and they kept both eyes closed, going about their tasks in the hope the monster wouldn't notice and single them out for his wrath.

Yes, Bolan thought as the truck drove on, the monster who enslaved these people went by the name of communism, and he was like some medieval dragon whose mere existence meant terror for peasant and king alike. The dragon's brothers might have been slain in Poland, Romania, Czechoslovakia and other formerly Communist countries across the globe, but in the Democratic People's Republic of Korea the dragon refused to die.

At one intersection a uniformed police officer was directing traffic in place of a failed stoplight. He looked up at the truck and did a double take. His hand shot stiffly to his brow in salute, but Bolan could see the quizzical look on his face.

Sang had warned him about military trucks being unusual in downtown Pyongyang, Bolan thought. He stuck his face through the window into the cab as Hwang returned the cop's salute. "Find an alley somewhere," Bolan said. "We'd better dump this thing like Sang suggested."

Hwang nodded, driving on down the street. Two blocks later he turned onto a rutted brick pathway between two dark buildings, then ground to a halt. Bolan moved to the slats, looking up and down the narrow alley to make sure there were no curious eyes. Satisfied, he opened the rear door, dropped to the ground, and hurried into the cab.

Hwang had almost finished changing back into his civvies when Bolan slid in beside him and handed him the slip of paper Sang had given him. "You know the way?" Bolan asked.

Hwang shook his head. "No. I had a map of the city... but it burned up in the Firenza." He shrugged, looking down at the paper. "We can find it, though.

Let's go ask directions. I'll pretend to be from Kaesong or something."

Bolan nodded. "I'm sure *you* could pull it off," he said. "But have you thought about how you're going to explain a big pale-faced round-eyes?"

The South Korean undercover specialist chuckled, then turned serious. "We could try the Russian routine—"

Bolan shook his head. "That was for out in the boonies," he said. "And even then, Han didn't buy it. Here in the capital we're likely to run into some fairly sophisticated officials. My Russian's good, but not perfect—especially for a Russian high enough up the food chain to be hired by your government."

Hwang nodded. "I see your point."

Bolan glanced out the window. "I'll stay here. You go back out on the street and get directions, then we'll stick to alleys and side streets on our way there."

"Okay," Hwang said. "Weapons?"

Bolan glanced at the assault rifles on the floorboard. There would be no way to conceal them. "Just the pistols," he said. "Nothing we can't hide."

"Okay." Hwang patted his side where he'd stashed one of the Type 68s, opened the door, then turned back. "You'll be here in the truck when I get back?"

A tiny voice in the back of his brain told Bolan not to stay in the truck, but to get out—and *fast*. "No," he said. He looked through the window and spotted an industrial-size white trash bin. "I'll be in there."

Hwang followed his line of sight and nodded, exited the truck and hurried down the alley.

Bolan dropped down on the other side of the vehicle. He knew part of his apprehension came simply from the fact that Sang had warned them about the truck drawing attention this far inside the city. The caution that tip had triggered had been further fueled by the police officer's reaction a few blocks back.

Bolan hurried across the broken bricks, lifted the lid of the trash bin and looked inside. Except for remnants of trash at the bottom, it was empty. He smiled grimly as he climbed over the edge.

Once inside, he squatted, then pulled the lid down over him. He breathed quietly, evenly, waiting for his eyes to adjust to the near-darkness. The only illumination was the few rays of the setting sun that made it through splits in the welding at the corners, but soon his eyes adjusted.

Bolan listened to the sounds of a city closing down for the day as he waited. Sang's warning and the cop's quizzical expression were both good reasons to increase caution. But there was more to his concern than that. Even if he hadn't been warned or seen the cop, the uneasy feeling would have been there.

Sometimes the well-trained soldier noticed tiny details and recognized them consciously. But more often than not, it occurred on a deeper level. The battle sense kicked in for no apparent reason. It was those times, Bolan knew, that the unconscious mind had picked up a threat and relayed the information to the brain. And the unconscious mind saw no reason to explain. It merely provided a warning.

Footsteps sounded at the end of the alley. His hand dropped instinctively to the Korean pistol at the small of his back. He turned slightly, trying to look through one of the cracks along the corner seam. Too dark. He could make out no details—just a silhouette approaching.

It could have been Hwang. The shadow was the right size, but Bolan's battle sense said no.

As the footsteps drew closer, he pressed his face closer to the corner of the trash bin. The dark form moving down the alley had left his field of vision, but he heard the distinctive sound of a flap holster unsnap. Steel brushed against leather as a pistol was drawn.

A voice spoke with authority in Korean, then silence fell over the alley again. The voice spoke again, louder, angry and a little frightened this time. A second later Bolan heard one of the convoy truck's doors pulled open.

He slid the pistol back into his belt and drew the COMTECH Stinger. It was a cop in the alley—the sound of the flap-holster snap had convinced him of that. It might even be the same cop he'd seen just before they left the street.

The truck door slammed shut, and there was a rustling sound. Then a radio squelch screeched, meaning a walkie-talkie had been turned on. The same voice that had shouted the orders spoke again, and was answered over the airwaves.

Transferring the Stinger to his left hand, Bolan pulled the Spyderco Centofante from his pocket, gripping the closed knife in his fist so that the ends extended top and bottom like a *yawara* stick. The officer had discovered the abandoned truck and radioed for backup. Soon the alley would be flooded with Communist cops. Canvasing the area would be a routine matter of procedure, and sooner or later they'd check the bin.

When they did, Bolan would have no place to run.

He gripped both hand-held weapons tighter. His only chance was for the cop in the alley to check the bin now, before his backup arrived. So far, the man had shown no interest in doing so.

That meant it was time for Bolan to create an interest.

He tapped lightly against the metal side of the bin. He felt, rather than heard, the unseen man in the alley turn toward him. From deep in his throat, he let a low moan of anguish escape his lips.

Footsteps started hesitantly his way.

The Executioner groaned again. The footsteps stopped just outside the bin. Bolan could hear the officer trying to control his breathing, could practically smell the fear that emanated from the man on the other side of the thin steel. Less than a foot away, Bolan knew he was trying to assess the situation and determine the proper course of action.

Normally a city policeman would wait for backup to arrive before risking a search of the alley. Yet this man clearly felt compelled to see if someone needed assistance. But it was dark and he was alone. Had he actually heard something, or were his ears playing tricks on him?

All these questions would be racing through the officer's mind as he tried to make his decision. Bolan helped him make up his mind by moaning again.

Slowly the lid of the trash bin began to rise. It moved up an inch, then shot back to clang loudly against the bricks of the building behind it. The barrel and front blade sight of another Type 68 pistol appeared above the rim. A split second later the policeman's frightened eyes moved into sight.

Bolan rose swiftly, bringing his right arm out to the side, then around in a vicious hammer-hand strike. The top of the closed Centofante struck the back of the cop's gun hand.

The police officer started to scream, but Bolan shot a straight left forward. The tip of the Stinger caught the man just above the bridge of the nose. The cop's eyes rolled back in his head, and he slumped to the ground, unconscious.

Bolan reached down and fished the cop's pistol from the garbage at the bottom of the bin. Then he was over the side, but hearing a sound at the end of the alley, he dropped to a squat, the Type 68 gripped in both hands.

Hwang turned the corner into view and jogged toward him. When he came to a halt next to the bin, he looked down at the cop, then back at the truck.

There was no need to explain the obvious. "Let's get out of here," Bolan said. "The guy already radioed in."

Hwang nodded, but as they turned back in the direction from which the Korean had come, four more uniformed cops suddenly appeared.

Bolan grabbed Hwang's shoulder and jerked him around toward the other end of the alley. They sprinted forward. One of the men behind them shouted, and another blew a shrill police whistle. Bolan and Hwang increased their pace.

Two shots exploded behind them. Bolan felt one of the rounds whizz past his ear before striking the brick wall.

As they pounded down the alley, the Executioner's eyes searched the exit to the street ahead. It was empty. Apparently all of the officers who had come as backup had entered the alley together.

Ten feet from the street, Hwang Su panted, "We'll make it, Pollock! We're gonna—"

The undercover man halted in midsentence as six new cops suddenly appeared and spread across the alley in a human wall that blocked their escape.

RHEE YUK LIFTED THE PEN to sign the last of the stack of State Department documents. He scrawled his name, then twisted in his chair to hand the forms to his new secretary and started to speak. The expression on the woman's face stopped him cold.

Rhee studied her briefly. *Fear*. What spawned it? He had seen it on her face ever since she'd arrived three days ago. It was more than the new job, and more than just the ongoing apprehension experienced by anyone who worked within the Communist system. It was something about him personally that terrified Li Fon.

Did she sense his secret?

Rhee decided to find out. "Fon," he said softly, "is there something about me that bothers you?"

The direct question surprised her. Her skin darkened several shades, and she turned her eyes away. He reached up, turning her face gently back to his, then removed his hand. "Please," he said. "You may speak freely."

The secretary kept her face where it was but cast her eyes down. "You are so—" she started to say, then caught herself and stopped, looking up in embarrassment.

"Please," Rhee Yuk said. "Go on."

Fon's eyes shot to the floor again. She took a deep breath. "Masculine," she said suddenly, then stopped.

"Please," Rhee said. "Your words will never leave this office."

"You are like a . . . like a *bear*," Fon almost whispered. "Big and strong and virile. I am . . . attracted to you!" Her head hung in shame.

Rhee reached out, taking her hand, relief shooting through his body like a heroin rush. Li Fon didn't sense his secret. Quite the contrary, she wanted him to seduce her.

"Thank you," Rhee said softly. "You are very kind, and I am highly complimented. You are quite attractive yourself."

Fon looked up and smiled.

"But you realize that we can never be . . ."

Rhee saw the hope that had suddenly materialized in the woman disappear just as quickly. It was replaced by confusion. "But . . . you are not married," she stammered. "I am single. You say I am attractive, then why can't—"

"Because the Party frowns on fraternization such as this between co-workers," Rhee said.

Fon looked back down to the floor. "They frown," she almost whispered. "They do not *forbid.*"

Rhee sighed. "No, they do not forbid it. But for me, a frown is enough. You must realize, Fon, that my first loyalty—my *wife*—is the Party."

Fon looked up, a tear forming in the corner of her eye. She quickly gathered the signed papers and hurried from the room.

Rhee stared at the door Fon had closed behind her as the anxiety suddenly returned in waves. His heart hammered against his chest, and he opened the top drawer of his desk for the bottle of sedatives. Two went down his throat with the liquid that remained in his teacup.

Traps, traps and more traps. They were everywhere, Rhee realized as the tension mounted in him. He couldn't risk romantic involvement. Li Fon might well be a government spy checking up on him, but even if she weren't, there were a thousand other ways a romance might give him away. Suppose he talked in his sleep?

Rhee turned to the clock. A sigh of relief escaped his lips when he realized the workday was over, but that sigh did little to relieve the trepidation in his chest. It was time to go home. But first he would make his daily stop at the post-office box. Perhaps the package he ordered had arrived.

The South Korean smiled. *That* would help alleviate the stress.

Moving quickly to the closet, Rhee grabbed his briefcase, hurried past Li Fon in the outer office and left the building.

He started down the street, zigzagging nervously through the crowd of workers on their way home. Today had been even worse than most days. At one point he had almost been convinced that even the janitor knew his secret. His brain had told him that was silly, but his emotions had screamed *No! The threat is real!*

Stress. Tension. He lived in daily fear for his life, and it seemed the line between reality and illusion grew thinner each day.

Rhee hurried down the sidewalk toward the post-office, dodging other workers on their way home. He passed a restaurant, and the strong odor of kimchi wafted out through the open door. He inhaled deeply, feeling hungry in his brain if not in his ulcerated stomach.

The South Korean mole felt momentarily dizzy, and the realization that he was overdue for another blood-pressure check crossed his mind. He considered, then discarded the idea of a fast detour to the clinic. The doctor would just change his medication from the old pills to new ones that didn't work, either.

Rhee smiled suddenly, a thought crossing his mind. One thing always worked to calm him down. But it was dangerous, even more dangerous than the post-office box. So dangerous that he reserved it for those days when he realized he was reaching the pop-off point.

Suddenly his heart hammered harder. His vision blurred, and he felt light-headed. He stopped in his tracks, trying to catch his breath, and as he did, he made his decision. Today was one of those days. He had reached his limit.

Glancing at his watch, Rhee realized he still had time. Yes, he could go to the club and still have time for a drink and a dance—perhaps even two. He could still make it to the post office before it closed for the night.

He cut down a side street, then another, before ducking into an alley. He looked cautiously both ways to make sure no one was watching, then hurried toward what appeared to be the rear entrance to a warehouse. Even in the cool evening air, sweat broke out on the back of his neck.

A small black buzzer was set just beside the door. His hand shaking, Rhee reached up and pressed it. A small window opened, and a set of feminine, heavily made-up eyes stared listlessly out at him.

The bolt slid back in the lock, and the door swung open.

Rhee hurried down the dark hallway to the stairs. Music, voices, and the sound of clinking glasses drifted down from above. The excitement in his soul began to chase away the anxiety as he mounted the steps, then darted into the rest room just outside the door to the club.

Here. This was the only place he could be himself. Here he could forget that he was Rhee Yuk, South Korean deep-cover intelligence agent, and at least for a few hours be the man he was meant to be.

He opened his briefcase with one hand as he loosened his tie with the other. The club had both formal and semiformal nights, but tonight the dress would be casual. And although the atmosphere was relaxed— accepting of individuality and even eccentricity—it was important to dress appropriately. Once he had changed, Rhee hurried into the club, checking his briefcase with the chubby middle-aged blonde at the window just inside the door. She handed him a ticket, the rough skin of her hand brushing his as she did.

Rhee winced. He liked blondes. But he liked them younger. The crone checking hats was definitely *not* his type.

His heart pounded harder, but now it felt good. It seemed that every pore in his body had been injected with some mild stimulant as he walked swiftly to the bar, ordered a Scotch and water, then turned back toward the tables.

Their eyes met immediately.

The blonde sat alone at a table at the back, looking directly at him. The features were Oriental, which told Rhee the hair had to be from a bottle. Maybe even a wig. He didn't care. Love, after all, was itself an illusion.

Still staring deeply into his eyes, the blonde uncrossed her legs, then languorously recrossed them in the other direction. In the brief instant that they were in motion, Rhee saw the shimmer of smooth flesh and a tiny triangle of hair.

"No panties?" he whispered out loud to himself. The lust that suddenly swept over him chased away more of his tension.

The blonde smiled, nodded and beckoned him across the room with a delicate wave of the hand.

The walk to her table took an eternity, but during it Rhee said goodbye to the last remnants of anxiety. By the time he sat down and took her hand in his, he had left the world of the double agent and entered another. A world that was far more pleasant. A relaxed world where he could be himself.

"Would you like to go into one of the back rooms?" the beautiful face asked.

Rhee nodded.

They rose and disappeared through a door.

When he emerged an hour later, Rhee Yuk's heart beat normally. His stomach no longer hurt, and his vision had cleared. He retrieved his briefcase and started for the rest room, then glanced at his watch and stopped.

He had spent more time at the club than he'd intended. He could still make the post office if he hurried, but he wouldn't have time to change.

The South Korean mole hurried out of the club feeling better than he had in days. His footsteps felt lighter as he went toward the post office, his mind still on the club. As he rounded a corner, two men suddenly shot past, forcing him against the building. They were followed a few seconds later by several police officers who looked far more tired than the men they chased.

Rhee reminded himself it was none of his affair and continued at the same quick pace. Ten minutes later he entered the post office and immediately went to his box. Stooping over, he inserted his key. The door swung open, and he was mildly surprised to see the receptacle empty. He had been certain the package would arrive today.

"Rhee Yuk."

The voice behind Rhee bore an unusual accent. French, but tinged with the Middle East, as well. Startled, Rhee straightened and turned to see a man who at first glance appeared to be Oriental. He wore the pants and shirt of the typical North Korean factory worker. A cheap jacket was folded over his arm.

The man smiled. "You may call me Katz," he said. His eyes traveled up and down Rhee's body. His restrained amusement was painfully obvious.

"I do not know you," Rhee said, looking back and inspecting the man. Actually, Rhee thought, the man looked vaguely Asian but also European.

"No, but I know you. We must talk. You have work to do."

All of the fear and stress returned suddenly as Rhee Yuk realized this man—whoever he was—knew. Knew not only his secret, but also knew that Rhee Yuk was a South Korean mole.

The man called Katz pulled a package from under his jacket. "You came for this?" he asked. "I picked it up for you. The lock was not difficult to overcome." He took Rhee by the elbow and led him toward the door, his eyes falling to the bright red high heels Rhee wore beneath his pleated beige skirt and frilly white blouse.

"Nice shoes," Katz said. "But they clash with the rest of your outfit." He handed the South Korean the package. "Perhaps these new ones will look better?"

HE WOULDN'T HAVE HAD TIME to stop if he'd wanted to.

Like a downfield blocker opening a hole for his running back, Bolan lowered his shoulder, driving it into the belly of the Pyongyang cop in front of him. The man's hand jerked away from the holster at his side as the forward thrust drove him back out of the alley to the street. Air rushed from his lungs as if a vacuum hose had been thrust down his throat, and the gun clattered to the pavement, then skidded beneath a car.

Bolan checked his momentum, regained his balance and pivoted back toward the alley. The cops sprinting forward from the other end had stopped shooting as soon as their six brother officers appeared in the line of fire. But that wouldn't make much difference if the ten or so still in action teamed up on him and Hwang with nightsticks, stun guns or pepper gas.

They had to get out of there, and quick.

As he rushed forward, Bolan saw that two of the cops had blocked Hwang's exit and now gripped him by the arms. The other three faced Bolan, their nightsticks up and ready.

He ducked low under the wild swing of the nearest cop, then brought the Stinger up in a vicious uppercut. The nose of the simple weapon drove deep into the attacker's sternum. The cop's eyes widened in shock. He coughed twice, blood spewing from his lips both times, then crumpled.

As he turned toward the other two officers, Bolan saw that one of the men holding Hwang was fishing into the handcuff case on his belt. Hwang took advantage of the momentary distraction to snap a foot into the officer's knee.

Bone crunched. Cartilage and ligaments tore. The cop dropped Hwang's arm and collapsed on the ground screaming.

The next officer's nightstick shot forward like a spear. Bolan parried the blow to his midsection, then twisted back and brought the end of the still-unopened

Centofante down on the top of the cop's head. The man dropped as suddenly as his partner.

Hwang now had one hand free. He used it to drive a hard reverse punch that started at his hip bone and ended in the jaw of the man at his other side. Another crack of bone sounded, and suddenly the South Korean undercover man was free.

The last of the six cops stepped back away from the big American, deciding that caution might be the better part of valor. Bolan glanced past him, back into the alley. The cops who had come from the other end were now less than twenty feet away. "Let's go!" he shouted to Hwang.

The undercover man didn't have to be told twice. Shoulder to shoulder Bolan and Hwang turned and sprinted down the street, weaving in and out of surprised men and women on the sidewalk.

A lone shot rang out, then an angry voice behind them shouted. Bolan knew what had happened. One of the cops had recklessly fired, endangering the pedestrians. His commander had put an end to that, and now the only sound from behind was that of the pursuing feet.

The first intersection appeared ahead, and Bolan led the way, Hwang falling a few paces to his rear. Sprinting off the curb into the street, Bolan narrowly missed a horse-drawn vegetable wagon. Wheels skidded, and the horse neighed in protest as the driver reigned to a sudden halt.

Hwang dodged and danced around the cart and horse and followed Bolan up onto the sidewalk of the next block. A half block back, seven of the police officers were still in pursuit, but two were holding their sides and had dropped to the rear of the column. Bolan pressed on, leaping high to jump a rack of hanging clothes a shopkeeper suddenly pushed out the door onto the pavement. He landed without breaking stride on the other side of the rack. Another quick glance told him Hwang had made the jump, but the cops had slowed to move around the obstacle.

The clothes rack increased their lead by another block. Bolan slowed slightly, letting his companion catch up. "We've got to ditch them somehow," he said. "Let's take to the side streets, then alleys." He led the way through the next block, narrowly missing a tall woman as he turned onto a side street.

When he looked back again two blocks later, only three of the officers were still in pursuit. Bolan turned on the steam, flashing past the windows of the storefronts. In the distance he heard a train whistle, and as it blew he noticed suddenly that there were no more pedestrians in front of the stores.

The fact was, there were no more stores. The area was open, providing a clear line of fire again for the pursuers behind them.

"Oh, hell." Hwang huffed behind him as the first shots rang out.

Bolan surveyed the lay of the land as he continued to run down the street. Ahead he saw the rail station. The whistle blew again, then was followed by more fire from their rear. Two hundred yards down the track, a locomotive was racing toward them. "Faster, Hwang!" he yelled at the top of his lungs.

Every nerve and muscle in his body strained as Bolan's arms and legs propelled him forward. He kept one eye on the oncoming train.

It would be close. But it had to be. If it *wasn't* close, the cops would make it across the tracks, as well.

Hwang's footsteps pounded behind him as 7.62 mm rounds from the cops' Type 68 pistols urged them on. The last stretch was an uphill grade, and Bolan's thighs and calves burned as if someone were holding a branding iron against them. His chest rose and fell with each painful breath, his lungs threatening to burst with each step.

When he crossed the tracks, the giant iron horse was less than twenty feet away. He slowed, turning in time to see Hwang leave his feet. The undercover man dived across the tracks a hairbreadth ahead of the engine, hit the pavement on his belly and slid a good ten feet before bounding to his feet.

For a moment Hwang stood staring glassy eyed at Bolan. His clothes appeared shredded from collar to cuff, and blood had already begun to seep on the palms of his hands, chest and thighs.

Bolan stared between the cars racing past and saw the blue uniforms grind to a halt. "You okay?" he asked Hwang as the two took off jogging down the street.

"Yes..." Hwang panted, a weak grin on his face. "I'm tough. Like...Johnny Cash."

They entered another commerce area, slowed to a walk and cut down a narrow pedestrian walkway. Bolan glanced at Hwang. "Johnny Cash? You pick up a liking for country-western music while you where in the States?"

The Korean undercover specialist looked at him, a smirk covering his face. "No, just a liking for Johnny Cash. He reminds me of me."

Bolan looked at him quizzically. He liked Hwang, and if the South Korean wanted to think he looked like Johnny Cash, he wouldn't argue. "Okay," he said.

"No." Hwang chuckled as they walked on. "You don't understand." He paused, his eyes twinkling. "I had to get tough or die back there," Hwang said. The smirk grew wider. "But hey, Pollock. I'm a boy named Su, too. Right?"

THE HOTEL STOOD atop a small rise like a haunted house in a B-grade horror movie.

Bolan and Hwang walked forward, leaving the street and starting up the cracked concrete steps to the front door. They had spent the past two hours making their way through the labyrinth of back streets and alleys of Pyongyang, stopping now and then to make sure they weren't being trailed. It appeared they had lost the police at the rail station, but at this point it wouldn't do to take any chances. There was the possibility, as well, that someone else had spotted the strange Caucasian and his bruised-looking companion, gotten suspicious and reported them.

Two old men huddled on a splintering wooden bench on the front porch of the hotel. Both smoked pipes. The ends of their long, wispy white beards had been singed brown from getting caught in the bowls. Their clothing looked as if it had not been washed during the past decade, and when they looked up at the strangers, both had a filmy residue over their eyes.

Bolan studied them as he mounted the steps. They looked no different than some of the other old men he had seen as they made their way through one of Pyongyang's many slum areas to the hotel—slum areas that Communist nations denied existed.

Hwang opened the rickety screen, then pushed open the rotting wood that passed as a front door. Bolan stopped behind him, turning back to look down over the neighborhood they'd just come through. Slum, ghetto, skid row, warren—call them what you would, these areas meant poverty, disease, violence and pain to those who endured them. The Communist governments could ignore them or try to explain them away all they wanted to, but that didn't make them disappear.

Hwang entered the hotel lobby. Bolan watched one of the old men reach under his ragged shawl sweater, then followed. The old-timers might look useless, but they served a purpose. Bolan didn't know exactly what the old man had reached for, but he suspected it was some kind of electronic transmitter. He'd done something to let the boys inside know the hotel had unusual visitors.

The hotel was just as dreary on the inside. Threadbare furniture formed a semicircle facing the wall, and perched on ragged chairs and couches were more old men mixed with younger ones. A game of mah-jongg was in progress, and all players took special care to appear as if they hadn't noticed the two newcomers. They did, though, and Bolan saw more than one hand move closer to the telltale bulges under sweaters, jackets and shirts.

Bolan and Hwang stopped at the front desk as a middle-aged man came through a door leading deeper into the hotel. Clean shaven and of medium height, he moved with the grace of a well-practiced martial artist, and had the long, sinewy muscles that come from lots of exercise but less than adequate nutrition.

He didn't smile. He didn't frown. He didn't speak. He just stared at Bolan and Hwang, and waited.

Hwang spoke softly. Bolan caught the word "Viking," and guessed that Hwang must have used the Korean words for "bird" and "talisman." The eyebrows of the man behind the desk rose slightly, and he glanced away from Hwang for a second to look at Bolan. Hwang spoke again, and this time Bolan picked up the names "Sang" and "Wonkwang."

The man behind the desk nodded before turning to the keys hanging from the wall.

"He is getting us a room," Hwang whispered out of the side of his mouth. "Someone will come there."

The desk clerk handed the key to Hwang. The undercover man started to turn, but a hand reached across the desk to grab one of his torn sleeves. Still holding Hwang with one hand, the man's other arm disappeared under the desk and reappeared holding a small wooden box.

Hwang took the box and nodded for Bolan to follow him. He led the way down a narrow, semilit hallway to a door, which he then opened.

Bolan stepped through the doorway to see a room even dingier than the lobby. A single bed stood against the wall, its filthy, ill-fitting mattress bunched in the center. Water stains covered the ceiling and walls, and the carpet and pad over the concrete floor had long ago worn out and been removed. Here and there fuzzy remnants around the cracks in the corners were all of the floor covering that remained.

Hwang took a seat on the bed, removed his shirt and opened the box. Bolan saw it was a first-aid kit. The South Korean didn't ask for help as he began treating the skinned areas on his chest and forearms.

A knock sounded on the door. With one hand on the Type 68 in the small of his back, Bolan reached for the knob.

A man stood in the doorway, his hand also invisible behind his back. His eyes dropped to Bolan's similar posture, and he chuckled, the hairs of his long, scraggly mustache dancing. "You have been sent by Sang?" he asked.

Bolan nodded. "He gave us your name."

"I am Wonkwang," the man said. "May I?" His eyes indicated the room behind the Executioner.

Bolan stepped back, letting the man pass. The visitor entered, nodded to Hwang and said something in Korean. Hwang glanced at Bolan, returned the nod and took a seat on the bed. He also spoke in Korean.

Then Hwang looked up at Bolan. "He speaks fluent English. Learned it at Berkeley, where he studied philosophy." He caught himself, laughed and shook his head. "So if he speaks English, why am I still translating? Habit, I guess."

Bolan turned his eyes to the man seated next to Hwang. "You went to Berkeley?" he asked.

"Yes."

"How is that?" Bolan demanded. "Last time I checked, we didn't have a foreign-exchange program with North Korea."

Wonkwang's smile was neither friendly nor cruel. "The government sent me," he said. "I was with North Korean Intelligence."

A momentary silence fell over the room. Bolan broke it. "You were the enemy," he said flatly.

Wonkwang's expression showed no affront to the statement. "*Was* is the operative word, Mr...."

"Pollock," Bolan said.

Wonkwang shrugged. "I was raised a Communist," he said. "It is a powerful doctrine full of idealism, and I did not see through it to the lies at its core until...later." He stared Bolan in the eye. "Perhaps you would have done so earlier, but I was unable to."

Bolan suppressed a smile. Wonkwang's words were a test to see how he would react. Just as Bolan's had been. And Bolan took no offense, either.

Wonkwang broke the new silence. "I do not fully understand why you are here," he said.

Bolan studied Wonkwang's face. The deadpan expression told him nothing. He wondered just how much the man could be trusted. Wonkwang appeared to be in his late thirties—not an uncommon time for men to open their eyes. It had taken many good men that long to see through the Communist propaganda they had been spoon-fed since birth.

But had Wonkwang really had a change of heart, or was he here with the Hwarang Warriors as a spy, just as he had no doubt been at Berkeley? And what of the Hwarang Warriors themselves? Bolan had heard of their existence before this mission, but they were a relatively new group that he knew little about. Resistance movements were like any other organization— made up of men both good and bad. Some cracked under pressure. In short, you couldn't trust every underground warrior you met any more than you could every single CIA agent, soldier or Marine.

He continued to study Wonkwang's face. The bottom line was he had no other way to contact Rhee. He would have to take a chance and trust this man. But at the same time he would keep his eyes open for any sign of betrayal.

"We're on a mission," he finally said. "One of great importance." Briefly he told Wonkwang about Curtis

Levi, then related what had happened with Lieutenant Han and Sang's men along the road.

Wonkwang smiled. "Word had already arrived that Han is dead, but we did not know exactly what had happened. May the crooked-faced bastard rot in hell. For your part in sending him there, we thank you."

"No thanks are necessary. But we need your help."

The Hwarang Warrior squinted. "What can I do?"

"There is a South Korean mole in the government here in Pyongyang," the Executioner said. "We need to contact him."

"What is his name?"

Bolan glanced at Hwang, who shrugged, meaning he also knew that there was no other way.

"Rhee Yuk," Bolan said.

Wonkwang gave an affirmative nod. "I do not know him. But I know who he is. He is with the State Department. *He* is a mole?" Wonkwang didn't seem that surprised.

Bolan nodded. "Can you contact him? Arrange a meeting?"

"Yes. But it may take time in order to be safe." Hwang frowned deeply. "There have been rumors about Rhee Yuk."

Bolan stared at him. "What kind of rumors?" he asked.

"Two kinds. First that he has a strange secret life."

"What kind of strange?"

Wonkwang shrugged. "Underground sex clubs and the like. I do not know the specifics, or even that the rumors are factual. But if they are true, I do not think it will affect our purposes.''

''What's the other type of rumor?'' Bolan asked.

''Just what you have told me. That he is with us, and that is the type of rumor that could become a problem.''

Bolan fell silent, reading the meaning behind the words. If the Hwarang Warriors already suspected Rhee of being a spy of some type, it would not be long until the Pyongyang government caught on, as well. There was a simple equation concerning underground operations and agents. The number of people who knew related directly to the length of time before *everyone* knew.

In other words, they had to get busy if they expected any help from Rhee Yuk. His days were numbered.

''I will arrange the meeting as quickly as is prudent,'' Wonkwang said. ''In the meantime, I suggest you stay here, out of sight. Word that an American and another man escaped the police this afternoon is already on the streets, and they will be looking—''

The sudden blast of a bullhorn cut through the air outside, drowning out the rest of Wonkwang's words. Rising as one, all three men in the room hurried to the window.

Outside in the street they saw two dozen uniformed troops. Hurrying around the sides of the hotel to block off a rear escape were two dozen more.

A man wearing colonel's bars held the bullhorn to his lips and spoke in Korean.

Hwang Su turned to Bolan. "Either we missed someone trailing us, or we've got lousy timing." He paused. "The guy just ordered everyone inside to come out unarmed and with their hands in the air." He paused again. "And he addressed the group as the Hwarang Warriors."

CHAPTER SIX

The tear-gas canister crashed through the window, exploding on the floor and shooting a foggy cloud upward throughout the room.

Wonkwang gasped, then coughed.

"Hold your breath!" Bolan shouted with the air still in his lungs. He grabbed Hwang with one hand, Wonkwang with the other, then propelled them toward the door to the hall.

He pivoted just past the doorway, slamming the door shut behind him as the sounds of more glass shattering echoed down the hall. "You have an escape route?" he asked Wonkwang, still gripping the man's upper arm.

Wonkwang had ingested just enough tear gas to choke off what he tried to say, so he nodded. Still coughing, crying and gasping for air, he took off down the hall away from the lobby.

Bolan and Hwang followed, hurrying through a series of twists and turns. More Hwarang Warriors emerged from rooms along the way and fell in behind Wonkwang. Some of the men carried firearms that ranged from an ancient wheel-lock pistol to recently seized government weapons. Others wielded swords, knives and traditional Korean martial-arts weapons.

Behind them the crashing of glass stopped. The gas assault was over, and the men outside the hotel were waiting for the gas to reach its ultimate effect.

With Bolan and Hwang at his heels, Wonkwang led the way through a kitchen and into another short hall. The men crowded behind in a tight group, whispering softly as they started down a staircase. Behind them the *rat-ta-tat* of automatic fire started as the siege of the hotel began.

The stairs ended in a dirt-floored basement, and once again the men crammed in next to each other. Wonkwang hurried to the wall and swung a calendar to the side, revealing a lone black button.

Wonkwang pushed the button, and a rumbling sounded in the wall.

A second later the wall began to swing inward. Through the opening a narrow tunnel was visible. Barely wide enough for one man, the portion just on the other side of the wall had been crudely sheathed in concrete. Beyond that, the walls were of dirt.

The inward swing of the wall forced some of the men out of the cramped basement and partway back up the stairs. Above them, the sounds of automatic fire drew closer. Wonkwang dropped the calendar back in place to hide the button and started waving the Hwarang Warriors into the tunnel. Tears still flooded his eyes as he turned to Bolan, but he managed to choke out, "Leads . . . short way only."

The men continued to bustle through the opening, and Bolan counted nineteen. Some had produced flashlights, and they led the way out of sight beneath the ground. Judging by the sounds upstairs, the attacking soldiers were meeting resistance, which meant some of the Hwarang Warriors had elected to stay behind and fight to give the others time for escape.

That meant two things. First Wonkwang's men had known an invasion could take place and planned ahead. And second some of them had decided to die in order that the others might live.

It was a good sign. It showed unity and strength of purpose.

Two elderly men who had guarded the porch were carried into the tunnel by younger men. Another good sign. The Hwarang Warriors were taking care of their people, and part of Bolan's doubt about the organization disappeared. He and Hwang waited until everybody else was through, then ducked under behind Wonkwang.

Wonkwang twisted the butt of a flashlight and stopped just inside the tunnel. He punched another button on the concrete wall, and the door panel began to swing back in place. By now he had recovered his breath enough to talk with greater ease, and he turned to Bolan. "We will emerge two blocks down. From there, we must scatter." He regarded Bolan with bloodshot eyes, then turned on Hwang.

Bolan could tell he was deliberating on just how big a part he wanted to take with the American and South Korean. Escape wasn't going to be easy for any of them, and it would be made even more difficult to have men along who weren't familiar with the area.

Finally Wonkwang said, "You should stay with me. I will show you the way. But if we should separate and survive, call this number. If I am not there, ask for Tang." He rattled off a phone number.

Bolan committed it to memory.

Without further ado, Wonkwang took off at a trot down the tunnel. Bolan pushed Hwang ahead of him and followed.

The tunnel had been dug almost in a straight line, and far ahead flashlights bobbed in the hands of the front runners. Dust motes floated downward through the bobbing beams of their flashlights. Dirt trickled from overhead, and Bolan squinted upward.

The tunnel had been dug quickly, with only time for rudimentary braces. With all the movement it was seeing tonight, it might give way at any time and bury everyone alive.

Roughly two hundred yards down the tunnel, the men had piled up again. Bolan slowed, then stopped, looking around Wonkwang and Hwang to see that the tunnel ended abruptly. But the diggers had come across a piece of luck during their construction of the escape route, and two feet off the ground, a drainage pipe gaped at the end of the passageway.

One by one the men crawled into the pipe. It was slow going, nerve-racking, particularly with the older men in tow. But like the well-disciplined fighters Bo-

Ian concluded they were, the Hwarang Warriors waited their turns.

Hwang turned to Bolan, a thin smile curling his lips. "Are we having fun yet?" he whispered.

Two men were still ahead of Wonkwang, Hwang and Bolan when the sound of running footsteps echoed down the tunnel from the direction of the hotel. Wonkwang raised his flashlight over his head and cast the beam that way.

A hundred yards away the shocked face of a soldier appeared in the beam like a startled deer.

Bolan drew one of the Type 68 pistols and squeezed the trigger. The tunnel walls rumbled with the blast but held.

The soldier pitched forward. Another NK regular, behind the first, tripped over the tumbling body and rolled to the ground.

The Executioner cut loose with three more 7.62 mm rounds, driving the soldiers frantically backward. The dirt walls shook again with the explosions as Bolan glanced behind him to see Wonkwang quickly entering the drainage pipe.

A return shot came down the tunnel, striking the dirt two feet from Bolan's face and raising a dust storm in his eyes. Squinting, he twisted back and fired twice more as Hwang ducked into the pipe. The Type 68 ran dry, so he dropped it, drawing the other.

His ears ringing, he aimed up at the dirt ceiling of the tunnel. He tapped the trigger, tapped it three more times in quick succession. All of the rounds struck the dirt just above the downed soldiers, and with the final round the ceiling began to cave in.

Screams echoed down the narrow passage as Bolan dived into the drainage pipe. As the tunnel filled, burying the enemy soldiers alive, Bolan crawled along in the darkness. The heavy smell of earth filled his nostrils. His eyes were so blinded with dirt that he didn't see the round hole until it was less than ten yards ahead.

The column of crawling men moved forward, stopping briefly each time one reached the end and exited the pipe. Bolan took advantage of each stop to wipe more of the dirt from his eyes with the backs of his sleeves.

When he reached the end himself, he climbed out of the pipe and found himself beneath a bridge. Beyond the concrete walls, he could see the grass of a steep embankment. Wonkwang and Hwang beckoned him forward, the others already dispersing into the night.

Bolan sprinted through ankle-deep water to the edge of the grass.

"This way!" Wonkwang hissed, then turned and clambered up the embankment to the street.

They were the last words the Hwarang Warrior ever said.

Bolan and Hwang were two steps behind when the full-auto volley of submachine-gun fire struck Wonkwang, twisting him obscenely into a macabre dance of death. Bolan reached out to grab Hwang and haul him back down beneath the bridge, but before his fingers made contact, Hwang spun a full 360 degrees. Holding his arm, he groaned, then dropped to the ground.

A third volley sounded, and a round ripped through the man known as the Executioner.

As soon as the phone rang, Boris Stavropol knew what the call was about. He'd known the call would come and—he glanced at his watch—he'd known almost precisely when. He had also known why.

Curtis Levi wasn't cooperating.

In many defectors over the years, Stavropol had observed the same psychological transformation Levi was experiencing. Personal problems mounted up, causing them to make the decision to betray their countries in rash moments of weakness. Then, when reality finally worked its way through the stars in their eyes, and they found that the country to which they'd sold out had no intention of turning them into minipotentates as promised, they began to regret their decision.

All of which, the former KGB man realized as he reached for the phone, was a fancy way of saying that Curtis Levi had had a change of heart.

The Russian pressed the receiver to his ear, hardly surprised to hear Dr. Kwison's voice. Kwison, North Korea's top missile engineer, was in charge of the three-man team that had been assigned to conduct Levi's initial debriefing.

"Yes, Doctor?" Stavropol said in Korean.

"We are encountering some difficulties," Kwison said.

Stavropol sighed silently to himself. "I suspected that would be the case," he said.

"Could we have your assistance?"

"Certainly," Stavropol said. "I will be right up." He dropped the phone in the cradle. Bracing his arms on the desk, he pushed himself up.

He went to the door and closed it behind him, then turned down the hall to the stairs. As he started up the steps, his knees began to ache. The former KGB man stopped to fish through his jacket for the bottle of painkillers. The prescription called for two, but he downed four, knowing even as he choked them down dry that they would do no good. On days like this, nothing stopped the pain. It was there, and the best he could hope for would be a diversion to take his mind away from it.

The two flights of stairs became a test of his strength of will. Finally he was outside Levi's room, and he paused to catch his breath. He didn't know what it would take to get the scientist talking, but it wouldn't do to have the American see *him* in pain. When he had composed himself, he twisted the knob and opened the door.

Levi sat in the straight-backed wooden chair that Stavropol had ordered placed in the middle of the room the day before. The American's clothes were disheveled, his hair wild and unkempt. He turned toward the door as Stavropol entered, his bloodshot eyes silently screaming *You lied!*

Three desk chairs had been rolled in on their wheels, and seated around the American rocket scientist were doctors Kwison, Chinp'yong and Chuhang. They were in white lab coats and held clipboards in their laps. One of them said something Stavropol couldn't make out, and Levi turned to him.

"Before we get into that," the American said, "we must discuss the combustion of liquid fuel itself. And in order to do that, we should first make sure that we all understand and *define* what a rocket is the same way. I have had conversations concerning the transport of nuclear-fission devices, gentlemen, that went on for hours before we finally realized that we were talking about different subjects completely. This came from the two parties not agreeing to basic definitions at the outset of the discussion."

Dr. Kwison excused himself and stood up, ambling across the room to the corner where Stavropol had taken up position. A portly man with a receding gray hairline, he folded his arms and clamped the clipboard to his belly. "This has been going on all day," he whispered. "He acts as if we are children who do not know what a rocket is. We ask a question, he talks in circles. Just listen."

Curtis Levi was talking louder now, and his voice was filled with nervous energy. Stavropol knew it was his presence that had caused the American's agitation. Levi couldn't know why the doctors had summoned the Russian, but he had to suspect it couldn't be good.

"The principle involved in rockets is simple," Levi said, his eyes flicking from the two men in front of him to Stavropol and Kwison across the room. "But it is vital that we agree in every detail as to *exactly* what they are. I like to think of it as if a toy balloon were filled with high-pressure hydrogen. The gas would press equally against every part of the balloon. Are we in agreement?"

Dr. Chinp'yong blew air from between his teeth in exasperation. Dr. Chuhang took off his glasses and began cleaning them with the tail of his lab coat.

"Now, if we should prick that balloon with a pin, the gas would begin to escape through the hole we made, driving the balloon away from the hole."

"Do you see?" Dr. Kwison said. "What he is saying is understood by students in every grammar-school science class in Korea."

"He is experiencing a very common emotion in situations like this," Stavropol said.

Kwison looked up, puzzled. "What is that?"

"Remorse," the Russian said.

"Ah," said Kwison, his eyebrows rising in understanding. "He is sorry he has come over to our side?"

Stavropol chuckled. "Wouldn't you be?" he said. "Levi acted hastily. At a moment of emotional weakness. That moment has passed, and he now realizes he is a traitor to his country. So—" Stavropol held a hand over his mouth as he yawned "—he is stalling. Trying to buy time without telling you anything."

Kwison's eyebrows lowered again. "But why? Does he suppose the U.S. will send a commando unit to rescue him? That is outrageous."

"Yes, of course it is. But he hasn't thought that far ahead. He is not stalling with a specific goal in mind. He is stalling simply because he no longer wants to help you build missiles."

Levi was still talking across the room. "You see, gentlemen, the rockets we build today are based on the same principle your neighbors the Chinese were using when they constructed fireworks displays a thousand years before Christ. And rockets have been used as weapons since the last years of the eighteenth century, when the Sultan of Mysore fired them at the English. The English themselves employed them against my country at Fort Henry in 1814, and..."

Stavropol turned a deaf ear to the American's drivel. There were many ways in which remorseful defectors attempted to delay the inevitable, and this was but one. He has seen them all far too many times to let it insult him anymore. If anything, it had begun to amuse him as he grew older. Each man who talked in circles seemed to think he had invented the idea. They were always shocked when someone like Stavropol finally entered the picture and explained it would no longer be tolerated.

Dr. Kwison turned back to Stavropol. "How long does this remorse usually last?" he asked.

The Russian shrugged. "If allowed to run its course without interference, sometimes days. Sometimes months."

Kwison's eyes widened. "Do you mean we may have to wait months to speak to him?"

Stavropol did his best not to laugh in the man's face. For all their brains, scientists could be so naive when it came to reality. "Sometimes," he said tauntingly, "the change of heart is permanent."

Kwison cursed in Korean. "Is there nothing we can do to change his mind?"

Stavropol chuckled again. "To change his mind? Probably not. But there are many things that can be done which will make him more eager to speak to you."

Dr. Kwison's eyes opened even wider now as he realized what Stavropol was implying. "Is there...no other way?" he asked, his voice trembling.

"Unfortunately, no."

"Must I...?" Kwison paused, looking down at the floor. "Is it...necessary that I...that any of us—" he indicated the other two doctors with a sweep of his hand "—be present?" Kwison looked up, his face pale.

"Of course not, Dr. Kwison," Stavropol said. He turned away from the man and walked across the room in time to hear Levi explaining the difference between rockets and jet propulsion. Nodding politely to the other two men in the lab coats, he said, "Gentlemen, perhaps it is time you took a break."

"But we haven't—" Chuhang started to say, but a look from Stavropol halted him.

Slowly the men in the lab coats left the room.

"You lied to me," Curtis Levi said as soon as they were gone. The American looked as if he was on the verge of tears.

Stavropol let the contempt well up in his heart, urged it on . . . reveled in it. Over the years he had found it to be a necessary element in hard interrogation, and had also found it to be a sensation not unpleasant. "*Lying* is such a harsh word," Stavropol said as he dropped down into one of the vacated chairs. "Perhaps we should say instead that you misinterpreted what was promised."

"You *lied*."

Stavropol shrugged. "Have it your way," he said. "But be realistic. Did you think you would be made some Oriental emperor?"

When Levi didn't reply, Stavropol rolled the chair nearer. "You are stalling. You believe you are doing it in a very clever way, but I have seen it many times in the past. That is the trouble with men like you—you believe that because you are very intelligent, everyone else must be stupid." He shook his head back and forth and made a clicking noise. "The doctors are tired of your double talk. They wish you to get serious and help them build a rocket capable of transporting nuclear devices across the globe. After all, that is why you came to us, is it not?"

Levi straightened suddenly in his chair. "You promised me wealth," he said arrogantly. "You broke your word. I am no longer under any obligation to keep mine."

Stavropol remained calm. "So you do not plan to cooperate as you promised?" he asked softly.

The KGB man's docility spawned a new boldness in Levi. The American smiled what Stavropol knew he must consider a cruel smile, and said, "Never! I will never tell them, or you, *anything!*"

Stavropol fought the urge to laugh. The American scientist had lived in such a soft world. In his world, when men lost their tempers with one another, they raised their voices. They sought revenge in political back-stabbing or other forms of palace intrigue. But they never struck one another. Never inflicted physical pain. And what went on behind closed doors, in back alleys, in warfare both hot and cold—these things were outside their realms of experience.

What was about to happen to Curtis Levi hadn't even crossed his mind.

The Russian shifted, and suddenly new pain shot through his knees. It came so suddenly that he jerked involuntarily. His teeth clamped together as the urge to laugh at Levi's innocence was driven from his soul.

Boris Stavropol reached into the inside pocket of his jacket and pulled out a pair of needle-nosed pliers.

The pain in his knees, back, hip and feet wasn't going to go away. Not today. But perhaps he could take his mind off it by introducing Curtis Levi to its world.

BOLAN HIT THE GRASS embankment on his side as a searing flash of pain shot up his thigh. Looking down, he saw that the leg of his slacks had been torn away and blood soaked the ragged remains.

He took stock of the surroundings. They had emerged from the drainpipe into a small neighborhood park. A picnic table, swing set and other playground equipment—all of stark stainless steel—glimmered in the moonlight to give the area a sterile feel.

A harsh voice barked in Korean, then suddenly three special-purpose soldiers appeared out of the shadows. Their Type 49 submachine guns were slung over their shoulders in assault mode.

Bolan lay where he'd fallen as a man whose dual shoulder badges identified a captain cautiously approached. Out of the corner of his eye, he could see one of the other two men standing over Hwang. The third special-forces soldier knelt next to Wonkwang.

He needn't have bothered. Bolan had seen the Hwarang Warrior take the steady stream of fire in his chest. He'd been dead before he hit the ground.

Turning his attention back to the Captain, he noted the stark red star on the crown of his khaki cap. The man stared down, his eyes black and emotionless. With the muzzle of his subgun centered on Bolan's chest, he jerked a walkie-talkie from his web belt and spoke into the mike. Static came back with the answer, then he reattached the radio to his side and shouted at Bolan in Korean.

Hwang spoke up from somewhere to his left. "He asked if you can walk."

Bolan breathed a silent prayer of thanks that Hwang was alive, then glanced around the park again. It was deserted, but the captain had already radioed for help. When that help arrived, the chance to escape would all but evaporate.

Unless they wanted to be shot, or spend the rest of their lives in a North Korean prison, he had to act now. "Tell him I think so, but tell him I'll need help getting to my feet."

When the answer was relayed by Hwang, a brief expression of concern came over the man's face as he weighed the risk of getting too close to the wounded man. Then he leaned over and extended a hand, his subgun still trained on Bolan.

Bolan let the captain pull him almost off the ground before, using his body weight as leverage, he jerked hard on the man's forearm. Simultaneously, he swept the other hand across his chest, knocking the barrel of the weapon aside.

A 3-round burst exploded into the grass. Bolan twisted beneath the captain, rolling to the side away from the weapon and tugging him facedown in the grass. Drawing the Centofante from his pocket, he slid his thumb to click open the blade. Pain shot through his leg as he moved over the captain and hooked the blade around under his throat.

The other two NK soldiers turned their attention his way.

Hwang took advantage of the distraction to reach up and grasp the Type 49 slung over the shoulder of the man guarding him. He jerked the weapon to the side, and the sling looped around the NK's neck. Rolling out and away from the man, the undercover specialist twirled the subgun, tightening the noose, then jerked hard.

A loud snap sounded in the park as the soldier's neck broke.

With his free hand, Bolan grabbed the back of the captain's hair. Keeping the knife to the man's throat, he pulled back and rolled away from the NK who had knelt next to Wonkwang. The captain's body now shielding him, Bolan yelled, "Tell him to drop the subgun or his captain's history."

Hwang spoke urgently, and the soldier stood frozen, trying to decide what to do. Hwang repeated the command, but instead of dropping the weapon, the NK began trying to align the sights on Bolan.

The big American jerked the captain back against him tighter and drew the Centofante's blade lightly across the man's throat. A thin trickle of blood dripped down over his fingers. "Drop the gun!" he shouted.

The special-forces man realized he had no choice. Loosening the sling from around his neck, he let the Type 49 fall to the ground.

Hwang dived forward, grabbed the weapon and swung the barrel up against the NK's cheek in one smooth motion.

"How bad are you hit?" Bolan called out.

Hwang shook his head. "I don't know," he said. "Upper arm. I don't think there's bone or nerve damage. But it hurts like hell."

The knife still at the captain's throat, Bolan struggled to rise on his wounded leg. The pain was acute, but he was lucky that it was only a flesh wound. The bleeding needed to be stopped as soon as possible, but unless he missed his guess, the bullet hadn't nicked or shattered any bones.

In the distance the sounds of vehicles racing their way grew louder.

"We've got to move out," Bolan told Hwang. "Ask our buddy here where he's parked."

Hwang moved in front of Bolan and his prisoner, shouting the words into the captain's face. The man mumbled a reply. "Follow me," Hwang said.

Bolan shoved the captain away from him, then stooped to retrieve the Type 49 the man had dropped. The barrel of the subgun tight against the man's kidney, he prodded him after Hwang.

The South Korean led them across the park at a jog to where a military jeep had been parked. Bolan pushed the captain into the passenger seat, then circled the vehicle and dropped behind the wheel. Hwang climbed into the back seat, training his subgun on their hostage.

"How long we planning to keep this one?" Hwang asked as Bolan started the ignition.

"Until we don't need him anymore." He heard the roar of engines as he pulled away from the curb, looked into the side mirror and saw two identical jeeps round the corner.

Four North Korean special-forces soldiers, bearing assault rifles, sat in each.

Bolan stomped on the gas. "Just until we don't need him anymore," he repeated. "But it looks like that might be a while."

In a few seconds a volley of fire punched into the back of the vehicle. It was accompanied by a loud, angry voice on a speaker system that came from the second jeep behind them.

Bolan floored the accelerator as they raced away from the park into a residential area. The captain huddled down, seeking cover from the onslaught.

Steering with his left hand, Bolan grabbed the back of the man's hair and jerked him upright. "Keep this guy's head up, Hwang!" he shouted over the explosions. "Let them know we've got one of their men!"

Hwang leaned forward and got hold of the man's collar. His other hand snaked over his shoulder and grabbed the front of his belt. With a quick tug, he hauled the man up and over the seat into the back.

Bolan stomped on the brake, taking a corner on two screaming wheels. He turned slightly as the jeep straightened out, righting itself again. Hwang twisted the captain to face their pursuers, and the salvos of fire suddenly stopped.

The voice behind them echoed over the speaker system again.

"They'd like us to pull over," Hwang said wryly.

Bolan's foot pressed the accelerator to the floor again, the pain from his leg wound shooting up his thigh. But Hwang's injuries concerned him more. Their mission was far from over, and while he was confident of his own ability to block out the pain, he didn't know how badly Hwang was injured.

The warrior pushed such thoughts from his mind. For the moment he had to focus on getting away, which meant some plan to lose the jeeps behind them. The special-forces men might have temporarily halted their assault, but they hadn't given up the chase. And they'd be radioing ahead to set up a roadblock.

Bolan raced on, followed closely by the other two jeeps. The voice over the speaker continued to scream orders, and as they sped past the shacks of the people of Pyongyang, men, women and children came out to watch the show. Roars of approval and encouragement rose up among the frustrated subjects of Communist Korea, and not a few fists of support were lifted amid the cheers.

A fork appeared in the road ahead. Bolan bore down hard on the accelerator, feinting right, then twisting the wheel violently to the left at the last second. The tires squealed their protest again as the jeep's front wheels hit the curb, then fishtailed down the street.

Behind them the first jeep followed the feint, its tires screeching as the driver hit the brakes. The second vehicle, farther back, had time to turn and pulled to the lead.

Bolan's mind whirled, searching for an answer. He knew that in minutes more vehicles would appear to block the road somewhere ahead. He had to do something before that happened. Something drastic.

The convoy shot out of the residential area into a light commercial district. Although he couldn't read the signs, Bolan recognized the marks of a plumbing shop, a car wash and several restaurants. A glance in the rearview mirror told him the jeep that had missed the turn was back in the game, but two blocks behind them. But the vehicle just to the rear had slowed, as well, and he wondered why.

He turned his attention back to the front. Squinting under the dim streetlight, he got his answer. A block ahead, the street dead-ended in front of a two-story office building. A circular drive formed a horseshoe in front of the edifice.

The warrior took a deep breath. Common sense screamed that he should hit the brakes. He and Hwang should flee on foot, taking their captive with them. But with their injuries how far would they get? By now the radio messages broadcast from the pursuit jeeps would be bringing more troops to the area.

But common sense was for common men, not warriors.

Waiting until the last second, he tapped the brake. The jeep almost fishtailed again, then straightened as they shot up into the circular drive. The tires wailed and the body of the jeep rose on its side as Bolan steered it around the curve.

The jeep skidded off the drive on the two left wheels, the right tires scraping against the brick front of the building. The stench of burning rubber filled the air as he fought to keep the vehicle upright. The jeep jerked violently to the left, then fell back upright, and a split second later they were shooting back out of the circular drive in the direction from which they'd come.

The voice over the speaker fell silent in awe.

"Get ready to fire!" Bolan shouted over his shoulder as he stomped the accelerator again. A moment later they had drawn even with the lead jeep, and Hwang opened up with the captured Type 49 from the back seat.

The driver of the first jeep folded over the steering wheel. The passenger next to him fell back. The two men in the back seat jerked spasmodically with the deadly impact of the 7.62 mm rifle rounds perforating their bodies.

Bolan didn't slow. Bearing down, he raced on down the street toward the second jeep. Gunfire now began on both sides, the NK special-forces men deciding that the captured captain's life wasn't worth their own. A burst of fire took out the windshield in front of Bolan, and shards of glass blew back over him like razor-edged hail.

In the back seat Hwang opened up with the assault rifle again, and a soldier in the oncoming jeep dropped his rifle over the side.

"Forget the men!" Bolan ordered. "Take out the vehicle!"

A steady stream of fire rattled behind him. Holes appeared in the grille of the NK jeep, and steam began to rise from the hood. The vehicle ground to a halt just as Bolan, Hwang and their hostage raced past.

Hwang emptied the remainder of the magazine into the driver, and they sped on down the street.

Bolan's eyes swept back and forth across the street. More special-forces troops would be on their way, and the jeep would flag them like some giant accusatory finger. They needed new wheels, and they needed them fast.

They had reentered the commercial area. A block and a half down the street a Toyota was parked in front of a restaurant. He hit the brakes, skidding the jeep that way. They squealed to a halt next to the Japanese auto as a man wearing a dark black suit got out, a puzzled look on his face.

Bolan leaped over the side of the jeep, his assault rifle in hand, and ripped the keys from the man's hand. Out of the corner of his eye, he saw Hwang circling the Toyota for the passenger door, clutching his subgun. Glancing behind him as he ducked into the vehicle, he saw the captain.

The man still sat in the back seat, staring sightlessly ahead. A lone, star-shaped bullet hole gaped in his forehead like some blood-filled third eye.

Bolan started the Toyota as Hwang slid onto the seat. He shot away from the parking lot as the South

Korean slammed the door, glancing into the rearview mirror.

The man in the dark suit stared after them, still looking as if he was trying to solve a riddle.

CHAPTER SEVEN

Bolan assessed the situation and knew his immediate goal was to get out of Pyongyang and into hiding somewhere before word reached the police that they were now driving the Toyota.

He glanced across the seat to the South Korean. His own wound had closed over, the bleeding coming to an abrupt halt on its own. He had lost blood, sure, and he felt slightly light-headed as he drove down the side streets. But they both needed to bandage their wounds before their physical activity prolonged the bleeding.

Bolan half turned to look at the seats in the back and saw several brown paper packages. "See what's inside," he told Hwang.

Hwang turned slowly, his eyes showing the beginnings of shock. "They have laundry marking on them," he said.

"Get them open and get your bleeding stopped," Bolan ordered.

Hwang ripped open one of the sacks and pulled out several freshly laundered white dress shirts. As Bolan drove on, the undercover man fashioned crude bandages for both of them.

Bolan considered stopping to change vehicles again, then discarded the idea. They'd been lucky with the

Toyota. Another transport switch was likely to take time—and would invite another confrontation.

"Take a left, next corner," Hwang said next to him. "There is a road that leads out of the city. Down to the river."

Bolan turned to him in the semidarkness, trying to gauge how much the injury had affected him. But Hwang's face remained deadpan, and Bolan learned nothing. "What will the traffic be like this time of night?" he asked.

Hwang shrugged. "Light. There is the curfew. We will stick out like..." He paused, looking up at the ceiling. "What is it you Americans say? A sore finger?"

"Close enough," Bolan answered. He drew a deep breath. "You see any other option?"

"No. Do you?"

The question had been rhetorical, and Bolan didn't bother to answer. He made the turn. Two blocks ahead he saw the road leading down off the bluff. He slowed as they reached the intersection, again turning to the man in the passenger seat. "You got something in mind when we get to the river?"

The interior of the Toyota grew darker as they descended the bluff. Hwang nodded. "River I know better than city," he said. "Fishing shack off road. Car camouflage in brush. We safe, I think—long enough at least tend injuries."

The Executioner had learned nothing by looking at Hwang's face, but the man's sudden change in speech pattern told him everything. The South Korean's command of the English language was excellent, but now he was lapsing into a weird form of "educated pidgin," dropping articles of speech as if he'd learned the language from semiliterate sailors along the river they were approaching.

The reason was simple. Hwang Su was suffering from shock.

Bolan leaned harder on the accelerator, guiding the Toyota on down from the rise. He had to maneuver a thin line, coaxing as much speed out of the vehicle as he could without screeching the tires around the curves and drawing the attention of the few other cars they encountered. Hwang had mentioned the curfew, and that meant the other vehicles on the road were likely to belong to government officials with passes that allowed them out at night.

In other words, bureaucrats who wouldn't hesitate to report a strange car.

The smell of water filtered in through the windows as they neared the Taedong River. The road flattened out, and soon a small harbor appeared in the distance. Bolan slowed, turning to Hwang.

The South Korean's eyes had closed.

"Hwang," Bolan said. "Hwang, wake up."

There was no answer.

Bolan reached across the seat, grabbing the man's shoulder. "Hwang!" he shouted. "Wake up!" He squeezed the undercover man's shoulder in iron fingers.

A short yelp escaped Hwang Su's lips, and he opened his eyes. "Where . . . where are we?" he asked.

"At the river. I need directions."

Hwang sat up straighter in his seat, peering through the windshield. "Right," he said. "A blacktop road."

Bolan saw the corner ahead and tapped the brake. "Hwang, stay awake," he said.

The man didn't move.

"Dammit, Hwang! Listen to me!" Bolan barked as he made the turn onto the blacktop. "I need your help. It's not like I can just stop and ask for directions."

Hwang nodded slowly. "I'm . . . sorry . . . Pollock," he mumbled faintly.

"Don't be sorry. Be *useful*. Wake up and tell me where the shack is. I can't find it on my own."

Hwang nodded his understanding and leaned forward again, his face almost against the windshield. "Another mile . . . maybe . . ." he said. "Then . . . right again."

Bolan accelerated, hurrying over the blacktop. They passed several more small dock areas, the buildings around them closed for the night. He wondered just how much time he had before even the iron will of the man next to him failed and Hwang succumbed to shock.

A heavily treed area appeared on the side of the road away from the river, and Bolan slowed. "This it?" he asked. "In there?"

Hwang's face was still against the glass. "I think so," he said.

Bolan cut the Toyota's headlights as the turn appeared. The vehicle left the blacktop and turned onto a dirt road leading into the trees. The tires bumped over deep ruts and furrows. Here and there large rocks and bricks had been dumped into some of the holes, but they made the going worse rather than better.

The trees on the sides of the road arched overhead, forming a dark tunnel. Above them the boughs swayed gently in the night breeze. The road wound around several curves, then suddenly opened into a clearing.

Bolan saw the shack on stilts in the center of the cleared area. He hit the brakes, stopping quickly at the edge of the trees. Hwang was asleep again, and he knew he'd found the site none too soon. The South Korean had been right on the money, though, guiding him here in spite of his clouded brain.

Bolan studied the shanty ahead. Hwang had done well. He had only made one mistake.

The shack wasn't deserted. Through the stained oil paper covering the windows, the Executioner saw a dim flicker of light.

Bolan knew there was no alternative to consider. There was no time to search out a better hiding place. He got hold of one of the assault rifles, then snapped the cover off the Toyota's dome light and unscrewed the bulb. The telltale interior light neutralized, he opened the door slowly, got out and closed it quietly behind him. The only sound was a short click.

Crouched low to the ground, the Executioner advanced quickly on the shack, stopping when he reached the rickety wooden stairs that led to the small porch above the stilts. They'd make noise; there was no way around it. There might be a better approach from the sides or rear, but even if there wasn't, he might get a look through one of the windows that would tell him what he was about to face.

Moving swiftly to the side of the crumbling shanty, Bolan pressed his face against more of the dirty oil paper that served as windowpane. He could see the same glow of light through the filmy substance, but no details of what lay inside. The window at the rear of the shack proved the same, but when he came around to the far side, he saw that a corner of the paper had been torn away and flapped softly in the evening wind.

Bolan moved close to the window, angling his head so he could get a view. Inside he saw a kerosene lamp in the middle of the floor. A few odds and ends—broken kitchen utensils and ragged clothing mainly—were scattered across the one-room shanty.

Three figures were asleep next to the lamp on the floor.

He studied the sleeping forms in the lamp's dull glow. Beneath filthy, moth-eaten wool blankets, the one closest to the window was a man. His face was almost emaciated. Next to him a woman in even worse condition lay huddled in a fetal position.

In her arms she gripped the third form. A baby.

Anger swept through the Executioner. The starving father and mother were bad enough, but the child got to him even more. He couldn't see the baby's condition, but he had to guess the infant couldn't be much better. This family—dying a slow death in the failing Communist economy—had moved into the deserted shack, finding what little comfort they could in lives that had to be living hell.

Bolan shook his head. Now he had no choice but to disrupt even what paltry relief they had found.

The anger was his reaction to feelings of helpless pity. Here, before him in living color, he saw the truth of the ''People's Paradise'' that communism always promised. Here was the equality that the proponents of socialism swore went beyond that of democracy to honestly make all men equal.

Well, it worked for a select few. But in the interests of forcibly maintaining a Communist state, starving men, women and children didn't matter.

Bolan slung the rifle over his back and went back to the front of the house. He hurried up the stairs to the front porch. The door stood slightly ajar, the lock that had once secured it and the knob long ago rotting out of the wood. He pushed the splintered wood inward and stepped inside to see the man roll out of his blankets and jump to his feet, holding a butcher knife.

He didn't bother to unsling the rifle as the gaunt man lunged forward on shaky legs. He stepped to the side, reached across his body and grabbed the bony wrist holding the knife. Careful not to snap the feeble limb, Bolan brought his other hand up and jerked the blade free of the man's fingers.

The homeless man looked up into Bolan's face. His expression showed no fear; rather it was beyond fear, and in his eyes Bolan saw almost a pleading that this stranger who had invaded his pathetic home would end his misery.

Bolan shook his head, tossed the knife behind him and glanced down at the woman and baby. They still slept, unaware of what was happening. Taking the man's frail arm, Bolan led him out of the house, down the steps and to the Toyota, where he opened the rear door and grabbed the laundry package. Handing it to the man at his side, he slammed the door and opened the front.

Hwang recovered to a semiconscious state, mumbling incoherently as Bolan lifted him out of the seat. Bolan was surprised at how heavy the smaller man felt, and reminded himself that his own injury had taken its toll.

The man standing next to Bolan looked at the blood covering the South Korean. Again his face was far past the point of showing emotion. But he seemed to sense now that the big stranger meant him no harm, and he reached out to close the car door.

Bolan hurried up the steps and into the house and deposited Hwang down on the blanket where the man had slept. The woman on the floor next to him stirred, opened her eyes, then abruptly sat up, clutching the baby closer to her breast. The fear that had been absent in her husband spread across her face, as conspicuous as the impoverished family's wretchedness.

The husband held out his hands, palms down, and shook his head. His wife nodded, but the trepidation in her eyes remained.

Bolan dropped to one knee, studying Hwang Su. How much blood had he actually lost, and was it more than a flesh wound?

Bolan looked up. "Water," he said. "Do you have any water?"

The man stared back blankly.

Cupping his hand around an imaginary glass, Bolan mimicked taking a drink. "Water," he said again.

A flicker of understanding showed in the dull eyes, and the man hurried out of the house. He returned a moment later carrying a bucket of water. The woman on the floor set the baby gently down, then rose and walked to a pile in a corner of the room. Returning with a tin cup, she handed it over.

Bolan dipped water from the bucket and held the cup to Hwang's lips. Half-conscious, the South Korean drank slowly, spilling more down the front of his blood-caked shirt than went down his throat. Bolan waited, gave him another cup, then pulled another laundered shirt from the package and tore off a sleeve. When both the fresh and dried blood had been wiped away, he could see the wound channel high on the biceps.

But the vital nerve endings of the area had been missed, and as Hwang himself had surmised earlier, the bone seemed intact.

Bolan continued to clean the wound, then looked up when he felt someone standing over him. The woman looked down, extending a half-full bottle of rubbing alcohol.

He nodded his thanks, tore a clean strip from the shirt and soaked it in alcohol. Hwang twitched as the liquid stung. His eyes opened.

The Korean smiled weakly. "It's not enough to get shot?" he said. "You've got to torture me, too?"

Bolan grinned. Hwang Su still had his wits about him. *Most* of them, at least. "Just call me Stavropol," he said.

He finished cleaning the wounds, then tore more of the shirt away and wrapped it snugly around Hwang's arm. Forcing more water down the man's throat, he turned his attention to his own leg.

He turned and sat down on the floor as a sudden wave of nausea flooded him. The light-headedness had returned, and he had to concentrate, forcing himself to tear another shirt apart. As he started to apply it to his thigh, the woman hurried forward and grabbed the cloth from him, rattling off something in Korean.

Bolan looked up at her as she dipped the rag into the water bucket. Her husband had retrieved the butcher knife from where Bolan had dropped it, and now moved cautiously forward. He pantomimed cutting Bolan's pants, staying well out of reach until he was certain his intentions were understood.

Bolan nodded his understanding, and the man squatted, jabbing the point of the knife into the bloody pants. His wife knelt next to him, gently running the damp cloth over the injured leg.

Anger swelled once more within Bolan. These were good, salt-of-the-earth people—people who didn't deserve to live in the squalor they'd been forced into by a government that claimed to care for its wards. As the woman switched from water to alcohol and the sting bit into his leg, he silently swore two things. First, while he couldn't save all of the poverty-stricken citizens of this, one of the last bastions of communism, he'd do something to help *this* family if he could. And he wished he could deal out some retribution to those who were responsible for this family's anguish.

The husband ripped up another shirt, soaked a strip in alcohol and tied it around Bolan's thigh. He wrapped a dry strip over it, then spoke again in Korean.

Bolan looked up at him, shaking his head. The man smiled and nodded, then his face seemed to change shape. The Executioner blinked several times, trying to clear his vision, but each time his lids opened again, the man's face grew fuzzier.

Bolan felt gentle hands on his arms as the man and woman gently eased him back on the dirty blankets that covered the floor.

THE TARGET WAS CENTERED in the cross hairs of his rifle scope. His finger moved back on the trigger, taking up the slack, ready to exert that final ounce of pull that would avenge the deaths of his family.

Then, a microsecond before the firing pin fell to begin his war everlasting, a homey aroma invaded Mack Bolan's nostrils. His trigger finger froze motionless. The cross hairs dimmed. The man just beyond them grew fuzzy.

Bolan opened his eyes and saw the tin cup in front of him. Broth. Chicken broth. As his vision cleared, he saw the woman who had treated his wound holding the cup out to him.

He sat up, his head pounding. As he took the cup, he turned to a window and saw the light of midmorning trying to penetrate the greasy oil paper. "Thank you," he said.

The woman smiled, and beyond the ravages of poverty and the premature wrinkles of despair, Bolan saw the beauty deep within. He held the cup to his lips and took a sip, drinking slowly, the near-boiling liquid threatening to scald him. Next to him, Hwang Su was stirring, and some color had returned to his face.

The sound of a crying baby broke the silence in the shack, and Bolan turned to see the child lying on more of the dirty blankets on his other side. As he sipped more of the broth, the mother took a seat on the floor, lifted the small form into her arms and eased her shirt aside. The baby's head leaned instinctively forward and he quieted.

Bolan turned to Hwang as the man sat up. "How are you feeling?" he asked.

Hwang shook his head and chuckled. "I had the strangest dream last night," he said. "We got shot."

Bolan smiled. Hwang sounded normal again, and while he was undoubtedly weak, he'd be able to go on. His attention turned to the front door as it suddenly burst open.

The ragged man who had helped him last night hurried into the shack breathing hard, his face red. He spoke rapidly in Korean, and the expression on Hwang's face become one of grave concern.

"Soldiers are coming up the road," Hwang interpreted.

"Coming here?"

Hwang nodded. "Has to be. This road leads nowhere else."

Bolan struggled to his feet, not surprised to find he was still weary. "What's the man's name?" he asked Hwang.

Hwang spoke, got an answer and said, "Jhoon. His wife is called Kimi."

"Tell Jhoon and Kimi to—" Bolan stopped in midsentence, remembering suddenly that Hwang's rifle and the spare clips were still in the Toyota. He had intended to hide the car and bring them in after attending to their injuries the night before, but in his weakened state had passed out before doing so. His rifle only had a partial clip, and it would be suicide to start a firefight they couldn't finish. The situation called for stealth, not firepower.

Hurrying to the window, he stared through the translucent paper to see the dark shadowy form of a jeep pull up next to the Toyota. A man got out and walked around the vehicle.

Bolan turned back to Hwang, who had struggled to his feet. "Either somebody saw us turn in here last night or there's been a report that these people are trespassing. But it doesn't matter. The soldiers will be here any second. We've got to move fast." He reached in his pockets, feeling the Spyderco Centofante and COMTECH Stinger, then glanced around the shack's single room. There were no closets, no cupboards, no furniture of any kind. Nowhere to hide. Looking up, he saw only the four-by-eight support beams that ran the length of the shack. They were too thin for concealment.

But they still might provide a momentary advantage. The Executioner hoped so. They had nothing else.

Hwang picked up the butcher knife that Jhoon had wielded the night before. Jhoon understood what was going on and hurried to a corner, lifting a battered frying pan.

Bolan shook his head. "Tell him to give you the pan," he instructed Hwang. "He's too weak to fight, and we'll need him as a decoy. Tell him and Kimi to lie down and act like they're asleep."

Hwang did as ordered, and Jhoon reluctantly gave up the pan. Bolan waved Hwang to the side of the front door as they heard the jeep drive up to the shack. Clasping his fingers together to form a step, Bolan hoisted the South Korean upward onto one of the support beams, then passed up his rifle in case they needed it as a last resort.

Bolan moved to the other side of the door. Extending his hands overhead, he jumped, grasping another beam. The effects of his own injury still haunted him, and he didn't have his customary strength or agility.

Reaching into his pockets, he extended the nose of the Stinger between the knuckles of his left hand. The Centofante flipped open in his right. Gripping the knife like an ice pick, he caught his breath as he heard footsteps mount the stairs.

They would have one chance, and only one. Their success would depend to a high degree on the reason the soldiers had come. If they'd been alerted to the fugitives' whereabouts, or recognized the Toyota from radio reports, they'd be ready for trouble when they hit the door.

But if they'd simply gotten wind of a trespassing family, and come to perform a simple eviction, their guard would be down. Bolan and Hwang would stand a chance.

Unless the first man through the door happened to look overhead.

The door opened, and a uniformed NK stepped through. His rifle was slung over his shoulder, the flap on his pistol snapped down. Bolan let relief course through him. They'd come for the family, with no hint that there might be resistance.

A moment later a man wearing sergeant's stripes stepped inside the shack, screaming orders in a high-

pitched voice. He strode past the first soldier to where
Jhoon lay feigning sleep, brought back a foot and
drove it into the man's ribs.

The Executioner remembered his vow of the night
before. He not only intended to help Jhoon and his
family, but he intended to make those responsible for
their condition pay.

Now seemed like as good a time as any to get started.

With a quick nod to Hwang, Bolan swung down
from the beam. His feet together, he drove them into
the small of the sergeant's back. The man jackknifed
backward with a grunt.

Bolan dropped to the ground, bringing the Centofante over his head as the sergeant turned. From the
corner of his eye he saw Hwang drop straight down on
top of the other soldier. Bolan employed a variation of
the old "one-two," first jabbing the Stinger into the
sergeant's throat, then driving the blade of the Centofante down through his carotid artery.

Bolan heard the loud clang of the frying pan as it
came down on the other soldier's skull. Blood spurted
from the sergeant's neck as Bolan turned to see Hwang
bring the butcher knife up into his opponent's sternum.

Both soldiers hit the wooden floor simultaneously.

Bolan stooped, cutting the leather sling from the
sergeant's shoulder with the Centofante and sliding the
man's rifle out from beneath his body. He hurried to
the door, peering out at the jeep.

The vehicle was empty. But another of the Type 58 assault rifles stood, barrel up, in the back seat.

Staying hidden to the side of the door, Bolan scanned the area in front of the shack. His eyes fell on the speck of khaki just inside the tree line. The third NK soldier faced away from him, his hands out of sight in front of his body. The man bobbed forward several times, then Bolan heard the faint sound of a zipper.

Bolan moved back from the door. He couldn't risk a shot. He had seen only the one jeep, but that didn't mean there weren't others in the area. Even if there weren't, the far-carrying report of the Type 58 could alert some citizen who'd feel compelled to report it. And Bolan wasn't ready to flee the cabin yet. He and Hwang needed to regroup and come up with a new plan of action for locating Curtis Levi.

Bolan leaned the Type 58 against the wall, palming the Centofante. He waited, watching the soldier walk calmly in the direction of the shack. But rather than come up the steps, he returned to the jeep and resumed his seat in the back.

Hwang had moved in to watch from the other side of the door. "Want me to call him up?" he asked.

Bolan shook his head. "If he doesn't recognize the voice, he'll come loaded for bear. I don't want any shots fired."

Hwang frowned. "What do we do?"

"Wait."

Five minutes went by before the first sign of the man's impatience appeared. He glanced at the watch

on his wrist, then settled back in. Five more minutes
found him checking his wrist again, and two minutes
after that he finally called out in Korean.

Hwang looked to Bolan.

Bolan shook his head.

The soldier in the jeep called out once more, then
cautiously got out. His rifle aimed forward, he approached the steps with watchful eyes.

The Executioner stepped back from the door, the
Centofante held in a foil grip. He listened to the footsteps as the man reached the porch, then moved on to
the door.

The rifle barrel came through the doorway first.

Bolan reached out, grabbing it with his free hand
and jerking the soldier into the shack. The man let out
a squeal of surprise as he twisted toward the am-
busher.

Bolan's knife hand came around in an arc, the Centofante's blade slashing down across the hand holding
the rifle's pistol grip. This time the NK screamed in
pain rather than surprise as his trigger finger was sliced
from his hand and hit the floor.

Hwang had stepped behind the soldier and swung his
good arm with the butcher knife around the man. He
drew the blade across the NK's throat, and the
screaming was silenced.

Bolan and Hwang dragged all three men across the
room and stacked their bodies in the corner. The Executioner watched both Jhoon and Kimi. They had sat
up in the middle of the floor, and Kimi clutched the

infant to her breast again. Their faces showed fear, but their eyes showed that the kind of violence they had just witnessed was hardly a new sight.

Fishing through the pockets of the dead men, Bolan found two billfolds and a money clip. He counted the *won* notes, coming up with the equivalent of more than five thousand dollars. A veritable fortune to the impoverished peasants of this bankrupt Communist land.

Bolan stared down at the corpses with contempt. The Democratic People's Republic of Korea appeared to be more democratic for some than for others. He didn't know how much money NK soldiers made, but it wasn't enough to provide that kind of pocket change. They were ripping someone off somewhere—probably people just like Jhoon and Kimi.

Bolan pooled all the *won* notes together, threw one of the dingy blankets over the men and stood up. Walking to Jhoon, he extended the money.

Jhoon stared at the clump of bills, his dead eyes suddenly widening. He looked up at Bolan in awe, and pointed uncertainly to his chest.

"He wants to know if it's really for him," Hwang said.

"I gathered as much," Bolan told him. "Tell him yes."

Hwang spoke and Jhoon answered.

"He says it's too much," Hwang said.

Bolan shook his head. Reaching down, he clasped the man's bony hands together and forced the money between them. "Tell him it's not nearly enough," he said.

Hwang spoke again, and at his words, the woman holding the baby began to cry.

CHAPTER EIGHT

In the far corner of the room, the baby breathed softly under the blankets. Jhoon sat next to it, holding a rattle and still crooning the Korean lullaby that had put the child to sleep. Kimi stood staring at the greasy paper over a window, and in the corner across from where Bolan and Hwang Su sat were the blanket-shrouded bodies of the North Korean soldiers.

"Others will come when these men do not report back," Hwang said. "We must leave."

Hwang was right, Bolan knew. More NK troops were likely to come looking for the missing men. But there was an even more important reason they had to get on with the mission immediately. Every second they delayed was another second in which Curtis Levi could give classified nuclear-missile information to the North Koreans.

Bolan stared at the wall, speculating on what secrets Levi might already have given up. It depended on whether or not the scientist had come down with a case of Traitor Remorse Syndrome. TRS affected some, but not all, of the people who betrayed their country, and it could only be hoped that Curtis Levi had contracted a healthy enough dose to slow his tongue until Bolan found him. But regardless of his willingness to cooperate with the North Koreans, Bolan knew that eventually he would cooperate.

One way or another, Boris Stavropol would see to it.

Bolan stood up, gingerly testing the weight on his wounded leg. They had to find Curtis Levi, and the only way that could be done was through finding Rhee Yuk.

Turning back to Hwang, Bolan said, "We've got to move, but we have to have a plan of attack before we go. Are you up to it?"

"The planning part or the attacking part?" Hwang asked with a grin.

"Both."

"I'm up to it. I may not have recuperated completely, but I'm still as good as a dozen NKs."

Bolan dropped the soiled strips of shirt to the floor. "That's fine, Hwang," he said. "But North Korea has a population of twenty-four million. That means we're outnumbered around twelve *million* to one."

Hwang's grin disappeared. "You aren't counting Rhee," he said, deadpan. "That drops the odds to eight million."

Bolan chuckled as he sat back down to inspect the wound in his leg. Clean and already starting to heal. "Okay, let's get serious," he said as he began ripping into a clean shirt. "How are we going to find Rhee Yuk?"

The tearing sound seemed to remind Hwang that he, too, had a dressing to change. He began unwinding the blood-soaked rags from his arm. "I had an idea last night," he said. "Then forgot it during everything." He took what remained of the clean shirt from Bolan, tore off the collar and soaked it in alcohol. "It came back to me in a dream."

Bolan waited silently as the undercover man swabbed the wound on his upper arm, then tore the remaining sleeves from the shirt.

"There is a man who could help us," Hwang said, wincing as he tightened the makeshift bandage. "If he will."

"Tell me," the Executioner said.

Hwang finished with his arm and sighed. His face changed to that of someone who'd just been to the funeral of a close family member. "His name is Myung Namsoo," he almost whispered. "He was once a special-forces officer like myself."

Bolan felt his eyebrows lower. "You said *was?*"

Hwang nodded. "Yes. An undercover specialist, too." He paused as if he was troubled. "The fact is, he was my partner."

Whatever the story was, it was clearly an emotional one. Bolan waited for Hwang to go on, but the wait did him no good. Finally he said, "Myung Namsoo defected?"

Hwang looked him in the eye, then shrugged. "Yes and no," he said. "In a sense, I suppose." His eyes moved overhead, and he paused.

This time Bolan didn't have long to wait.

"He was undercover in Pyongyang. Not a mole like Rhee, but a lengthy assignment nevertheless. What is that called in English?"

"Deep cover?" Bolan said.

"Yes." Hwang nodded. "Deep cover. We had an opportunity to plant two men in the North Korean Bureau of Internal Transport—an agency that has two functions. They make travel arrangements for government officials, and also act as a state tourist agency for foreign travelers. In actuality this means it is a cover for keeping track of the activities of both citizens and visitors. Our superiors saw it as an occasion to learn more about how the bureau operated. They planned on sending both me and Myung." He stopped.

"Why didn't you go?" Bolan asked.

"At the last minute it was decided not to risk the exposure of two agents. Instead of accompanying Myung, I was sent to your Stony Man Farm for training." The sorrow Bolan had seen earlier on Hwang's face now seemed to change to guilt. "While he was there, Myung met a woman. They fell in love."

Silence fell over the fishing shack. Hwang was thinking, clearly choosing his next words carefully. Finally he said, "You must understand, Pollock, that while I am angry with Myung, I would bet my life that he has never 'rolled over,' as you Americans call it. Reports say he simply took his undercover identity on permanently, married the woman and has remained at the Bureau of Internal Transport."

Bolan stood up, walked to the package of shirts still on the floor and lifted it. Two still remained intact, and he tossed one to Hwang as he unbuttoned the blood-stained cloth that covered his own shoulders. "The NK government still don't know who he really is?" he asked.

"Not according to our Intel. And as you might guess, we keep close tabs on him through other agents." He began painfully inserting his injured arm into the shirtsleeve.

"How about Myung's wife?" Bolan asked.

Hwang shook his head. "She knows nothing."

"Okay. The way I see it, we need four things."

By now Hwang was buttoning his own shirt with his good arm. "Yes?" he said.

"First, clothes that fit well enough to keep from advertising that we stole them," Bolan said. "And wheels. We can't take the jeep, and by now the Toyota's been across every radio wave in Asia." He looked briefly at the bodies in the corner, then to Jhoon and his family at the back of the room. "And we've got to get *them* out of here before more NK regulars show up."

Hwang nodded his agreement. "We can walk back to the port area. There is a laundry not far from here. And appropriating a vehicle will not be difficult. As soon as we have done that, we can drive them into the city and drop them off." He stood up on legs that shook but held. "That was three things. You said four."

Bolan turned to face him. "Four is the hard one," he said. "Somehow we've got to contact Myung without getting burned. It should be easier to get into the internal-transport bureau than the State Department, granted, but the cold, hard fact is that I stick out like a sore thumb in this country."

Hwang shuffled toward Bolan, the now-familiar grin covering his face. "Unless your heart is particularly set on seeing the Bureau of Internal Transport building, I suggest another plan of action."

"What?" Bolan asked.

"Let's just go to Myung's house," Hwang Su said. "Our intelligence people have his address on file."

Bolan frowned. "They gave it to you?"

"Not exactly," Hwang said, the grin now bigger than ever. "I got it . . . well, kind of like I got the colonel's military ID, and the Firenza, and the weapons we started out with and the—"

Bolan couldn't stifle his laugh. "I get the picture," he said. "Let's go."

IT TOOK NEARLY AN HOUR to walk the two miles back to the port road.

Bolan would have preferred to go after more clothes and a car alone, letting Hwang rest at the shack with Jhoon and his family. But that hadn't been possible. Hwang had traded his blood-drenched trousers for the rags Rhee had worn, and while he looked every part the beggar, at least he showed no signs of violence that would attract the attention of the authorities.

Besides, Bolan thought as they walked on, Hwang was a proud descendant of Korea's ancient warriors, and forcing him to stay behind would have meant a loss of face. The undercover specialist was of the Oriental mind-set, meaning face came right under honor at the top of the priority list. And it was so far above death that death lost all meaning whatsoever.

A quarter mile from the port road, Bolan led the way off the packed dirt into the trees. Ahead in the distance he heard the sounds of traffic. He led Hwang to the edge of the foliage, then stopped.

Peering between the branches, he scouted the port area in the noonday sun. It was larger than it had looked at night, and he saw that they were directly across from a dock with a loading bridge. Transit sheds lined the other side of the dock, with a small quayside railway circling the entire area. Just on the far side of the rail tracks were several small office buildings. A few cars and trucks were parked in a lot to the side. Other vehicles went about their business on the roads that crisscrossed the port area.

"There." Hwang pointed through the leaves to the office buildings. "The laundry is roughly in the middle."

Bolan studied the terrain. He wasn't sure which of the buildings housed the laundry facilities, but it didn't matter. Even the closest stood a good hundred yards away, across an open area where anyone walking or running would be clearly visible. The bottom line was that there was no way a Caucasian, a head taller than anyone else, wearing blood-caked pants and a shirt six sizes too small, was going to leave the trees and enter the laundry without drawing attention.

Hwang put his thoughts into words. "I'll have to go alone," he said.

Bolan nodded. He led the way through the trees once more, paralleling the road until they were directly across from the office buildings. He turned to Hwang. "Just get in, get out and bring me the biggest clothes you can find," he said. "We'll go after transport as soon as I look less conspicuous." He paused. "Got it?"

Hwang nodded. "No big deal," he said. He stepped from the trees and walked across the road to a ramp leading down to the port area.

Bolan settled in for the wait, taking a seat in the soft grass. His stomach growled, reminding him he had eaten nothing but Kimi's chicken broth for a day and a half. Body fuel would have to become a major priority soon, both to keep up their stamina and to aid in recovery from their injuries. But for the time being that, too, would have to be put on hold.

He watched Hwang shuffle past a stop sign at the top of the ramp to the parking area, cross between two cars and step up on the sidewalk in front of the offices. A couple of cars raced by on the port road, and several vehicles passed Hwang as he walked on, but none of the drivers or passengers showed interest in the ill-dressed civilian.

Hwang ducked inside the third doorway from the end, and Bolan studied the cars in the lot. Most were Japanese, but here and there he saw aging ZILs—remnants of the age of the Soviet Union. He heard another vehicle slow as it neared the ramp, and looked through the trees to see a four-door Hyundai sedan.

The driver wore a khaki eight-point cap with a short plastic bill, and the glint of steel on his chest sparkled in the sunlight as the Hyundai turned down the ramp.

A premonition of trouble washed over Bolan as the Hyundai parked in front of the laundry. The door opened and the driver got out.

The sparkle had not been an illusion. The man wore a khaki security uniform with a bright silver badge on his chest.

The security officer opened the rear door and pulled out a basket of dirty clothes, kicking the door shut again with his foot. A second later he disappeared inside the laundry.

Two seconds later he was back out on the sidewalk, his weapon in the small of Hwang Su's back.

An armload of clothes fell from Hwang's arms as the security officer bent him over the hood of the Hyundai. Bolan shook his head in disgust. Of all the rotten timing, they had picked the exact moment when one of the dock cops decided to do his laundry. The man in the khaki uniform had walked in to see a beggar stealing clothes, and was now making what might well be the biggest arrest of his week.

The security man slapped handcuffs around Hwang's wrists. For a brief moment the South Korean looked up the ramp, to the exact spot where Bolan sat hidden. Slowly Hwang shook his head. Then the dock cop threw him into the back seat of the car. The security man paused long enough to gather the clothes Hwang had dropped, then slid in behind the wheel.

As Bolan scanned the area, he could see what Hwang's head-shake had meant. It would have been an exercise in futility to sprint down the steps and across the parking lot. The entire area was open, and the man in the eight-point cap would have more than enough time to see him coming.

The Executioner glanced through the leaves and limbs to the stop sign. He had one chance, and one alone.

Another vehicle whizzed by on the port road as the Hyundai started up the ramp. He rose, stretched his legs and felt sharp pains join the constant ache in his thigh where the bullet had passed through. He dropped lower into a crouch, ignoring the stings, finally putting both hands on the ground in front of him like a sprinter about to burst off the blocks. His timing would have to be perfect—he couldn't come out of the trees and expose himself until the car was committed to stopping at the sign. But if he waited even half a second too long, the car would be gone before he reached it.

The Hyundai neared the stop sign and slowed. A split second before it came to a complete stop, Bolan shot from the trees. Three short, choppy steps took him from the grass to the port road, and four more breezed him past a suddenly honking Isuzu that shot past on the pavement. Missing him by less than an inch, it whizzed on down the port road.

The Isuzu's horn drew the attention of the security officer behind the wheel of the Hyundai. The man looked up in surprise.

Bolan drew the Type 68 pistol two steps before he reached the car. Holding it above his head, he swung the butt against the driver's window. Glass crashed down around his arm as he felt the butt strike the security man in the jaw.

Reaching through the hole with his other hand, Bolan grabbed the security officer by the throat and thrust the pistol into his face. "Tell him to take the car out of gear, put on the emergency brake and scoot over," he told Hwang.

From the back seat of the vehicle, Hwang passed on the instructions.

The man in the eight-point hat stared at Bolan, then did as he'd been told. A moment later Bolan was behind the wheel.

He reached around the dock cop, unsnapped the man's flap holster and pulled an ancient Type 64 pistol from the leather. He tossed it next to Hwang in the back seat. "Tell him to take off your cuffs, then put them on him," he said.

Hwang leaned forward, turning his back to the front seat as he spoke again. With Bolan's gun still in his face, the dock cop wasted no time unlocking the cuffs. Without a word he turned his back so Hwang could snap them around his wrists.

Bolan threw the car into gear but kept his foot on the brake. "Now take one of our old shirts and blindfold him," he said.

When he was satisfied their captive couldn't see, he took his foot off the brake, turned and drove quickly back to the road that led to the shack. Five minutes later he parked in front of the ramshackle structure, got out and opened the passenger door. He hauled the security man out and led him up the steps to the front door. Hwang followed, carrying the clothes he had found at the laundry.

Jhoon and Kimi both sat against the wall. They looked up as the door opened, but their faces showed no expression. Hwang chuckled. "They're getting used to this stuff, Pollock," he said.

Bolan kicked the blindfolded man's legs out from under him and let him fall to the floor. He ripped off the tiny shirt he'd been wearing and picked up the larger of the two blue chambray work shirts Hwang had appropriated. Hwang lifted the other shirt, but Bolan shook his head. "I think you'd be better off as a cop," he said.

Hwang Su nodded, dropped to one knee and unbuttoned the dock cop's shirt. The blindfolded man froze in terror, but when the South Korean began to unbuckle his gun belt, he suddenly kicked up with both legs and began screaming in Korean.

Hwang drew back a hand and slapped the man across the face. "They hire morons to guard the docks in North Korea," he said in disgust. "The fool thinks we're going to rape him."

Bolan picked up a pair of denim pants from the floor. "Tell him to relax, he's not our type," he said.

Hwang laughed, then spoke calmly. The man settled down, but his arms and legs remained stiff as oak.

The uniform fit Hwang almost perfectly. As soon as he was dressed, Bolan said, "Get Jhoon and his wife and baby ready. We leave in two minutes." He gathered up the rest of the weapons they had accumulated from the soldiers and walked out of the cabin toward the Hyundai.

THE DRIVE BACK UP the bluff was uneventful. Bolan slouched low behind the wheel, keeping the visor over his face to shield himself from the busy afternoon traffic that crowded the road.

The road rose steeply, and Bolan looked down to see the gently flowing waters of the Taedong River they had just left. The peaceful ripples that drifted along the shoreline stood out in bold contrast to the tidal wave of violence he knew lay ahead. They entered the city proper, driving silently through the commercial area, past canneries, factories and rice- and corn-processing concerns. All was government owned, and the men and women Bolan saw going about their business had no private interest in the success or failure of each enterprise, and they came and went with the same listlessness he had seen in the people elsewhere.

They entered the old section of town and turned into the market area. Here he saw booths with scrawny chickens, wilting produce and stringy-looking slabs of meat. A parking lot stood on the corner, and he pulled in, sandwiching the Hyundai inconspicuously between two cars near the center.

Bolan turned to Hwang next to him. The uniform fit well, and the South Korean looked the part. But a dock guard in the city might draw attention. Questions might be asked about what he was doing this far away from the port during working hours.

Reaching into his pocket, Bolan pulled out a roll of *won* bills. "Ask Jhoon if he minds doing a little shopping for us."

Hwang rested his injured arm over the seat as he spoke. Jhoon answered. "He says it is the least he can do after the money you gave him," Hwang translated.

Bolan nodded. Scrounging through the glove compartment, he found a dirt-stained notepad and broken pencil. He sharpened the tip with the Centofante, then handed the pad and pencil to Hwang. "Write this down for him. Food. A conservative business suit that will fit you, and one for me. He should get himself and Kimi some new clothes, too, and whatever he needs for the baby. But tell him not to turn this into an all-day shopping trip, either."

Jhoon nodded repeatedly as Hwang translated. When the South Korean handed him the list, the homeless man kissed his wife on the cheek, patted the baby's head and got out. Bolan watched him disappear on the crowded sidewalk amid the other shoppers. Hwang's dressing in the port-security uniform had freed the other denim pants and chambray shirt, and while Jhoon hardly looked affluent, at least it seemed credible that he had money to spend.

Bolan turned to study the woman holding the baby. He smiled. She smiled back. Bolan saw that some of the tension had left her face, but the smile was restrained, as if she wasn't getting her hopes up—not yet, at least.

"What's the baby's name?" he asked the woman.

"Hung," she answered.

"Hung," Bolan repeated. "As in King Chin Hung?"

Hwang nodded. "The monarch of Silla, the ancient kingdom of southeast Korea." He paused. "The name reflects both her hopes for the child's success, and a desire to escape the North."

Bolan reached over the seat, patted the baby and then turned back toward the front. A moment later Jhoon appeared again, loaded down with packages and walking excitedly. Gone were the denim pants and chambray dock worker's shirt, and the North Korean now wore a startlingly white suit, a black shirt open at the collar and a smile of pride from ear to ear.

Hwang chuckled softly as the man approached the Hyundai. "Good Buddha," the South Korean grunted under his breath. "You've created a *Saturday Night Fever* monster, Pollock. Next time we see Jhoon it'll be on the pages of *GQ*." He got out and helped Jhoon deposit the packages in the car.

The odor of strongly spiced food set off hunger pangs as Jhoon began distributing several white cardboard containers. The Executioner set his in his lap and opened it, taking the chopsticks that were handed over the seat. Steam rose from the carton as he looked down to see what appeared to be a mixture of meat, fish, eggs and vegetables.

"*Sinsollo*," Hwang said, answering Bolan's unasked question. "Not my favorite, but hey—who's complaining?"

Jhoon and Kimi ate as if they hadn't had a decent meal in years, and indeed, Bolan thought, they probably hadn't. Kimi breast-fed the baby as she shoveled the food into her mouth, and when they had finished, Jhoon lifted a brown-paper-wrapped package from the floor and handed it to her.

For the first time since Bolan had seen her, the woman's eyes seemed to sparkle as she broke the string. She pulled out a new red skirt and sweater, and then suddenly broke into tears. She handed Hung to her husband, then unashamedly tore the rags from her body and put on the new clothes.

Bolan pulled out of the parking lot, letting Hwang direct him to a downtown hotel. They said goodbye to Jhoon and his family, and watched them go up the steps.

"How long will the money last in this economy?" Bolan asked the South Korean.

Hwang shrugged. "Depends on how wild they get. Several months, though, if they're careful."

"Then what?" Bolan said.

Hwang turned to look at the big American but said nothing. He didn't have to. They both knew the answer.

Finally the South Korean broke the silence. "You are a brave man, Pollock," he said. "A good man. And you have helped them." He stopped to take in a breath. "But there is a limit to what even you can do."

Bolan threw the Hyundai into gear and pulled away from the hotel. "Maybe," he said. "Let's go find your friend Myung."

IT WAS THE LAST THING they had considered. But it was in front of them before they could turn around.

Bolan slowed the Hyundai at the end of the line of cars, staring forward at the temporary metal guard shack that had been set up at the side of the street. Around it stood a half-dozen North Korean special-forces troops of varying rank. A sergeant with a clipboard stood next to the driver's-side window of the vehicle two cars ahead.

Bolan glanced into the rearview mirror. More cars had pulled up behind them, blocking them in. The street was too narrow for a fast U-turn. Quite simply, flight was out of the question.

"This standard procedure?" Bolan asked Hwang. "A checkpoint in the middle of town?"

The South Korean fidgeted in his seat. "Only when they're hunting for someone."

Bolan didn't have to ask whom they were looking for—a tall American and an Oriental. Hwang looked official in his uniform, and Bolan figured that gave them maybe a fifty-fifty chance of bluffing their way through the checkpoint. The uniform might well get them through—but it might just as easily work against them. Everything hinged on whether or not the security officer had been found in the fishing shack yet.

The man had been left gagged, blindfolded and his hands cuffed behind his back, but it wouldn't be long before he was found by soldiers who came to investigate the disappearance of the other three men. Had they found him yet? There was no way to know. But if they had, word would be out over the radios that the two fugitives were now driving the Hyundai, and that one might be dressed as a port-security officer.

But, Bolan realized as the next car in line was waved forward, there were no other options. They'd have to try their bluff, and if it didn't come off, they'd play it by ear.

The sergeant with the clipboard bent into the window of the car just ahead. A moment later a chubby Korean wearing a black suit and matching bowler hat struggled out from behind the wheel. He produced a set of keys, opened the trunk and stepped back.

Bolan watched the guard search through the items in the trunk. The car ahead had been waved on without such a thorough vehicle check. Something had made that happen—maybe a properly impressive ID or a recognized face. Whatever, they would have to hope Hwang's uniform did the same for them.

In the rear of the Hyundai, covered only by blankets from the fishing shack, were the Type 58 assault rifles.

A thousand questions raced through Bolan's mind as he waited. Were North Korean port-security officers issued rifles? If so, were they the standard Type 58s, one of the many variations, or something different altogether? If they did have rifles, did they keep them in their private vehicles or check them back in after their shift? And if they kept them in their cars, how likely would they be to bring them into the city?

All of these unanswered questions—these tiny details that Bolan and Hwang had no way of knowing but of which the NK soldiers were likely to be aware—would come into play in a few moments. If the details added up, they would corroborate their cover story. If they didn't, the little discrepancies would mean their arrest, and likely their deaths.

The sergeant slammed the trunk shut and waved the car ahead on.

"Same song, second verse," Bolan said out of the side of his mouth as he drove slowly forward. "I'm a Russian consultant. This time I'm here to advise your government about the housing problem."

The scratchy sounds of a two-way base radio drifted toward the car from the guard shack as the sergeant stepped up to the car. Bolan got the answer to one of his questions immediately. A muscular man in his early fifties, the sergeant had gray hair sticking out from under the ear flaps of his khaki cap. The red star in the center of the crown looked down at Bolan as accusingly as the eyes below it, but the man made no motion toward the pistol at his side.

The dock cop hadn't been found yet. At least if he had, word hadn't yet been radioed here.

The sergeant frowned at the driver before him and spoke sternly in Korean. Bolan forced an embarrassed smile and shrugged as Hwang leaned across the seat to speak through the window.

The sergeant saw the uniform, and his face softened slightly as he listened. Finally he broke into a smile. "Ah," he said in Russian. "A chance to practice my second language. Good." He reached through, shaking Bolan's hand. "You are here to help us with the housing?"

Bolan returned the smile. "I'm here to try," he said.

"Good. This is very good," the sergeant said, his head bobbing up and down. "We have many people with no place to live." The smile turned briefly into a frown of concentration, then returned. "I suppose I should check your car more closely, as we are looking for two men who match your description. But the one man is American, rather than Russian." He chuckled. "You are not American, are you?"

Hwang leaned farther across Bolan. "We confess!" he said with mock dramatics. "This man is the famous American gangster, Al Capone!" He held his arms up as if he were cradling a Thompson, and said, *"Ra-ta-ta-ta-tat!"*

The sergeant laughed and stood up. "Have a nice stay in Pyongyang." His hand had moved back to wave them on when an excited voice suddenly blared over the radio in the guard shack.

The man's hand stopped in midair. He turned toward the radio, then swiveled back toward the Hyundai as he reached for the pistol on his belt.

A half-dozen assault rifles swung toward the Hyundai as Bolan threw it in gear and floored the accelerator.

CHAPTER NINE

Curtis Levi awoke screaming.

The American rocket scientist lay flat on his back. Above he could see the cold stone ceiling, and for a moment he thought it had all been a nightmare. Then he tried to move his arms, but they were tethered on short leather straps that bound him to the bed. The most excruciating pain he had ever experienced shot through his body.

Levi screamed again. Not so much from the pain this time, but from the realization that it hadn't been a dream at all.

The monster with the needle-nosed pliers had been real.

For a few moments Levi's brain tried to deny the memory. He told himself it couldn't possibly have been real. The monster with the pliers couldn't have done the things Levi remembered him doing, because no human being could be that cruel.

No, it hadn't happened. And if it had, he would be dead. No human being could endure and live to recall the torture his mind continued to deny.

He shifted slightly, and again the agony shot through him. He froze, realizing the source of the pain was the white sheet that covered him. Each time he moved, it scraped his skin as if made of sandpaper rather than linen. The mental metaphor brought back another memory, and tears began streaming down his face. Sandpaper. That was why his skin hurt so. As well as pliers, the monster had used sandpaper. And there had been a cigar, tweezers, a razor blade and . . .

Suddenly Levi was screaming again. But the voice seemed not to come from his throat. It was more as if it originated far away, rebounding off the stone walls and ceiling as it neared his ears. He lay still, trying to stop the spectral shrieks, but the scream issued forth again and he knew it must come from him. He tried to raise a hand to cover his mouth, but the strap held it back.

My God, Levi wondered. What *had* Stavropol done to him? He couldn't even remember it all. What had the man done that had been so terrible his mind refused to register it?

"And what have *I* done!" Curtis Levi howled at the top of his lungs. He cried now, from both the pain in his body and the pain in his soul.

Finally his shrieks subsided to sobs. He listened, trying to hear any other sounds within the room. Nothing. Silence. It was as if he were the only human being left on the face of the planet. That thought brought another, an even more frightening, possibility.

Perhaps he was *not* on this planet anymore. Perhaps he was dead. Perhaps the pliers, the sandpaper and the other instruments that had violated every square inch of his body had finally finished their business by taking his life.

Perhaps this was the reception room to hell, and even now he was waiting to be welcomed by the devil himself.

The sound of a door opening caused Levi to turn his head toward it. Somebody entered the room, but he saw only a fuzzy, indistinct form. He tried to focus his eyes. An elderly man. Caucasian. The face grew clearer, and a greater horror than he'd ever before experienced suddenly filled his heart.

"Stavropol!" the American screamed.

Boris Stavropol was pushing one of the office chairs across the floor on wheels. He stopped it next to Levi's bed and sat down, his face wreathed in a smile like some kindly country doctor making a house call. Mixed with Levi's memories of last night, the Russian's amiability made him seem even more appalling.

Levi began to gasp for air. He felt as if he were choking, and each new spasm rubbed the sandpaper bedclothes harder across his body.

"Oh, come now," Stavropol said, looking mildly irritated. "It's not all that bad."

Levi's breathing slowed. Finally he got a grip on the stomach that threatened to turn wrong side out. He stared at Stavropol, but now he could see beyond the kindly appearance to the demon that inhabited the man's soul. He blinked his eyes, and when he opened them, Stavropol's head and face had grown longer to the point of being grotesque. A goatee had grown on his chin, and horns had sprouted from his head.

The American looked down at Boris Stavropol's feet. His shoes were gone, and where they had been, furry cloven hooves now grew out of the cuffs of his slacks.

Curtis Levi knew it had to be a hallucination brought on by the trauma. Nevertheless, this time it took a good five minutes before the screaming stopped.

Stavropol waited patiently.

Finally the delusion evaporated, and Levi's screams dropped once more to the sob of a wounded animal. He turned his face away from the man at his side.

"Are you rational once more, Curtis?" Stavropol asked.

Curtis Levi opened his mouth to answer, but the words wouldn't come out.

A knock sounded at the door. Levi heard Stavropol rise from the chair and shuffle away. He wanted to look—to see what new monster might have arrived to assist Stavropol in his never-ending torment—but he was afraid if he turned, the horns and hooves would come back.

The door opened, and a voice Levi recognized as Dr. Kwison's said, "How is he?"

Stavropol's voice drifted across the room. "He will be all right by this evening. I am afraid I misjudged his pain tolerance, and also his reaction to the stimuli. He retreated early—a little too early for the techniques to become effective." There was a pause, then the Russian went on. "He has less courage, less tolerance for discomfort, less *character,* if you will, than even I had imagined."

"Will he be ready for questioning by tonight?" the doctor asked.

"I should think so," Stavropol said. "At least, sometime tonight he will tell you whatever you wish to know."

The doctor snorted. "We thought that before. What if he still refuses?"

Stavropol's chilling laughter echoed against the cold stone walls in answer. "He *will* talk, Doctor," Stavropol said. "But if by some stretch of the imagination he still persists in being uncooperative . . . if he is resistant again, then our American friend will consider last night quite pleasurable compared to what he will experience tonight."

THE HYUNDAI BURNED fifty feet of rubber before the volleys of the 7.62 X 39 mm rifle rounds exploded. Bolan kept his foot against the floor as the rear windshield shattered. Bullets flew through the car, taking out the front windshield and striking the dashboard.

The rear tires exploded simultaneously, and the back of the Hyundai dropped six inches. The vehicle slowed as the wheels hit the concrete. Sparks trailed the skidding car like the tail of a shooting star.

"Hold on!" Bolan yelled as he fought to keep the wheel under control while Hwang Su braced both arms against what was left of the dash.

The front tire struck the curb, bounced off and sent the car fishtailing down the street. From behind came the roar of jeep engines turning over. Bolan swerved around a parked Datsun, then the careering vehicle struck the rear fender of a Nissan. Bouncing off the other car, it spun across the street and up onto the sidewalk as pedestrians dived for cover.

A street sign slowed the Hyundai further, and Bolan felt something hard strike the back of his head. For a moment he thought he'd caught a round, then one of the rifles from the back dropped onto the seat between them.

The street sign sent the car sliding across the front of a building, and sparks flew as metal scraped brick. Bolan stood on the brake, trying to rein in the unyielding vehicle, but a rifle round had found the brake cable and the car raced on as if with a mind of its own.

He wrenched on the wheel, getting the car back toward the street. After crashing through a vegetable stand, they skidded on toward the intersection.

As the Hyundai drew even with the corner, an ox-drawn wooden cart also appeared, right in their path.

A split second later, the front bumper struck the cart and sent man, animal and cart flying.

The ox's weight finally stopped them in the middle of the intersection. The engine died. Bolan twisted the key, but the engine only coughed. Grabbing the rifle that had hit him in the back of the head, he looked over at Hwang.

The South Korean had been thrown around the interior of the car. His wounds had reopened, and he was again covered with blood.

"Can you run?" Bolan asked.

Hwang nodded, and Bolan reached behind him for one of the rifles and checked that the Type 68 pistol was tucked into his belt.

"Then let's go!" He leaped out of the Hyundai and turned toward the overturned ox cart. The driver jumped to his feet, shaking his fist and yelling.

From behind them came the roar of racing jeeps. A split second later more automatic fire issued forth from the rifles of the special-forces troops.

The bullets made the old man end his tirade as he dived behind his cart. Bolan and Hwang sprinted down the alley. Hwang was fading, and fading fast. He was as tough as a steel machine, but machines sometimes broke down and needed repair.

Footsteps sounded behind them, and Bolan stopped, pushing Hwang on. Twisting back to the mouth of the alley, he saw several soldiers attempting to enter. A steady stream of fire from the Type 58 drove them back for cover around the corner.

Bolan turned and saw Hwang slowing, then he halted altogether. Bolan pulled up next to him and saw why.

The alley dead-ended against three adjacent buildings.

The footsteps sounded behind them again, and Bolan turned, firing once more to stall for time. His eyes rose upward to see that the shortest of the structures was at least twelve stories high. Above an alley door, he saw a sign in Korean. Reaching out, he tried the knob. Locked.

On both sides of the door were heavy metal containers marked with the international sign for infectious material. Bolan turned to fire another burst down the alley to keep pursuit at bay, then swung back to Hwang. "What is this place?" he asked, indicating the sign.

Hwang staggered forward, pressing his nose almost against the sign. "Hospital," he panted. "Burn center."

A light bulb suddenly blazed in Bolan's brain. A burn center would likely have a helicopter to transport emergency cases. While his idea was a long shot, at this point in the game, there wasn't a "short shot" available.

Without explanation, Bolan twisted and shoved the undercover specialist against the wall for support. Pressing the barrel of his rifle against the lock, he pulled the trigger, discharging the last round in the magazine. The door swung open to reveal a dark hallway.

Bolan threw the rifle aside since he had no extra clips. Then he stepped inside, pulling Hwang with him. He closed the door behind him, and they made their way past what appeared to be administrative offices, then turned down a hallway. When Bolan saw the stairs, he shook his head to himself.

They were headed for the roof, and if it were up to him, his legs would carry him there. Elevators were death traps, but considering Hwang's condition, twelve flight of steps would do him in even more quickly.

"Keep your eyes open," Bolan said as they moved on down the hall. "We're looking for an elevator."

Hwang Su pointed to a sign overhead. "Left...next hallway," he said, his voice reflecting his fatigue.

Behind them Bolan heard the sounds of men cautiously entering the building from the alley. He and Hwang turned the corner and saw the elevator. By now Hwang's feet were beginning to drag. Bolan stopped in front of the car, pressed the Up button and waited.

After what seemed like an eternity, the elevator doors slid back. As Bolan was about to enter, a flash of blue caught his eye.

He looked up to see a uniformed security guard stepping off the elevator. The man's mouth dropped open in surprise. His eyes moved from Bolan to Hwang, then his hand fell to his gun.

The Executioner didn't hesitate. A right cross into the jaw dropped the guard as if he'd been hit between the eyes with a sledgehammer. He fell to the floor, still inside the elevator. Bolan scooted him out of the way with his foot and told Hwang, "We want the roof."

Hwang stared at the Korean letters next to the buttons. He shook his head. "It doesn't go all the way to the roof," he said, gritting his teeth against the pain from his injury. "The top floor is storage and a laboratory. You have to reach the roof by the stairs or use the special elevator that goes straight from the operating room.''

Bolan jabbed the top button on the row. The doors closed, and the car began to rise. He knelt and used the guard's own handcuffs to secure his hands behind his back, lifted the Type 64 pistol from his holster and jammed it into his belt.

The uniformed man began to come around as they rose through the air. Bolan cocked his fist again, and a second later the guard returned to sleep.

Finally the elevator stopped, and the doors swung back on a tile-floored hallway. The lights had been dimmed, and the laboratory was obviously closed for the night.

''Hwang, which button stops this thing?'' Bolan asked.

Hwang Su stared at the buttons, then his arm moved out as if made of lead, and he punched one just to the side of the floor buttons.

In the hall Bolan stopped long enough to call the other two service elevators up. Poking the same buttons he'd seen Hwang punch in both other cars, he froze the elevators on the top floor.

It wouldn't stop the pursuing men—they could always take the stairs. But it would slow them down.

With Hwang in tow, Bolan made his way past several offices, seeing the hospital's crest—a fire-breathing dragon wearing a stethoscope—imprinted on each of the glass doors. He spied what looked like a stairwell at the end of the hall. The door was unlocked, so Bolan grabbed the undercover specialist under the arms and backed up the steps. As he neared the top, the wind charged down the stairwell, whipping his hair around his face. Below he heard the pounding of feet as the soldiers finally arrived on the top floor.

In the center of the roof, he saw the helipad. The only problem was, the pad was empty.

He felt cornered and fought the feeling off. There was another way off the roof. There *had* to be. He just had to find it. And he had to find it fast.

Down the steps behind him, the door to the lab floor opened. He drew the Type 64 pistol, dropping the front sight on a black combat boot as it started into the stairwell. The little pistol erupted in his fist, and the boot jerked back.

He fired once more to make sure they knew he was there. The round struck the concrete floor and ricocheted around the narrow stairwell.

Bolan handed the Type 64 to Hwang and said, "Keep it aimed down the stairs. Fire one round whenever your hear something. *One* only. We don't have ammo to waste."

The warrior rose and sprinted to the retaining wall at the edge of the roof. Looking down, he saw the building adjacent to the hospital. It was a four-story drop to the roof. No way they'd make it—not with Hwang's condition.

Bolan circled the roof, checking each of the adjoining buildings. All of them were shorter than the burn center, and to reach them would require both strength and climbing ability. He didn't know how much climbing ability Hwang had, but he knew he didn't have strength.

A shot sounded at the top of the stairs, and Bolan drew his Type 68. He sprinted back to see Hwang aiming his pistol down the steps.

A khaki-clad body was sprawled lifelessly at the foot of the stairs. Hwang looked up at the big American. "Any luck?" Hwang asked.

Bolan had started to answer when the flopping rotor blades of an incoming helicopter sounded above. He looked up to see the chopper a half block away. Squinting in the darkness, he strained to make out the shape. A converted military chopper. But as it neared, he spotted the dragon insignia on the chopper's sides.

Bolan helped Hwang to his feet and started leading him toward the helipad. By the time they reached the center of the roof, the chopper had set down. Four men in white uniforms wheeled two gurneys down a ramp from the loading door. They ignored Bolan and Hwang, speaking excitedly as they hurried the burn victims away from the helicopter.

Not so the pilot. Through the glass, Bolan saw that the man's eyes were glued to his. He didn't move. Bolan started to move toward the ramp, but a sudden voice behind him froze him in his tracks.

Three troopers had finally braved their way to the roof. They now stood just beyond the stairs, the stocks of their Type 58 assault rifles against their shoulders.

He drew the Type 68 again, pulling Hwang along. They were in a direct line of fire to the helicopter, and he doubted the men at the stairs would risk a shot with their penetrating rifle rounds.

Bolan aimed his pistol toward the pilot. "Hwang, tell the man to stay put."

Hwang shouted the order. The man heard.

And decided to call the Executioner's bluff.

The chopper engines roared, and a second later the helicopter began to rise. Bolan turned quickly, seeing that in another second the special-forces men would have a clear shot. Shoving the Type 68 into his waistband, he grabbed Hwang around the waist with one arm and reached up with the other, hooking an elbow around the skid.

The chopper jerked them off the roof, and suddenly they were sailing over the dark city of Pyongyang.

Hwang looked up at Bolan, his eyes suddenly wide. "Are we doing what I think we're doing?" he asked incredulously. "Or am I hallucinating from fatigue?"

Bolan's shoulder had already begun to ache. Fighting both his and Hwang's body weight and the bounces the chopper was taking in the air currents, he knew he couldn't hang on long. "Hwang," he said, "loop your belt through mine. Do it *fast.*"

The helicopter bobbed gently in the night wind as the South Korean unfastened his buckle and threaded his belt through Bolan's. Wrapping both arms around the Executioner's neck, he held on for dear life.

Slowly Bolan let go of the undercover man and reached up with his other hand, grasping the skid. The fresh arm took some of the strain off his throbbing shoulder, but even with both hands now supporting their weight, he knew their time in the air was limited. Sooner or later his strength was going to give out.

Somehow he had to get the pilot to set the chopper down.

Bolan looked back down at Hwang. "Hwang, if I get you close enough to the skids, can you hold on?"

The answer was honest. "Who knows?"

"We're going to find out. It's our only hope." He took a deep breath. Then, looking up, he began to pull.

Slowly, an inch at a time, they began to rise. The muscles in Bolan's shoulders, arms, and back screamed in pain as he "chinned" his way up to the bottom of the chopper. When his head was over the skid, he yelled, "Grab it!"

Hwang made a grab for the skid, got hold of it and wrapped his hands around it.

Bolan reached down, grabbing the man by the back of the collar and pulling. Hwang got his chest over the skid, balancing precariously as the chopper continued to bob in the air. The warrior paused, catching his breath. He wasn't finished—not by a long shot.

Now he had to get up on the skid and face the pilot.

He unclipped the Centofante from his pants pocket, thumbed open the blade and sliced through his belt. Releasing Hwang's buckle again, he secured the belt around the skid. Now, if he fell, at least the belt would catch him, unless it snapped in two.

Bolan glanced at the undercover man's face as he closed and reclipped the Centofante. The man hadn't had much strength to begin with, and Bolan had called upon him to perform a feat most people couldn't pull off on their best day. The bottom line was, Hwang Su was fading fast.

With another deep breath, Bolan reached up and grabbed the boarding step. Again his entire upper body screamed in pain as he hoisted himself upward. The chopper hit an air pocket, and he dropped back down. For a moment he felt the grip of both hands slipping, but his fingers curled back around the steel skid and rubber-covered step.

By now his breath came in short, hard pants. Hwang wasn't the only one fading, and he knew that if he didn't make it up on top of the skid with the next effort, he wouldn't have the strength to try again. Closing his eyes briefly, he pulled.

Bolan shot up onto the skid, his foot slipping, then wedging against the cross support. He hauled his other foot up onto the boarding step, drew the Type 68 and stood up, grabbing the window frame with his free hand.

The pilot turned to look at him with an expression that could only be called awe.

The Executioner drove the butt through the glass, then set the business end of the weapon against the man's head. "Set her down," he ordered.

The pilot might not have understood English, but he seemed to understand just what he had to do.

IT WAS MIDMORNING by the time Bolan and Hwang found the street on which Myung Namsoo, aka Kim Sang, lived. The pilot had set them down in a park on the edge of the city. Wanting to get out of the area as quickly as possible—the downed chopper was already drawing too much interest—Bolan had left the man bound and gagged and then hot-wired the first car he'd seen. The Honda Civic had helped put several miles between themselves and the pilot before they'd abandoned the vehicle.

But they'd been seen taking the car, and Bolan had no doubt that by the time he dumped it in a back alley closer to town, the police had the description and were on the trail.

The Mitsubishi had been sitting in a driveway. In the wee hours of the morning, no prying eyes had seen Bolan crack the steering column and drive away. At least the Mitsubishi wouldn't be associated with the big American and his Oriental partner who'd been wreaking havoc on the capital of North Korea for the past day and a half. But even though there wouldn't be nearly as much "heat" on the Mitsubishi, Bolan intended to get rid of it as soon as they made contact with Myung.

He turned the corner and drove by several boxlike houses. Constructed of brick and wood, they appeared to be one-bedroom units designed by an architect whose primary deficiency was a lack of imagination. They looked no different than tract housing in any other city of the world.

But there *was* a difference. In the U.S., Great Britain, France or any other free nation, these houses would have been inhabited by lower income families. But in a Communist country like North Korea, the inhabitants of this level of home were the elite—meaning the government bureaucrats. The little cracker boxes Bolan saw before him now were as good as it got.

Next to him Hwang opened his eyes. He needed rest, pure and simple.

"Which one?" Bolan asked.

"12313," Hwang said drowsily. "The fourth one on the left, I would guess."

Bolan drove slowly past the house, taking it in, as well as scanning the neighborhood for nosy neighbors. Myung's home looked no different than its neighbors. The curtains were drawn over the front windows, and it looked as if no one was home.

At the end of the block, Bolan cut around the corner, pulled to the curb and glanced at his watch. Almost 1000 hours. Myung would have been at work for some time, and assuming he kept regular government hours, wouldn't return until somewhere between 1600 and 1800. Bolan turned to Hwang. "Does Myung's wife work?"

"Only part-time, if I remember correctly."

Bolan thought for a moment. "Okay, we're going to kill two birds with one stone here. We've got to wait on

Myung anyway, so we'll go on in and grab something to eat. That'll give you a chance to get some rest, too."

Hwang grinned. "You said *I* could get some rest. Tell me, aren't you even tired?"

"Closing my eyes for a few hours wouldn't kill me." He got out and walked across the street to the alley, with Hwang following sluggishly the rest of the way to the rear of Myung's house. The backyard was a small postage stamp of yellow grass that led to a one-step back porch. Bolan ducked under the clothesline and stepped up to the screen door.

The screen opened easily, but the door to the house was locked. The top half comprised a dozen small windowpanes. With a final quick scan of the area, Bolan drew the Centofante, tapped the pane closest to the knob and watched it fall out. Reaching through the opening, he twisted the bolt.

He led the way into a small kitchen, then moved on to conduct a quick room-by-room search to make sure the house was vacant. When he got back to the kitchen, Hwang had already opened the refrigerator and was piling plates and containers on the table. "Make yourself at home," he said, handing Bolan a set of porcelain chopsticks. "I'm sure my old partner won't mind." There was an unmistakable tinge of sarcasm in his tone.

Bolan dropped into one of the chairs and dug into what appeared to be a chicken-and-vegetable concoction. He watched as Hwang's strength appeared to return a little more with every bite.

But the man was frowning. He had something on his mind, and Bolan suspected he knew what it was.

"Out with it," he said.

Hwang looked up, surprised. "It shows, huh?"

"All over your face."

Hwang nodded slowly. "I'm trying to decide how I feel about what Myung has done," Hwang said around a bite of chicken. "We were partners. And he was my best friend." He stopped chewing and looked at the wall. "So, is Myung Namsoo a traitor to my country or not?"

Bolan didn't answer. Hwang was really talking aloud to himself, trying to sort out in his head what had happened between him and his old partner.

"Part of me—the South Korean special-forces soldier—says yes, Myung Namsoo is a traitor. He deserted the special forces, and South Korea. Myung had a mission, and by choice he did not complete it. But the other part of me—the part that was Myung's friend—reminds me that even though he did not complete the mission, neither did he reveal any information about us to the enemy." He lifted the chopsticks, then paused with them halfway to his mouth. "If Myung were discovered to have once been a spy, he would still be executed. There is no way he could ever convince them that for the sake of a woman he had given up the business and assumed his undercover identity for good."

"He's in a tough spot," Bolan agreed.

Hwang set his chopsticks down. "What do *you* think, Pollock?" he asked. "Is Myung Namsoo a traitor?"

Bolan shook his head. "What Myung did wasn't right," he said. "But if he's just working for the Bureau of Internal Transport, I wouldn't call that aiding and abetting the enemy very much. We're into one of those many 'gray' areas of life, Hwang. I'm not sure you can call Myung a traitor, at least not in the strictest sense." He saw the confusion still on the undercover specialist's face. "Men do strange things for love sometimes, Hwang. Things they wouldn't dream of doing otherwise." He stood up. "Let's get some rest while we have the chance."

Hwang Su dropped the chopsticks back to his plate and nodded. "My appetite is gone," he said.

Bolan began gathering up the plates. "Go on back and find a bed," he said. "I'll take care of this. In case Myung's wife comes home, I don't want her first sight of the kitchen to tell her somebody's been in the house."

Hwang nodded and disappeared down the hall. With a careful eye to detail, Bolan put things to rights again, then returned to the living room and dropped down onto the couch.

The breakneck pace of the past two days suddenly rushed over him in a wave of fatigue. He leaned back and closed his eyes, knowing he might not get another chance to sleep until the mission was over. Yet, at the same time, he told himself he could not afford to lose touch with the waking world entirely.

Soon he drifted into a state of semiconsciousness. How long he was there, he couldn't say, but suddenly he heard soft female voices outside the front door. At first he thought they were part of a dream. Then the sound of a key sliding into the front door roused him further, and suddenly he was on his feet and racing down the hall to the bedroom.

The front door was already opening as Bolan cupped a hand over Hwang's mouth, then the women stepped into the living room. Hwang understood what was happening immediately, and he rose silently from the bed. The chance to rest had done him a world of good; his eyes were clear and his step steady as he followed Bolan.

The friendly chatter continued in the living room, and Bolan moved toward the closet door.

The closet door creaked quietly as he opened it and waved Hwang inside. He looked past the undercover man to see two clothes bars filled with hanging garments. Hwang disappeared behind them.

Bolan squeezed in after him, closing the door. He dug through the forest of clothes and took up a position next to Hwang. "Myung's wife," he whispered. "And a friend."

He sensed rather than saw Hwang's nod in the darkness. No further words were spoken. There was no sense taking the chance of being overheard. Bolan glanced at the luminous face of his watch—1644 hours.

Unless he wanted to scare the wits out of these two women by holding them prisoner until Myung Nam-soo returned, all they could do was wait.

Myung and her friend continued to chat excitedly, then tea-making sounds came from the kitchen. Roughly thirty minutes later, after what sounded like goodbyes, the front door opened and closed. Soft footsteps padded down the hallway to the bedroom.

Through the door Bolan heard the sound of a zipper. The swish of clothing coming off followed a moment later. Myung's wife was undressing, which probably meant a trip to the closet.

Bolan wasn't mistaken. The closet door opened, the light from the window streaking in. The Executioner froze, hoping both he and Hwang were hidden.

Through a small gap in the hanging clothes, Bolan saw a startlingly attractive Oriental woman in a beige bra and matching lace panties. Draped over one arm was a plain blue dress. The other hand pulled a hanger from the bar in front of his face. The woman softly hummed a half-familiar Oriental tune as she slid the dress down over the hanger, then pulled a floral-print robe from the bar.

Bolan held his breath. A moment later Myung's wife had slipped into the robe, returned the empty hanger to the bar and closed the door. She padded back down the hallway, and the sound of pots and pans clinking against each other came from the kitchen.

He felt an elbow in his ribs. "Close call," Hwang whispered in his ear.

Bolan nodded in the darkness. "I'm surprised she didn't see us."

"That's not what I meant," Hwang said.

"Huh?"

"I meant, that it is a close call as to whether or not I myself would have left the South Korean special forces for a woman who looks like that."

CHAPTER TEN

When Myung opened the closet door himself two hours later, Bolan and Hwang didn't hide.

Bolan rose behind the lower clothes bar, and before Myung could verbalize the shock that registered on his face, one of Bolan's hands was behind his head jerking him into the closet while the other covered his mouth.

Hwang shoved the barrel of his pistol into Myung Namsoo's ribs. He spoke softly yet forcefully in English for Bolan's benefit. "Send your wife on an errand, old friend. We must talk."

Although Hwang's face was still hidden behind the hangers, it was obvious Myung recognized the voice. He relaxed, and Bolan risked dropping the hand that covered his mouth. "Hwang Su," Myung whispered. "Is it you?"

Hwang's face held the same confused expression that Bolan had seen earlier. "Send her away," he said.

"You were sent to kill me?" Myung asked. His voice sounded more curious than frightened.

"No," Hwang said. There was a long pause, then in a sad voice he added, "But I will if I must."

Myung nodded in the semidarkness and started to turn. Hwang grabbed his shoulder and held him back for a second. "Remember that we will be listening," he whispered. "We would not like to hurt you...*or her*."

Myung smiled. "You would never hurt her," he said.

"Do not be so sure," Hwang said. "You cannot know."

"I can." Myung nodded. "I know *you*." He turned and walked out of the room.

Bolan and Hwang followed him as far as the bedroom door. They heard him speak in the kitchen.

Hwang turned to Bolan. "He is sending her for wine. She says, 'Why? We have nothing to celebrate.' Now he says, 'Every day with you I celebrate.'"

Bolan heard the woman giggle.

A moment later the front door closed. Myung appeared again in the bedroom. He smiled at Hwang. "It is good to see you," he said.

"Is she gone?" Hwang asked.

"Yes. Thank you for letting her leave." Myung glanced to Bolan. "May I assume your friend is American, and that we are speaking English for his benefit?"

Hwang's voice was harsh. "You may *assume* nothing, Myung Namsoo," he said. In his fist he still gripped the Type 64 Bolan had given him, the barrel pointed at his former partner's belly. "Assuming anything is always a mistake. I once assumed that you could be trusted—that you were loyal to South Korea, the special forces...and me."

Moisture appeared in Myung's eyes. "Hwang Su..." he said, but didn't finish the thought.

"We will go into the kitchen," Hwang said, indicating the hall with his gun. "There is tea?"

Myung nodded, turned and led them down the hall.

Bolan and Hwang took seats at the table while Myung got three cups and the teapot. He poured in silence, gathering himself together, then joined them at the table.

"So," he said. "If you are not here to kill me, there is something you need."

Bolan looked at him. "There is," he said. He proceeded to explain about Curtis Levi, Boris Stavropol and Rhee Yuk. He finished by letting Myung in on the fact that, unless they got Levi out of the country soon, North Korea would have the technology to launch nuclear weapons across the globe.

Myung listened attentively, nodding now and then. When Bolan had finished, he blew air through his clenched teeth with a low whistling sound. "Then you want me to help you locate Rhee Yuk, who in turn can take you to where Curtis Levi is held?"

"And it has to be done fast. For all we know, Levi is spilling his guts right now. But even if he isn't, he will be. Boris Stavropol is an excellent interrogator, if you get my drift."

"Yes, I remember Stavropol from his KGB days," Myung said. "Some of the stories about him make even the most hardened soldier weak with nausea. This Levi has no chance to resist unless he is very tough."

"Well, he isn't," Bolan said. "I could always be wrong, but he's not likely to hold out long." He paused, then said, "Levi and you are in similar situations, Myung. He made a mistake—a mistake I suspect he highly regrets by now."

Myung didn't answer, but Bolan could see by his face that he'd hit home.

"So you will help us?" Hwang asked.

Myung turned to him. The moisture Bolan had seen earlier in the man's eyes was back. "Hwang Su," he said softly. "Of course I will help you. I am not a traitor. I have told the North Koreans *nothing*. They do not even know I was once a SKSF operative. If they did, I would be dead."

The strain of mixed emotions showed on Hwang's face, but his voice remained hard, professional. "What is your wife's name?" he asked.

"Sachiko," Hwang said.

Bolan saw Hwang's eyebrows rise at the Japanese name.

"Her father was from Tokyo," Myung said. "Her mother, Korean."

"Does she know your secret?"

"No," Myung said, shaking his head. "She knows me by my undercover name, Kim Sang. And that is how I wish it to remain. Telling her would place her in too much danger and—"

The sound of the front door suddenly opening caused him to stop in midsentence. A voice called out cheerily, and then Sachiko appeared in the doorway. Her smile changed to a look of surprise as her eyes moved from Bolan to Hwang, then to her husband.

She spoke, and Hwang and Myung both looked to the counter where a black leather purse sat.

"She forgot her purse," Hwang said.

Bolan turned back to Myung. "Does she speak English?" he asked.

Myung shook his head.

"Then you can make something up, or you can come clean and hope for the best."

Sachiko frowned at her husband. "Sang?" she asked quizzically.

Myung glanced at his wife, then back to Bolan. "I have never been able to fool her on anything," he said. He shook his head as he stared down at the table. "Except *this,* which, of course, is *everything*. Perhaps it is time for the truth." He turned back to his wife and pointed at the empty chair across from him.

The baffled look still on her face, the beautiful Oriental woman sat down.

Still staring down at the table, Myung Namsoo began his story. Hwang translated softly for Bolan's benefit, skipping some parts he guessed were personal and irrelevant to the mission. Bolan watched Sachiko's face change from bewilderment to concern, then finally to anger. Finally she reached across the table and slapped her husband across the face.

Myung's expression didn't change. He continued to stare at the table as his cheek reddened.

Now Sachiko began to speak, her voice angry and pleading in turn.

Suddenly she leaned across the table and threw her arms around her husband. She sobbed into his neck, whispering something that Hwang started to translate, but Bolan held a hand up, palm out, and shook his head. Whatever it was, it was personal.

Finally Sachiko sat back. Myung took his wife's hand as he turned to Bolan. "I will help you," he said. "I will help you find Rhee Yuk because I am ashamed of what I have done. And I demand nothing in return. But when this is over, there is a good chance I will finally have been exposed. I would like to ask a favor."

Bolan waited.

"I would ask that you help me and my wife escape to your country." He paused. "I do not think I will be welcome in mine."

Bolan frowned. "I'll do the best I can," he said. "But understand that once we snatch Levi, things are likely to get pretty chaotic. I can't guarantee your safety... or hers."

Myung turned back to his wife, drawing her close to him. He spoke and she nodded. "She understands," he said. "And she agrees."

Bolan stood up and looked from Myung to Sachiko to Hwang. "Then let's do it," he said.

THE FALSE WALL Myung had built into his closet raised his wife's eyebrows far higher than it had Bolan's or Hwang's.

Both Bolan and Hwang knew few men said good-bye to the warrior life without taking part of it with them. The warrior—be he front-line soldier, clandestine operator or police officer—knew firsthand the violence of which men were capable. He might start selling insurance, managing a drugstore or even making travel arrangements for North Korean bureaucrats, but he continued to take precautions.

Once a man had "seen the elephant," he never forgot that elephants were out there.

From his hiding place Myung produced two Daewoo Precision Industries Tri-Action semiauto pistols—one in 9 mm, the other chambered for .40 S&W. He unwrapped a blanket, and Bolan saw a K1A1 carbine, also from Daewoo. Two 30-round 5.56 X 45 mm box magazines accompanied the carbine. Bolan accepted the .40-caliber Tri-Action and relegated the Type 68 he still had to backup duty. Myung shoved the 9 mm Daewoo into his belt. The carbine's collapsible stock was retracted and the weapon wrapped innocuously in a blanket, which Bolan placed next to him in the back seat of Myung's Volvo 240.

Myung had also produced a cheap body-mike transmitter that operated over FM radio waves. "It's prehistoric," he said. "But it's all I've got."

"Bring it," Bolan said.

Myung grabbed a bottle of Japanese saki from the cabinet on the way out of the house and kissed his wife goodbye.

The drive to the Bureau of Internal Transport in downtown Pyongyang took almost an hour. No one spoke as they drove, and Bolan rested his head against the back seat. Work hours were over for the day, and he couldn't afford to wait until morning to contact Rhee.

No, they needed Rhee tonight. The problem was, none of them had a clue as to where he lived.

Myung, however, felt certain he could access the address by tapping into the State Department personnel files from his office. Like their American counterparts, South Korean special-forces soldiers specialized in one field of training, but cross-trained in other specialties. Among Myung's many fortes had been computers.

In the front seat Myung and Hwang passed the saki bottle back and forth, taking sips to be sure their breath smelled of alcohol. Bolan stared out the window as they drove quietly through the night. He'd have liked to have had Kurtzman from Stony Man Farm hacking his way into the State Department files, but Myung would have to do.

The next problem lay in the fact that Bolan couldn't enter the building. Hwang was to be presented to the desk guard as an old friend. Their cover story was that they had been out drinking and wanted to sober up on coffee before going home to face their wives. A Caucasian simply didn't fit into that picture, and they could think of no other picture that would legitimize taking Bolan into the building after hours. So he had decided to wait in the car and listen to the transmitter over the FM radio while they tracked down Rhee's home address.

The Bureau of Internal Transport lay in a modern office complex in the heart of downtown Pyongyang. Bolan slid below window level as they parked. "Turn the radio on, but keep it low," he said.

In the front seat he heard the switch turned on. Snatches of Oriental music came from the speakers as Myung twisted the dial to find the frequency on which the transmitter was set. Then Bolan heard Hwang say, "Testing, one-two-three-four." The words were accompanied by loud, scratchy feedback from the close proximity of the mike to the receiver.

"We're ready," Hwang said.

"Then take off. Don't take any longer than you have to, and don't take any chances. Keep me informed of your progress as best you can, but again, don't take any chances."

Hwang looked over the seat and grinned. "Relax, Pollock. Myung and I have done this drunk routine so many times we could do it *drunk*." He poured a little of the saki onto the front of his shirt and handed the bottle to Myung, who did the same. The interior of the car began to smell like a Japanese geisha house.

Hwang handed the bottle over to Bolan, then turned to Myung. The confusion caused by his changed relationship was still evident on his face. The expression slowly changed as he finally made his decision. "Ready, partner?" he asked Myung.

Myung looked as if a thousand-pound load had just been lifted from him. He smiled a smile that could only be called grateful, then said, "It's like old times."

The two men exited the vehicle and crossed the street to the door of the office building. Through the glass front on the first floor, Bolan could see a gray-uniformed guard reading a newspaper behind a desk. Spread out across the desktop were a variety of pastries, a pen set, several stacks of paper and a hand-held walkie-talkie. A small shelf was fastened to the wall directly behind the man, and on top of it were potted plants, paperback books and a small transistor radio. The man looked up as Myung stuck a key in the door.

The two undercover partners staggered inside and went into their routine, playing jovial, friendly drunks. But even as the amused guard greeted Myung, a vague uneasiness settled on Bolan.

He couldn't say what, but something was wrong. Everything had gone smoothly, yet his battle sense had suddenly gone on alert.

Myung and Hwang reeled to a row of elevators and disappeared a moment later. But a second after the doors closed, Bolan heard the FM radio screech. Then Hwang's voice said, "Like our performance, Pollock?" His voice was much fainter in the elevator.

Bolan monitored the sounds as they made their way to the computers and started their search.

He relaxed a little. Maybe he'd been wrong. Maybe his battle sense was simply working overtime—still tired from a fast pace with little rest. Hwang and Myung were doing an excellent job. They were pros.

"There!" Myung said in a forceful whisper suddenly. "I have it!"

In a minute Hwang responded. "Pollock, we are finished. We are coming down."

Bolan breathed easier as he heard the men leave the office. Whatever had bothered him earlier seemed to have been a false alarm. It happened sometimes, and this looked like one of those times.

Shifting slightly in his seat, Bolan turned his eyes back to the guard on the other side of the glass. The man had given up the newspaper and was now eating. With his mouth full, he suddenly swiveled in his chair toward the shelf behind him.

The elevator doors opened as the guard swiveled back, holding the transistor radio. He twisted the dial to change stations as Myung and Hwang emerged into the lobby.

Bolan held his breath, suddenly realizing what had triggered his battle sense earlier. He stared through the glass as Hwang and Myung ambled toward the front door. Their steps showed better coordination than when they'd entered, but they still looked like men who'd just drunk the town dry.

Bolan shook his head, wanting to yell at them not to say anything, not good-night, not goodbye! But he knew it would do no good.

He watched, helpless, as the two men stopped in front of the guard's desk and Myung said something cheerful sounding.

Bolan heard the words. So did the man in the gray uniform.

The Executioner heard them over the FM radio in Myung Namsoo's Volvo, and with them he heard the same screech of a transmitter too close to a receiver that he'd heard when Hwang had tested the unit.

The man sitting behind the desk heard Myung speak both in person and over the transistor radio in his hand. For a second he stared at the small black box in confusion.

Then what had happened sank in, and he leaned back in his chair and drew the revolver from the holster at his side.

CURTIS LEVI SHRIEKED at the top of his lungs. Then his eyes clouded over, and he stared straight ahead as if watching something happen several miles away. "Mary had a little lamb, little lamb..." he sang in a voice that sounded like death itself.

Boris Stavropol wiped the pliers on his handkerchief, squeezed the handles together and returned them to the inside pocket of his coat. He studied the man before him with the look of a chemist observing an interesting experiment.

The American rocket scientist had become an enigma to the Russian. Oh, Stavropol had encountered many men tougher than Levi. Men who held out longer, a few all the way through a slow and painful death. But he had always at least suspected these men would be tough before he began.

With Levi, Stavropol knew he had made a mistake—a mistake he hadn't made in years. Before he had begun the interrogation, he would have wagered his life that the American would be talking within ten minutes. But Levi had held out for two nights.

"The lamb was sure to go!" Curtis Levi screamed at the top of his lungs. His eyes closed, and his head fell to his chest as if his neck were broken. Blood dripped from his face to his lap.

Stavropol grunted. "Curtis," he said softly.

Levi's head shot up again. "Mary had a little lamb!" he bellowed. "Little lamb, lit—"

"Curtis, you can quit singing," Stavropol said. "We are finished for this evening."

Levi's head dropped back to his chest, and again droplets of blood splashed down over his lap and legs.

"You surprise me, Curtis," Stavropol said. "I would never have expected you to resist me for so long. I suppose you are to be commended for bravery beyond what I expected," Stavropol said. "But you must realize, it will be very bad for you in the long run."

"M-I-C," Levi began singing, "K-E-Y..."

Now Levi was singing the song from the Mickey Mouse Club. The former KGB officer had seen similar things in the past. Some men regressed to childhood during torture, their minds reaching out to plead for a more pleasant, pain-free period of their lives. He had listened to more cries for "Mommy" than he could remember, but all of Levi's psychological defenses seemed to center around song.

Interesting. Very interesting. Stavropol frowned. Perhaps he would study this phenomenon further and even write a paper about it after he retired.

"Forever may we wave your banner high..." Levi sang.

"Curtis," Stavropol said. "Curtis, you must—"

"M-I-C," Levi interrupted.

Stavropol reached out, grabbing Levi's neck with one hand and cupping his other over the man's mouth. "Curtis, listen to me!"

The American stared into Stavropol's eyes, his own still clouded and distant.

"Curtis, you must understand that so far I have relied only on what I refer to as level-one interrogative techniques. Level one is designed to inflict enough pain to encourage cooperation without causing permanent damage." He took his hand away from Levi's mouth and looked down at the blood covering his palm. "Curtis, do you understand what I just said?"

Slowly, almost imperceptibly the American nodded.

Stavropol wiped his hand on the handkerchief. "Level one has not been successful," he said. He watched to make sure the man in the chair was still listening, then said, "Do you know what that means?"

Just as slowly as he had nodded, Levi shook his head.

"It means, Curtis, that tomorrow I must move to level two." Stavropol dropped the handkerchief to the table next to him. "Level two is no more painful physically, but psychologically it is devastating. So far, nothing has been done to you from which you cannot recover. But tomorrow that will not be the case."

A flicker of interest suddenly showed behind the clouds in Levi's eyes.

Stavropol waited a moment to let the tension mount, then went on. "At Level two, we begin doing things from which you will not heal. And you will be aware of that fact as these things are done. Perhaps I will begin by amputating all of your fingers one by one. Sometimes I start with the penis, sometimes the testicles. It depends upon my mood." He shrugged. "But it makes little difference where we *start,* Curtis. What matters is where we end level two. If you continue to withhold your cooperation, when I finish, you will have no arms or legs. No ears or nose. You will be unable to hear and you will be blind."

Now the clouds drifted away completely, and Levi stared at Boris Stavropol with the same terror the Russian had seen when they'd begun the night before. Stavropol smiled inwardly. Good. He had found the man's weakness. Level two it would be.

The former KGB man sat back in his chair. For a moment he considered returning to his office for the tools he would need for level two. He glanced at his watch. No, it was late and he was tired. He needed to get a good night's sleep so he'd be fresh for tomorrow. There was no rush.

Or was there? Stavropol's mind flashed back to Seoul and the big American who had tried to snatch

Curtis Levi from his clutches. He had lost the man easily, and in some ways that was disappointing. On the other hand, rumors were flying around the North Korean capital that a man fitting the American's description had teamed up with an Oriental—probably a South Korean agent of some type. They were wreaking havoc in the streets, and possibly were in league with the Hwarang Warriors.

The former KGB man shrugged his shoulders. The chances of locating Curtis Levi were one in ten million.

He leaned on the arms of the chair and pushed himself to his feet. With one final look at the tormented human being before him, he went across the room. Grasping the doorknob, he turned back to the man strapped into the interrogation chair. "Think about what I have told you," he said. "There is still time for you to cooperate. Do so, and no more harm will befall you."

Stavropol twisted the knob, said, "Good night, Curtis," and started through the door.

Behind him he heard a weak and quivering voice whisper, "M-O-U-S-E."

BOLAN DIDN'T WANT TO KILL the desk guard. Not if he didn't have to. The old man was well past his prime, and had obviously been put out to pasture at a job where he wouldn't get in the way.

The guard walked Hwang and Myung to the wall with his revolver, his hands shaking. With the new interference from the man's transistor radio, reception over the Volvo's FM was too garbled to make out. But here and there Bolan caught snatches of the man talking nervously.

Leaning over the front seat, he opened the glove compartment. Digging quickly through the contents, he came up with a small plastic map case roughly the size of a billfold. He frowned. What he had in mind might or might not work. He hoped it did. If not, he would have no other choice than to break through the glass door with guns blazing.

He fished into his pocket for the Stinger, then exited the Volvo and sprinted across the street. By now the man in the gray uniform had Myung and Hwang facing the wall, their hands clasped behind the backs of their heads. With the Stinger in his left hand and the map case in his right, Bolan rapped loudly on the door.

The glass around the frame rattled and shook. The guard turned to look.

Bolan let out a breath. He had half hoped either Hwang or Myung would take advantage of the small diversion to whirl around and disarm the guard. But the elderly guard was staying well out of their reach, his revolver aimed at the small of Hwang's back. He shot a look across the lobby at the entrance, then turned quickly back to check his prisoners as he tried to decide what to do.

Bolan banged the map case against the glass, silently praying that the shadows were right to keep the guard from making out any details. The miniature map holder was close to the size of a badge case, and with it hanging open as it was now, he hoped the man would mistake it for one. That would add to his confusion, but Bolan still had to do something to explain the fact that he was obviously not Korean.

Taking a deep breath, he began shouting through the glass in Russian. "Let me in!" he demanded. "I am Colonel Petrovsky, and these men have escaped custody." He paused, knowing it was unlikely that the guard would understand his words. But the confused man should at least recognize the language, and would know that many former Soviets had been taken on by North Korean Intelligence and police agencies.

The guard continued to hesitate, then slowly he began backing toward his desk, heading toward the walkie-talkie.

"I demand you let me in *immediately!*" Bolan shouted through the glass in a commanding voice.

The guard smiled faintly and nodded toward the door, making it obvious he hadn't understood a word. But he appeared to realize that the man at the door was an ally of some kind because the revolver never moved away from Hwang and Myung. Lifting the walkie-talkie with his left hand, he spoke into the radio, then set it back on the desk.

Bolan rattled the door again. "Let me in!" he demanded.

The guard backed toward the door slowly, the gun in his hand still trained across the room at Hwang and

Myung. Bolan folded the map case and stuck it back in his pocket.

When he reached the door, the man turned quickly to the glass and spoke. Bolan shook his head and shrugged his shoulders. The guard checked his prisoners again, then reached into his pocket with his free hand, pulling out a wallet and holding it up against the glass.

The intimation of his pantomime was unmistakable. He wanted to see Bolan's credentials up close before he unlocked the door.

For a brief second Bolan pretended not to understand. This close there was little chance the map case would be taken for anything other than what it was.

Which meant the time for subterfuge was over. The time for action had begun.

Bolan drew back his fist and drove the nose of the Stinger through the door. The glass exploded into huge, razor-edged chunks that shattered into smaller fragments as they hit the concrete entryway.

The shocked guard turned to face the door, his mouth dropping open. The revolver fell from his hand as Bolan stepped through the door frame.

Running footsteps sounded down the hallway by the elevator as he used the free fingers of his Stinger-filled hand to grab the guard by the collar and lift him to his toes. With his other hand he lifted a light uppercut into the guard's sternum.

The man fell to the floor coughing as two more guards appeared in the lobby, revolvers drawn.

These men were younger, fit and ready to fight. Both carried Type 68 semiauto pistols as they halted in the middle of the lobby.

By now Hwang and Myung had drawn their weapons from concealment, and they teamed up to take out the guard. Hwang fired a double-tap of 7.62 mm lead into the chest of a slim NK with bristly black hair.

Bolan drew his Daewoo as Hwang's twin rounds drove the guard back three steps. A look of surprise came over the young man's face, but he didn't fall, and no blood appeared on the front of his gray uniform blouse.

Hwang knew the reason as well as Bolan did. He lifted the sights of his pistol slightly, and the next round bypassed the ballistic nylon vest and took the man squarely in the throat.

Myung had presented his own Daewoo from concealment, and he and Bolan double-actioned their triggers at the same time, wasting no time with body shots. Taking careful aim, Bolan sent two of the .40-caliber rounds into the head of his target. Myung, firing almost dead on, got his man with his first shot, just above the bridge of the nose.

Myung and Hwang hurried across the lobby. They vaulted over the old man on the floor, followed Bolan through the door and sprinted across the street.

The Volvo was already a block from the internal-transport offices when the first siren sounded in the distance.

"The old man still alive?" Myung asked.

"Yeah. He'll be all right," Bolan told him.

"Good," Myung said as he squealed the tires around a corner. "He's a good old-timer. I've known him ever since I started work there." He guided the Volvo down the street. "One thing's for certain, though."

"What's that?" Hwang wanted to know.

"I won't be going back to work there anymore."

CHAPTER ELEVEN

In Rhee Yuk's apartment there was a note on the table.

Striker,
Hal sent me to button-hole Rhee and get him
ready. Unfortunately he's suffering from *big-time*
battle fatigue—useless to anyone right now. We've
gone to a place he goes to "relax." Back around
0400, or meet us there—400 block, Kanggye
Street, downtown. Alley entrance only. Ring bell.
   Can't wait to see your face. You'll see what I
mean.

Katz

Mack Bolan studied the note on the kitchen table,
wondering exactly what Katz meant. Though Katz had
retired from active field work as the Phoenix Force
leader, he carried on in an advisory capacity at Stony
Man Farm. And on occasion decided to handle some
special jobs, and here he picked and chose. His note
made several references that led Bolan to believe there
was something unusual about Rhee. He could only
hope that whatever it was wouldn't have an adverse
effect on locating Curtis Levi.

Bolan looked up from the table at Hwang and Myung, then handed the note to Myung. "Any ideas where this place is?"

"Downtown, like it says, of course. I know Kang-gye Street. But the alley entrance means it concerns something illegal or at least frowned upon by the government."

"Drugs?" Hwang asked.

Myung shrugged. "Perhaps," he said. "There are opium dens hidden around the city. But it might just as well be a church or something outside the norm."

"So," Hwang said, "do we go or wait?"

Bolan glanced at his watch. The appointed time was still hours away—hours during which Stavropol might be skinning Curtis Levi alive or holding an electric cattle prod to his testicles. "We go," he said, pointing toward the door.

A few minutes later they were on their way. Myung took back streets and kept the headlights off, not wanting to draw the attention of local authorities looking for curfew breakers.

Bolan stayed low in the back seat. His mind drifted to Yakov Katzenelenbogen. He hadn't expected to meet up with him here in North Korea. Brognola had obviously contacted the Israeli and dropped him in to round up Rhee while Bolan and Hwang made their way north.

The Executioner felt himself frowning, trying to decipher the cryptic nature of Katz's note. The battle-fatigue part he could understand. Unlike other undercover officers, moles lived their parts twenty-four hours a day. They had little contact with their associates, and sometimes began to lose their real identity as if it were part of some past life. Other times the daily stress of worrying that they'd be discovered—with no immediate relief in sight—caused them to turn to the bottle, drugs or other forms of stress relief.

Myung found Kanggye Street easily, and then the 400 block. He pulled into the alley and parked.

They got out of the car and walked along the darkened alleyway. Myung produced a small pocket flashlight and shined the beam on each back door as they passed. No buttons or doorbell devices of any type appeared.

They came to a turn in the alley and followed it on past more darkened doors. Finally Myung's flashlight paused on a door. Just to the side was a red button. Bolan leaned forward and pushed the button.

There was a window set in the door, and Bolan stepped aside. Whatever was inside was illegal under Communist law. That meant anyone seeking entry was well looked over before being allowed entry, and a couple of Korean undercover men would stand a far better chance.

The window slid open. For a second no one spoke. Then Myung, standing directly in front of the door, said something in Korean. A feminine voice at the window spoke back. There was a question-answer exchange, with the responses from inside clearly becoming more negative at each stage. Finally Myung shook his head, still smiling. He turned to Bolan and Hwang.

Bolan nodded.

In one smooth movement Myung lifted his foot and drove it forward into the door. The voice shrieked through the window as the door flew open. Myung charged through, followed closely by Bolan and then Hwang.

The door had struck the woman, and she now lay on the floor dazed. An angry red welt was growing on her forehead. Bolan stooped to look at her closer.

Despite the feminine appearance, she had a large, masculine Adam's apple and a neck that looked as if it belonged on an NFL linebacker.

Stepping over the body, they started toward the stairs at the end of the dark hallway.

A slow rendition of "The Girl from Ipanema" drifted down the steps as they mounted them. Bolan reached the second-story landing, passed the door to a foul-smelling rest room and stepped into a large ballroom.

The odor of perfume filled the air as if it had been dumped into the duct work. The band—dressed in Caribbean garb—was centered on a stage against the far wall. Just in front of the stage was the dance floor. Some of the men dancing wore tuxedos. Others wore sequined evening gowns that sparkled with each pass of the ceiling strobe lights. Regardless of what they wore, the dancing men floated lightly to the soft Caribbean beat.

"I have always been a Buddhist, Pollock," Hwang said. "But I must now concede that you Christians are right."

"How's that?" Bolan asked.

"There really *is* a hell, and I have died and am in it."

Bolan chuckled. Directly in front of him, between the dance floor and the stage, were several dozen tables where men dressed as men, and men dressed as women, sat drinking, talking and laughing. Bolan scouted the tables left to right, his eye finally falling on the middle-aged man who sat alone at a table near the front.

He led the way to where Katz sat sipping his drink. The Israeli faced the dance floor and didn't see Bolan approach.

"What's wrong, Yakov? You're not dancing."

Yakov Katzenelenbogen turned in his chair. He laughed, then shook his head. "It is not because I have not been asked. Please, you and your friends sit down. Fill the chairs. *Please*. You would be surprised how many odd Koreans seem to have a penchant for older Jewish men."

Bolan laughed as he dropped into the chair next to Katz. The band went into a fast-paced rumba as Hwang and Myung took the other two chairs.

Katz looked out across the dance floor. "Do you see the, er, *person* wearing the black floor-length gown with the silver sequins and pearls?" he asked.

Bolan followed his gaze, seeing an Oriental in the described costume dancing with a man who wore a black tux. As he watched, the man leaned forward and said something, and the figure in the gown threw back its head and laughed coquettishly.

"Tell me you're joking," Bolan said.

"I wish I could," the Israeli said. "But since I can't, meet Rhee Yuk." He grinned mischievously. "Your new partner."

Myung turned to Hwang. "And I thought *you* were bad," he said.

Hwang nodded. "I should have listened to my mother and become a doctor," he said.

Katz leaned in close. "Seriously now, Pollock. Rhee Yuk is on the edge, and the edge is crumbling fast. You've got to be aware of that—the pressure has just about done him in." He took a deep breath. "I latched on to him last night and I thought he'd lost his mind— a textbook paranoid. I had to make him call in sick at work today, and by tonight he was climbing the walls. He's convinced the North Koreans know who he is."

"This seems to help him?"

Katz nodded. "Pretending to be a woman lets him be somebody else for a while. Someone who isn't at risk of being executed as a spy."

Bolan looked Katz square in the eye. "We need Rhee to locate Curtis Levi," he said. "Can he pull it off, or is he too far gone?"

Katz shrugged. "Hell if I know," he said honestly. "It's not like he forgets his name or undercover identity or anything like that. But I'd keep a close eye on him. If you look up the term 'loose cannon' in the dictionary of slang, I suspect you'll find his picture in the margin." The Israeli grinned. "Probably wearing a dress."

Bolan nodded. "Where are you headed from here?" he asked.

"Little island due west off the coast," Katz said. "Just the other side of Nampa." He tapped a coat pocket. "I brought a radio, and Grimaldi's going to do a touch-and-go as soon as he hears from me."

Bolan frowned. He could use the Israeli's help if he was free. "Is there a job waiting?" he asked.

Katz shrugged. "David and the others got one on hold. Hostage situation in Barcelona. So far, negotiation seems to be working. But Hal wanted the team there just in case, and I'm in a special advisory capacity on standby." He paused, adding his own frown to Bolan's. "You need something? Grimaldi won't be back for me until tomorrow."

"Then you've got time for a little side trip?" Bolan asked.

"You need something, I'll *find* the time."

"I do. I'll tell you about it later." He looked out across the dance floor to where Rhee and his partner were now engaged in a wild tango. "Now, if you'll collar Rhee, we'll get out of here." He cleared his throat and kept his face emotionless. "Unless you're starting to have too much fun."

The muttered response was in Hebrew, and Bolan didn't understand it. But he doubted it was complimentary.

Katz stood and made his way through the dancers to Rhee Yuk. The South Korean mole looked longingly at his date, shrugged and returned to the table with Katz.

After brief hellos, they all stood and trickled toward the door. In a few more minutes they were outside, the music already fading behind them.

DAWN BROKE over Pyongyang, and light began to streak in through the window of the kitchen.

Seated at Myung's table were Hwang, Rhee Yuk, Myung and Bolan. The men were silent, each lost in private thought as the new day began and the moment of truth neared. By this time tomorrow, they knew one of two things would have happened.

Either they would have already snatched Curtis Levi back, or one of the last Communist nations of any consequence on the planet Earth would have the ability to transport nuclear devices across the globe.

His thoughts turned briefly to the assignment he'd sent Katz off on before heading for the island where Grimaldi would pick him up. It shouldn't be difficult, or take long, and the Israeli would be in the air and on his way long before Bolan accomplished his own tasks of the day.

He had considered asking Katz to stay to help him evacuate Levi. Another gun would have helped, and there were no better guns than those fired by Katz, but Katz needed to return to Stony Man Farm.

Bolan felt his heavy eyelids threatening to drop again. He would have liked nothing better than to retire to the couch again for a few more hours of sleep.

Which, of course, was the last thing he could afford to do.

Cued by the whistling teapot, Sachiko rose from her chair and moved to the stove. Bolan looked at the men still seated around the table. They had stopped by Rhee's apartment again after leaving the cross-dressing club. Rhee had washed the heavy mascara and eyeliner from his face and changed clothes. Dressed now in a conservative gray business suit, he looked as if he were already up for the day and about to leave for his office at the North Korean State Department. Instead, he sat with his eyes glued downward at his hands, which were folded on the table.

Sachiko circled the table, setting a cup and saucer in front of each man. She moved back to the stove and lifted the teapot, retracing her steps to fill the cups.

Bolan continued to study the men. Myung Namsoo looked tired. In his eight-to-five job managing interior travel, he had grown unaccustomed to late hours. His eyelids dropped heavily as he lifted the cup to his lips.

To his side, Hwang looked up and smiled as Sachiko poured his tea. His face was drawn and weary, as well. Bolan had watched him recover maybe eighty percent since being shot, but the South Korean undercover specialist was still dragging his tail.

As Sachiko filled the teacups and set fresh biscuits on the table, Bolan spoke up. "We don't have much time," he said, breaking the silence. "We've got to locate Curtis Levi and get him out of here *today*. Now—" he looked to Rhee "—I'm open to ideas."

Rhee Yuk was helped by the conservative business attire he'd changed into, but his face still reflected that he was struggling with embarrassment. "I would like to explain—" he began.

Bolan shook his head, stopping the man in midsentence. "Look, Rhee," he said. "Unless it has to do with finding Levi, I don't want to hear it. I have no interest in what you do behind closed doors. Now, let's get on with your idea."

The man nodded his understanding, then turned to Myung. "It occurs to me that your office would have travel vouchers for the trip Stavropol and his assistants made to Seoul. If you could find them, it would begin a trail that would lead back to Pyongyang and connect with *my* office—the State Department will be in charge of keeping Levi once he is here. I should be able to find out where he is being held through our own paperwork."

Myung nodded. "We would have the records somewhere," he said. "Obviously I can't go back to my office after our visit last night, though I could perhaps access the records from one of our satellite offices. Travel expenses must be cleared and paid. But a mission such as that would be highly classified. It would be veiled as something else in our record books."

"Like what?" Bolan asked.

Myung raised his hands, palms up. "Almost anything," he said. "A trip to somewhere else. Perhaps a series of several trips whose expenses all totaled up to the same amount as the actual journey to Seoul."

Bolan frowned. "There's got to be some kind of cross-reference. Some place where the actual use of the money is written down in order to keep agents from padding their expenses."

Myung nodded. "Yes, but that is kept within the intelligence units themselves. I do not have access to it—even by computer."

"Would the phony documentation be dated the same as the real trip?" Bolan asked.

Myung nodded. "Probably," he said. "Since my office does not have access, there is no reason to disguise it further."

"Then all we can do is figure up roughly what we expect a mission to Seoul would cost, then look for something in the records that comes close. Can you some up with an educated guess of expenditures?"

Myung smiled. "That has been my profession here in Pyongyang."

Bolan turned to Rhee. "There may be more than one expense claim that could be the trip to Seoul," he said. "You'll have to cross-reference them to see which is the right one. Can you do that?"

"Yes, but how long it takes will depend on how many false leads there are."

Hwang leaned forward to make his point. "Locating Levi is the easy part. We must then get him out of wherever he is. I have thought long and hard about this," he said. "Do you know how difficult it will be to get this man out of the country?"

"Close to impossible," Bolan remarked.

There was a long silence. Then Hwang said, "Your mission is to ensure that the North Koreans do not learn Levi's missile technology, correct?"

Bolan nodded.

Hwang took a deep breath. "There is an easier way to keep this scientist from talking once we locate him," he said.

Bolan knew what he meant—he and Brognola had already discussed it. He shook his head. "That's a last resort," he said. "Levi is still valuable to the West. We've got to try to get him out alive. If it turns out we can't, we'll consider your idea."

Hwang nodded.

Bolan took two biscuits from the plate and spread a thin layer of butter across each. The men ate in silence. When they had finished, he glanced at his watch. "Rhee, you get started for your office. Myung, be careful at your satellite office. We don't know what the surviving guard from your regular office told them, so be on the lookout. You two find out what you can. We'll stay in touch through Sachiko, here at the house. Use pay phones so we can't be traced or listened in on. And talk in generalities."

"You and Hwang will be here?" Myung asked.

The Executioner stood up and shook his head. "We've got another small job to attend to," he said.

CHAPTER TWELVE

The Honda two-door hatchback made its way down the side of the bluff. It seemed to Bolan that he had been up and down the road to the Taedong River at least a hundred times since he and Hwang had first arrived in Pyongyang.

Bright rays of morning sun filled the car, and again Bolan found himself hunching below window level. Traffic was heavy as people hurried to work, and word would be out on the streets about the Caucasian and his Oriental partner, still wanted by the police.

And the government paid an ample reward for reporting illegal aliens. Particularly those who shot their soldiers.

Behind the wheel Hwang suddenly said, "Does it ever get to you, Pollock?"

Bolan turned toward the undercover specialist. "I'm not ready to start wearing a dress, if that's what you mean."

Hwang burst out in laughter. "No, that's not what I meant. Unless I've misjudged you, you could be certifiably insane and still not turn to cross-dressing." He gave a final stifled chuckle, then turned serious. "The things we do, I mean." He tapped the steering wheel.

"Like killing people. And stealing this car, and all the others we've stolen along the way."

Bolan looked back out the window as the trees along the curving road raced past. "I've never killed anybody who didn't deserve to die," he said. "And when I can, I leave cars I have to take where they'll be found and returned to the owners," he said.

"What about when that's not possible?" Hwang pressed. "What about when they get totaled out? It kind of bothers me."

Bolan smiled. "Then I tell myself the owner doesn't mind."

Hwang chuckled again. "As a freshman at the university, I studied psychology," he said. "What you just said is called 'rationalization,' I believe."

"And you think all rationalization is bad?" Bolan asked.

"The professor taught us that rationalization was how people excused many things they wanted to do. They did them simply because they wanted to, then went looking for a reason that didn't sound so selfish."

Bolan nodded as they neared the river. "Sometimes that's the case," he said. "But the root word of *rationalization* is *rational*. Do you know the definition of that word?"

Hwang frowned. "Well . . . *reasonable,* I guess. *Sensible.*"

The warrior nodded again. "That's right. Now let me ask you a question. What will happen if North Korea actually develops the technology to send nuclear missiles to the other side of the world?''

"Well," Hwang said as the road flattened out and the bridge appeared ahead, "I suppose eventually they'll launch them at the U.S."

"And what do you think the U.S. will do?"

"Return the favor, I suppose. Blow the hell out of North Korea." Hwang paused. "They wouldn't have much choice."

"Correct again." Bolan looked out the side window as the Honda started over the bridge. Below, the brown waters of the Taedong drifted along in peaceful waves that seemed to contradict this discussion of nuclear holocaust. "So if you were the owner of this Honda we grabbed fifteen minutes ago, and you had the chance to stop a nuclear war by donating your car to the cause, would you do it?"

"Or get blown up?" Hwang said quickly. "Of course."

"Me, too. I'd call that rational, reasonable and sensible. And if whoever owns this car is of the same mind, I'd guess they'd say the same thing."

"I see your point and I agree," Hwang said. "But it's still difficult sometimes. I was taught that stealing is wrong, and that two wrongs don't make a right."

Bolan yawned. "I was taught the same things," he said. "Wouldn't it be nice if the world worked that smoothly?"

They fell into silence as they left the small village at the bottom of the bluff and headed north. Bolan closed his eyes, taking advantage of the drive to catch a little more rest. What lay immediately before them might be an easier task than rescuing Curtis Levi.

But that didn't mean it would be easy.

Two years earlier Hwang Su had been in the village of Wonjang, a few miles north of the Pyongyang bluff. He remembered the small police substation, and had noted the lax security around the small building. It housed an armory that served several of the small villages of the region, and could outfit those substations in the event that civil unrest cut them off from the capital. But the harsh dictates of communism eventually made discord among the citizens unlikely, and the regime had grown lazy in guarding their weapons.

Bolan reached under his shirt and let his fingers fall on the .40-caliber Daewoo Myung had given him. It was a good gun, but it wasn't enough. They would need heavier arms if they intended to go up against the North Koreans guarding Levi, and Wonjang offered the perfect opportunity to obtain the necessary weapons.

Hwang slowed as the tiny village appeared in the distance.

"How many men you suppose will be on duty?" Bolan asked.

"Unless things have changed since I was here, six, maybe seven," Hwang said.

Bolan glanced outside to the tiny shacks that now lined the roads. Here and there he saw ox-drawn carts.

A few people rode rickety bicycles. "Seems like a lot for such a little place," he said.

"For the U.S., yes," Hwang said. "Or for South Korea, or for any free country for that matter." He drew a deep breath and what he said next came out almost as a sigh. "But the Communists like their police as visible as possible. Not to control the criminal element but to remind the average citizen that he's being watched."

Soon the police substation appeared on their left as they drove slowly by. It was a one-story affair, and pale institutional green walls and a few wooden benches were visible through the open front door. To the left side of the door was a window where a man in uniform sat.

"We should do it and do it quick," Hwang said. "This is like any small town. A strange car makes good gossip."

Bolan nodded. "Circle the block and drop me off," he said. "Then give me two minutes before you go in the front."

Hwang started to turn down an alley behind the station, but Bolan shook his head. "It'll draw too much attention," he said. Down the street was a row of small fruit-and-vegetable stands. "Turn there. I'll cut back and cross the alley on my own."

A moment later Bolan opened the door and started to get out. Hwang reached across the seat and grabbed his arm. "There are several other colorful expressions I picked up in the U.S.," he said. "One will fit you as soon as you step out onto the sidewalk. You will stick out like a turd in a punch bowl, so *hurry.*"

Bolan smiled. "I'd planned to," he said. "Just give me a good enough show to keep the people in the front busy." He stepped out of the vehicle and onto the dirt-packed street as the Honda hurried to the end of the block and turned the corner.

Dozens of pairs of eyes turned toward the stranger. Hushed and nervous chatter prattled up and down the street.

Speed was of the essence now that he'd been seen. Communist North Korea mandated that anyone who failed to report suspicious characters or behavior was as guilty of a resulting incident as the perpetrator, and possibly it wouldn't be long before someone headed into the police station.

Cutting between two of the vegetable stands, Bolan crossed the alley behind the police station. The back door was propped open to allow ventilation, and he silently thanked the officer in charge for his careless-ness. He ran a hand across the Daewoo under his shirt, but reached into his pocket for the Stinger instead. The pistol was there if he needed it. But with any luck, he'd accomplish his goal silently.

Pressing his back to the brick wall beside the open door, Bolan peered around the frame. Inside he saw an empty room with two tables, a cabinet and sink—a break room. He glanced at his watch. It was still early, too soon for breaks. The men inside would be going about their morning rituals.

With a final glance up and down the alley, he slipped inside the break room. From this new vantage point he saw a closed door to his left and a padlocked cage to the right. Beyond the heavy crosses of wire that covered the cage, rifles and other weapons stood in racks against the wall of the darkened enclosure.

Another open door leading toward the front of the building gaped in front of him, and he made his way silently to the wall next to it. Through the opening he could hear the quiet tapping of a typewriter. Then a sleepy voice spoke, and was answered by another. Someone slurped from a drink, and then the room fell into silence.

He dropped to one knee and leaned forward to the edge of the door frame. In the room beyond he saw three desks. Two faced his way, while the other was pointed toward the front of the building. The desk nearest him was empty, but men sat behind the other two. Both were typing, their eyes glued to the task.

Through an opening that led to the front room, Bolan could see the green walls and benches of the lobby. The window where the front-desk officer had sat was out of sight to the side.

The Executioner pulled back around the corner, rising to a squatting position. Hwang should appear in the lobby any second now. His task was to go to the window, begin an excited account of some fictional crime, then suddenly go into a faked epileptic seizure that would demand the attention of anyone in the first room. In the meantime Bolan would go to work on the officers in the back.

The old adage about the "best-laid plans of mice and men" raced through Bolan's mind as he heard a toilet suddenly flush behind him.

He rose, turning toward the sound. It had come from behind the closed door across from the weapons cage. As the flush died down, it was replaced by the screech of air in the pipes as water began to run in the sink.

Bolan sprinted back through the room toward the alley.

He was a split second too slow.

The man who came out of the rest room caught a glimpse of the tall figure that flashed by from the corner of his eye. He turned, his mouth dropping open in surprise.

Bolan saw the reaction. Reaching up with both hands, he checked his momentum on the door frame, then spun back toward the cop as the man finished tucking his uniform shirt into his pants.

The Stinger shot out into the man's sternum, stifling the cry that had started on his lips. But the muffled sound still carried, as did the thud of his body on the floor. Bolan swung his foot sharply against the officer's head, knocking him unconscious.

But the damage had been done. Excited voices came from the room with the desks, then the scraping of a chair scooting across tile floor. Bolan was already back across the room. Retaking his position beside the door, he gripped the Stinger in his left hand as his right curled around the butt of the Daewoo.

A moment later an overweight officer stepped through the door. He saw his comrade on the floor and Bolan at the same time, and his hand dropped toward the flap holster on his belt.

Bolan stepped forward, driving the nose of the Stinger into the man's jaw. A sick mashing sound echoed throughout the room as the bone splintered, followed by a muffled scream.

Drawing the Daewoo from his belt, Bolan brought it down on the back of the officer's neck. The man collapsed without making another sound.

From the front of the building came Hwang's excited sputtering. Nearer, Bolan heard the other chair scoot back from the desk. He waited until the footsteps that followed were about to enter the back room, then stepped into the doorway and released an uppercut.

The punch landed directly under the third officer's chin, the Stinger's point driving up into the soft palate. The man's eyes rolled back in his head as he dropped to the tile.

Bolan stepped over the man as he heard someone hit the floor in the front room. Through the opening he saw Hwang foaming at the mouth and thrashing madly about on the floor.

As he made his way forward, two uniformed men knelt beside Hwang. One grasped his arms while the other dug a tongue depressor from a pouch on his belt.

Bolan shot into the lobby as the man jabbed the tongue depressor into Hwang's mouth. Raising the Stinger high over his head, Bolan brought it down in a hook that caught the man at the base of the neck and sent him plummeting over Hwang.

The other kneeling officer groped for the pistol at his side. Still on his back, Hwang launched his legs up and out, encircling the neck. Then Hwang's legs snapped back like a giant set of scissors, and the Communist cop's neck snapped as he hit the floor.

Bolan turned his attention to the reception window where the desk officer sat stupefied. Coming out of the trance, he lifted a telephone to his ear with a trembling hand.

Bolan aimed the Daewoo at the window and cocked the hammer for effect. "Don't," he said.

The North Korean police officer understood the meaning, if not the word.

MYUNG NAMSOO SAT BACK from the computer terminal, laced his fingers together and cracked the knuckles. The sound echoed hollowly off the walls of the office he'd "borrowed." He glanced through the open door to the reception area, then looked to his watch.

Myung smiled to himself as he stared at the computer screen. He had sent the secretary to fetch more coffee after he spilled the container by the office coffee machine. Obtaining coffee in Pyongyang was different than it was in Seoul. In South Korea you went to the store, bought what you had come for and went home. In North Korea, or any Communist country for that matter, you went to the store and then stood in line for a few hours to receive a chit that allowed you to transfer to the purchase line, which would be just as long. Then, unless they had run out of what you wanted before your turn came, you finally picked up the item for which you'd come.

In any case, the secretary wasn't likely to be back before noon. Upon arrival, he'd told her he would be working there for a few days while the authorities investigated some incident at the main office. The secretary had merely nodded and offered to make coffee so he would feel at home.

Myung's smile widened. He was tired, dead tired after being up all night, but his weariness couldn't keep his good mood down. He felt as if a huge burden had been lifted from his shoulders—a burden that weighed as much as the whole southern half of the Korean peninsula. His decision to stay with Sachiko had not been made lightly, and not a day had gone by since that he didn't question it.

Was he a traitor to his own country? He thought not. He had not completed his mission, but neither had he sold out to the North. He had, rather, entered a sort of twilight limbo where he was neither deserter nor patriot. He had been a man without a country.

Until last night.

Prying his mind away from the events of his personal life, Myung leaned back toward the screen. He moved the cursor on down the list of vouchers that he'd handled in the past two days. The North Korean system called for any representative about to travel to file an estimate of expenses and have it approved by his office. The Bureau of Internal Transport then issued a claim voucher to the NK treasury, who issued that amount to the person who had filed. Differences between estimated and actual expenses were rectified with another system of vouchers after the trip had been completed.

He continued to move the cursor slowly down the screen, stopping occasionally when something caught his eye. He had done his homework on paper before spilling the coffee, and knew within approximately a thousand *won* the total amount of money that would have been requested for the trip.

Stavropol always worked with a team of five men—he remembered that bit of intelligence from his South Korean special-forces days. And Myung had to assume they would have crossed the border at least two days before the scheduled pickup in order to recon the area and lay out their route of escape. That meant gasoline for two vehicles, food and hotel accommodations for six men for at least two nights, maybe three. He was betting on three, since the snatch had gone down at night. They would have kept the rooms after normal checkout time in order to have a base from which to conduct last-minute preparations.

Myung's smile became a frown as he stopped the cursor on an endorsement one of his staff had signed for the Department of Commerce. The file reflected a request for funds to send two men to Wonson to greet a delegation of Japanese businessmen. He could tell at a glance that the request was inflated. Even with the lavish treatment the spoiled Japanese expected, it was apparent that whoever had filed the request was looking to slide a few extra *won* into his pocket.

Myung studied the total. Yes, far too high. But still not what it would take to send six men to Seoul for three days.

He continued to look for suspicious vouchers. The next entry concerned three delegates who'd traveled north to the Chinese border to escort a grange expert who was to address the Department of Agriculture. The expenses seemed in line this time—maybe even on the light side. He moved on.

His fingers wavered for a second, and his mind drifted back to what Sachiko had told him a week before—information he had not yet shared with anyone. She was pregnant, and the knowledge filled his heart with such joy that he thought surely it would burst.

Myung stopped the cursor and let the love flood through his chest. After the initial joy that Sachiko was with child had worn off, his guilt had intensified. Was his son—or daughter—to be born a slave to communism? He had decided that at the first opportunity, he must tell his wife the truth, then make plans to flee the country with her. But that problem had been solved for him with the arrival of Pollock and Hwang.

The cursor stopped suddenly as Myung saw that he had personally okayed a withdrawal of several thousand *won* so that six men could take two vehicles to Kaesong. The request had once again come from the Department of Agriculture, and the purpose listed was a gathering of farm representatives from the lower provinces.

Although Myung knew full well where Kaesong was located, he glanced reflexively at the wall map. Kaesong. The historic battle site of the Koran War was as far south as you could go without entering South Korea itself.

Six men.

Myung scrolled past the itemized estimation of expenses to the total. He turned to the paper where he had made his own estimate of the trip to Seoul. His eyebrows lowered. The total was a good two thousand *won* short of what the trip to pick up Curtis Levi had to have cost.

Myung Namsoo sat back against his chair, still staring at the screen. *This was it.* He knew it. His heart told him so. But what of the discrepancy of total funds?

The front door of the outer office opened and shut. Myung cursed silently as he heard the secretary start the coffee machine. She had made it back early, which meant he would have to be careful.

Cracking his knuckles again, Myung studied the file for more clues. Six men. It had to be Stavropol and his crew. But what if it wasn't? What if it really was just a meeting of the Department of—

Agriculture. That was it. The Department of Agriculture was the common link for which he'd been looking.

Myung shot the cursor back up the screen to the file concerning the Chinese agricultural expert. Going straight to the total request, he jotted it down on the page where he'd made his original estimate. Then, dropping back to the voucher for the trip to Kaesong, he added that amount below it and added the total.

Myung Namsoo smiled as he saw he was less than a hundred *won* below the total expenses he had calculated for Boris Stavropol.

He reached for the phone at his side, then thought better of it. Pollock had warned them to use safe phones, and that was good advice. Who knew when the Party might be listening in, and this was no time to take chances. No, he would go to a phone booth and call from there.

Rising from behind his desk, Myung Namsoo reached for his briefcase, then stopped. Why? What would he need his briefcase for now? Nothing. He would never return to this or any other internal-transport office.

He glanced through the open door to where the secretary sat. It would be better to take it, just the same. It might look unusual if he did not, and again this was no time to take risks.

The briefcase under his arm, Myung walked into the outer office, stopped in front of the secretary's desk and looked down at her. "I am feeling ill," he said, his hand moving to his throat.

"There is flu going around," the woman said.

"I will take an early lunch," Myung said. "Unless I feel better after eating, I will not return."

The woman smiled as he turned to the door. If she was anything like his secretary, Myung knew she would whip out her reading before he reached the elevator.

He rode the elevator down alone, offered an official-looking nod to the guard on the door, then he left the building without turning back again.

BOLAN GAVE THE GO-AHEAD, and Hwang rolled to his feet and drew the Type 68. Moving quickly to the window, he stuck the gun through the hole and barked in Korean at the desk officer.

A second later there was a buzz, and a door next to the window swung open.

Bolan stepped into another office area and pointed the Daewoo at the frightened man behind the desk. "Tell him to take his weapon out slow and leave it on the desk," he told Hwang.

At the command, the desk officer—a sergeant by the stripes on his sleeves—unsnapped the flap on his holster and slid out what looked like a GI Government Model .45 pistol.

Bolan waved the man away from the desk and lifted the pistol curiously. His question was answered by the inscription on the side of the slide. Model Of Thc

1911A1.45 Automatic, it read, and below that on the frame, Made In China By Norinco.

Bolan pulled the slide back far enough to see that a round had been chambered, then laid his Daewoo down on the desk. The .40 S&W was a good caliber—sort of a split between the great knockdown power of the .45 and the high capacity of which 9 mm pistols were capable. But the .40-caliber pistol was a rarity in North Korea, and when he ran out of the ammo Myung had supplied, there would be little chance of finding more.

Thumbing the Norinco's safety down to Fire, Bolan turned it toward the sergeant. "Ask him if they've got any more of these," he told Hwang.

The sergeant looked at the big .45-caliber bore of his own weapon and nodded.

Bolan reached out and grabbed the man, keeping him in front as he made his way back through the lobby and the middle offices to the locked cage at the rear of the building.

Two of the men on the floor were coming back around as they entered the room. A swift kick to the head by Hwang sent them back to dreamland.

Bolan pointed to the big padlock on the cage door and shoved the muzzle of the .45 against the side of the sergeant's neck. The man didn't hesitate, reaching into his pants pocket and coming up with a key ring. A moment later the lock fell open.

Opening the gate, Bolan pushed the sergeant inside the cage. Hwang also stepped in, and they began surveying the piled boxes and lockers.

"What do you want me to do with this one?" Hwang said.

He had a good point. It would take both of them to load what they needed, and that left no one available to baby-sit. "I think it's time for his morning nap," Bolan said. "Then go get the car and pull it around to the back door."

A quick chop to the neck took care of the guard, then Hwang hurried out.

Bolan flipped the Norinco back on Safe and shoved it into his belt. He had no idea what the Korean letters printed on the boxes before him meant, but a pry bar he found leaning against the wall worked as translator. Flipping open the lid of a rifle-length crate, he found a dozen new Type 58 assault rifles. Pulling out four, he stacked them against the wall.

In an already opened wooden crate were appropriate magazines for the rifles. The box was marked with the number 50, and no more than a half-dozen could have been removed from the top. Considering the fact that he was arming eight people, that meant they had roughly five to six magazines a piece.

If that didn't turn out to be enough, a hundred more wouldn't make any difference.

Bolan carried both boxes out of the cage and set them next to the alley door. He returned to the cage and pried the lid off another crate. Inside he found a dozen or so vest-style canvas magazine carriers. He counted out eight once more and piled them to the side.

A row of dark green lockers stood against the concrete wall. All were locked, but a flip of the pry bar was all it took to open them. In the first were two dozen first-aid kits. He frowned. There was a limit as to how much they could carry, and as soon as they snatched Levi it would be a mad rush for the border. There would be little or no time to treat wounds. Medical treatment would have to wait until they'd reached the safety of South Korea, and then doctors would be available.

If the wounded survived that long.

Moving on to the next locker, Bolan flipped the lock and opened the door to find row after row of plastic-bodied hand grenades in "egg carton" containers. The FAMAE GM 78-F7s were of Chilean origin, and had already been fitted with coils of notched steel wire that would produce shrapnel upon explosion.

He remembered Hwang's words that this armory was here in case of civil unrest. It looked as if the North Koreans had no qualms about shredding their own people.

Again Bolan hesitated. He didn't yet know where Levi was being kept. It might, or might not, be an environment in which the grenades would be useful. But assuming they found the rocket scientist and got him out, chances were there would be ample opportunity for a few ground explosions on the way back to Seoul.

Counting out sixteen grenades, he piled them on top of the vests.

The next locker had housed several dozen stacked pistol boxes. Opening the one on top, he found Norinco .45s identical to the one he now carried in his belt. The pistols were still packed in creosol, and came with an extra magazine and cleaning kit.

Eight of them went to the pile.

Hwang appeared behind him as Bolan moved to the corner and what appeared to be an ammunition box. He pointed at the letters on the side. "What's it say?" he asked the undercover specialist.

"It's ammo for the rifles you left by the door. I just loaded them."

"Well, load that, too. What about the case to the side?"

"It's .45 hardball," Hwang said. "You find more of the Norincos?"

Bolan nodded, drew the .45 from his belt and handed it butt first to Hwang. He nodded toward the pistol boxes. "I'll get another one ready on the drive back," he said. "Take this one. But remember they're new. Unfired. Be ready for a few jams until they loosen up."

Hwang shoved the Norinco in his belt, lifted the case of rifle ammo and started for the alley. The Executioner hoisted the .45s and followed.

The South Korean had already raised the hatchback, and the two men shoved their loads into the back. They returned to the cage for the grenades and vests, then snapped the hatchback shut.

"Ready?" Hwang asked.

"Almost," Bolan said. He strode back into the building and into the lobby, lifting the first of the unconscious men from the floor and carting him to the cage. Hwang caught on and dragged another man inside the wire. They moved to the middle desk area, added those men to the ones inside the armory and finished with the officers who had fallen in the break room.

Bolan snapped the padlock shut, locking the cops inside the cage. Hwang followed him out of the police substation, and they got into the car.

"I feel like I've done this before," Hwang said with a grin.

"What's that?" Bolan asked.

"Locked the cops inside a jail cell and made my getaway." He shrugged as Bolan twisted the key and pulled away from the curb. "On the other hand, maybe I just saw it in an old Western."

CHAPTER THIRTEEN

Locked in the small rest room just off his office, Rhee Yuk gripped the sides of the sink. His arms began to tremble, and he squeezed the porcelain harder. The unbearable anxiety that had gradually mounted within him over the years was about to come to a head.

And when it did, he knew he would spin out of control, his personality disintegrating into an unconnected jumble.

Rhee stared at his reflection in the stainless-steel mirror over the sink. For a split second he wondered if it were a one-way glass the Communists used to spy on him. Then he was sure of it.

Rhee looked up at the light fixture above his head and realized it might contain an eavesdropping device, and a moment later he was convinced that it did.

And the chairs, the desks, the picture frames on the wall . . . all hid cameras and transmitters and—

The timid knocking on the door jerked him momentarily back to reality.

"Mr. Rhee?" Li Fon said. "Are you *certain* you are all right? I could call the doctor—"

"I am fine!" Rhee almost shouted. "Just sick to my stomach. Please leave me alone!"

Rhee heard his secretary's footsteps pad away. He looked back into the mirror and felt his chest contract. He felt as if perhaps he should not breathe—as if the *way* that he breathed might give away the fact that he was an undercover agent. He held his breath for as long as he could, then gasped for air.

Over the years Rhee Yuk had worked his way up the bureaucratic ladder to a position of authority in Pyongyang. But how could that be done without making some mistakes along the way—mistakes of which he was not aware? The answer was, it could not. Somewhere he had left clues to his real identity. It was humanly impossible not to have done so.

A flash of lucidity settled in his brain, and suddenly shame replaced his paranoia. He stared into the mirror. Who was he? What had he become? At first he had handled the stress through movies and novels and pretending to be one of the characters in the stories. Then he had tried alcohol, then prescription drugs and then even the opium and heroin smuggled across the border from China.

All had worked for a while. A *short* while. Then the novelty of each escape wore off, and he was unable to use such devices to chase away the maddening fear.

The knock on the door was louder this time. "Mr. Rhee," Li Fon said. "Please. A man insists on talking to you. He says it's urgent."

Rhee turned toward the door. "What is his name?"

"He did not give a name. But he is with the Bureau of Internal Transport and very insistent."

The knowledge that he should have left the office for a safe phone and called Myung's house long ago crept from the back of Rhee Yuk's brain to the front. Horror flooded through him. He looked down at his watch and saw that he had been locked in the rest room for nearly three hours. *Three hours.* His failure to follow the plan had forced Myung to call here.

"Just a moment!" Rhee said. "Tell him I will be there in a moment." He turned back to the mirror, reached down into the makeup kit on the sink, and pulled out a jar of cold cream. Hurriedly he wiped the eyeliner, mascara and rouge off his face with a wash-cloth and inspected himself in the mirror.

Turning back to the door, he unlocked it and hurried to his desk.

"You did not call," accused Myung on the other end of the line.

Rhee started to answer, then realized there was nothing he could say.

"Write this down," Myung ordered. He gave Rhee the information about the Department of Agriculture trips, then said, "Do not force me to call again. Do your job. Then meet us at the place we agreed on."

"Yes." Rhee listened to his voice tremble as he spoke, then hung up. He turned to his computer and fed in the information Myung had given him.

It didn't take long to find the link. The Department of Agriculture had recently acquired office space in an ancient castle that had been built in the days of Koguryu, Silla and Paekche, the three kingdoms that

eventually united to become Korea. Uninhabited now
for several centuries, the crumbling structure was cur-
rently under historical restoration. Part of Koguryu
Castle had already been completed and was being used
to house government offices.

Rhee sat back. He had passed the castle on his way
into work every morning since being planted in North
Korea. He had done so this very morning. He had even
noticed that the renovation seemed almost complete,
but he had never dreamed that he was within a hundred feet of the American rocket scientist. He pictured
the castle in his mind. It was small as such structures
went—only four stories if he remembered correctly.

The South Korean mole *felt* rather than saw Li Fon's
eyes on him. He looked up from his desk to see his
secretary standing in the doorway, her lower lip
drooping in surprise. He followed her line of sight
across the room to his desk, then down to his hands,
folded in front of the computer.

Rhee Yuk almost screamed as he saw the bright red
fingernails and realized he had forgotten to remove the
polish.

THE CITY HAD BEEN founded over three thousand years
ago, and like many other early settlements that had
endured the test of time, Pyongyang had preserved
some ancient structures that still stood among the more
modern buildings around them.

His face partially hidden by the sun visor, Bolan
lifted the cheap binoculars he had found in the Honda's

glove compartment. He looked out across the park to Koguryu Castle. He and Hwang had arrived at the park only a few minutes before, having made it back to Myung Namsoo's house with the weapons shortly after Rhee arrived with the news that Levi was being held in the castle. He had been a total nervous wreck, barely capable of speech. Babbling, he talked about transmitters hidden in the sink at his office and the fact that his secretary had seen him in nail polish. What was real and what was fantasy was difficult to determine, and Bolan wasn't convinced they could trust the information that Levi was in the castle.

In fact, Bolan was certain of only one thing in regard to the South Korean mole. The man was quickly coming unglued. From now on, everything Rhee said would have to be sifted through a filter for authenticity and, if possible, verified from a separate source.

The Executioner stared through the lenses at the activity around the castle. As Rhee had advised, renovations on the building's south side seemed to be complete. To the north and east, however, wooden scaffolding rose from the ground up along the rock walls. Masons were busily reinforcing the concrete between the stones. Workers came and went through the doors carrying brushes, paint and building materials.

Lifting the binoculars higher, Bolan squinted at the stones as if trying to see through them. The renovation part of Rhee's story checked out. But was Levi really in the castle, or was that part real only in Rhee Yuk's distorted mind?

Hwang had brought the car to a halt along a drive that wound through the green trees, park benches and picnic tables. They had a good view of three sides of the castle, but they dared get no closer. Armed with submachine guns, uniformed special-forces soldiers stood watch at all entrances. Armed guards were hardly unusual at Communist government buildings, but Bolan had never seen such a heavy guard unless there was good reason.

He had also spotted three uniformed North Korean foot-patrol officers strolling through the park, and there had been at least two cops in plainclothes. None of them had been there for family outings, and they carefully scrutinized the people who passed by.

The reason was simple. The authorities were still looking for him and Hwang.

"We are in what you Americans call a quandary," Hwang said behind the wheel. "We cannot be sure Levi is inside, and we cannot get close enough to find out. Even if we *knew* he was there, we do not know in which part of the castle to look." When Bolan didn't answer, he went on. "What if we tried to get in as workmen?"

Bolan dropped the binoculars to his lap and shook his head. He pointed toward three men carrying paint cans as they stopped in front of the guards. "They're checking IDs."

"We could capture some of the men when they leave," Hwang said. "Take their identification and—"

"That might work for you, but the IDs will have descriptions. Maybe even pictures. We don't have time to wait for a worker who could match my description."

Hwang nodded. "Then I must go alone," he said. His eyes followed a man in white overalls who was leaving the castle and starting across the park. "I'll get his ID and overalls, and report back to you." He started to open the door.

Bolan reached across the car and grabbed his arm. "Sit still. That idea has too many holes in it." He paused, then explained. "Those are special-forces soldiers, Hwang. They aren't stupid, and neither are the cops. They're looking for two men who match our descriptions, but they know we could split up." He shook his head. "Let's think a minute. There's got be another way to do this."

Hwang shrugged. "I will think," he said, and turned back to the castle.

Bolan heard the hum of a vehicle and watched a white delivery van arrive in front of the castle. Two men in khaki work uniforms jumped out and opened the sliding side door. As they unloaded three small boxes, he spotted several larger containers inside. The men carried the smaller boxes up the steps to the porch leading into the castle.

A special-forces guard with an unusually thick mustache stepped forward and spoke. The taller of the two workmen shrugged. The guard shook his head violently and pointed back to the van.

Hwang grunted. "At least we know now what happens if you *don't* have identification," he said.

A short argument ensued, then the guard finally pulled a walkie-talkie from his belt.

Handing Hwang the binoculars, Bolan said, "What's in the boxes?"

"Tools. The bigger of the three is a small circular saw—like you'd use to cut wallboard or small pieces of wood. Nothing of interest to us."

The stand-off at the door continued, and it became apparent that the guard had radioed inside for someone to verify the delivery. Finally a hunched figure stepped outside and spoke to the guard.

Bolan squinted toward the figure as he took a clipboard from the guard, scribbled across it with a pen, then pointed the delivery men inside. Something about the man seemed familiar.

Next to him Hwang Su was still looking on with the binoculars. Suddenly he started with surprise. "You won't believe this," the undercover man said.

"Try me."

Hwang handed the binoculars across the seat. "See for yourself."

Bolan managed to focus just as the figure on the porch turned to face him. His heart skipped a beat as he recognized the wizened face and hunched shoulders.

Boris Stavropol.

The Russian followed the deliverymen back inside.

"I'd like to think he's given up his old profession and is helping cut Sheetrock," Hwang said. "But something tells me that's not the case. And something tells me the circular saw is not for floor joists."

"Something tells me you're right," Bolan agreed.

The deliverymen reappeared and walked back to the van.

"Let's go," Bolan said.

"Back to Myung's?" Hwang asked.

"Eventually. But first we've got a delivery van to hijack." He nodded toward the men as they got into the vehicle.

"But we still don't know for sure if Levi's here," Hwang argued.

"He's here," Bolan said confidently. "If Stavropol's here, so is Levi."

"But *where?* That's a big castle, Pollock. We've seen a good two dozen guards, and there could be twice that many inside. We can't just go in and start knocking on doors. We've got to have at least some idea which part of the building to search."

"We will have," Bolan said. "Start the engine before we lose the van."

Hwang shrugged and twisted the key in the ignition. "I'm afraid I don't understand," he said as he pulled out.

"You will. We'll use the van to get inside, but it just came to me how to recon this place beforehand. The cops are looking for two men—one Caucasian, the other Oriental. We've been concentrating too much on the race part. They're looking for *men,* Hwang, and that's the key. We're going to send in a *woman.*"

The Honda fell in behind the van. "Sachiko?" Hwang said. "Forget that. Myung would never stand for it. Besides, she's got no experience at this sort of thing."

"I don't mean Sachiko," Bolan said.

Hwang looked across the seat. "Excuse me. Maybe I've missed something, but as far as I know, we don't have any other women we can..." His voice drifted up as his eyes suddenly lit up with understanding. "You've got to be kidding," he said.

Bolan shook his head.

"Pollock, he's *crazy.*"

The Executioner shrugged. "I don't see that we've got any other choice. If you can come up with something better, I'm all ears, Hwang. But in the meantime we'll grab the van. Then find us a telephone. We'd better call and tell Rhee to start getting his makeup on."

Hwang shook his head and blew air through his pursed lips in exasperation. Finally he grinned. "Good idea," he said. "You know how long it takes women to get dressed."

THE SUN WAS DROPPING toward the Pyongyang bluff as Rhee Yuk climbed the steps to Koguryu Castle. He felt as if his bladder would fail him any second. Ahead he saw the two special-forces soldiers watching him. He moved carefully, methodically, making sure his step was correct. Feminine, not masculine.

It wasn't easy. The new black pumps were already forming blisters on his feet.

Rhee moved on, looking modestly away as the men ogled his legs, then his padded breasts. He felt as if his heart would hammer a hole through his rib cage, and forced his thoughts back to the whirlwind events since he'd left the office that morning. He had returned to Myung Namsoo's house only moments before Hwang and the American had arrived with enough small arms to start a revolution. Hwang and Pollock had left again to scout out the castle, and he had fallen asleep on Myung's couch, exhausted.

Sachiko had awakened him what seemed like only seconds later. Pollock and Hwang had called.

Sachiko and Rhee had gone shopping.

The guards continued to watch as he neared. He saw the lust in their eyes, and knew he must look good in the smart new skirt and matching blazer Sachiko had helped him pick out. That was *some* consolation for the terror in his heart, he supposed.

Rhee stopped in front of the guards, reached into his purse and pulled out a stack of documents from the Bureau of Internal Transport. "These must all be signed by Department of Agriculture representatives and returned *today*," he said, making sure he pitched his voice above normal.

One guard, a strikingly handsome man, took the papers. He tore his eyes away from Rhee's chest long enough to give the pages a cursory glance, then handed them back with a leering smile. "And you are...?"

"From the Bureau of Internal Transport, *of course,*" Rhee said, letting his tone grow slightly bitchy.

The second guard stepped forward. He was less attractive but no less interested in Rhee's build. He glanced instinctively down at the slit in the skirt, then his eyes rose back to eye level. "Is this customary procedure?" he asked.

Rhee let out a disgusted breath. "No, it is *not* customary procedure," he said. He threw back his head, sending the bangs of his wig away from his eyes. "And if the Department of Agriculture had followed the customary procedure, I could be back at my office doing what I am paid to do rather than making up for *their* mistakes."

The first guard handed the papers back and nodded. "You may pass," he said.

Even though his heart was filled with terror, Rhee couldn't resist the impulse that now overcame him. As he turned, he let the stack of papers fall from his hand to the ground. Then, before either of the guards could bend down to help him, he stooped at the waist and began gathering them back up.

As the skirt rode up, Rhee felt the men's eyes again on his legs. He stifled a giggle. How surprised would they be if they could see higher?

Rhee Yuk entered the castle, his high heels clicking along the stone floor past several men who were installing a window. Although the outside of the castle was being restored as close to the original as possible, no such attempt was being made on the inside. Glass, wallboard and metal were being added to the wood and stone, and when finished, the rooms would be fully functional, modern offices.

Rhee turned down a hallway to the south side of the castle, where work had been completed. He looked into the windows of each office as he passed, but saw nothing that would lead him to believe Curtis Levi might be held captive inside. When he came to the stone steps, he mounted them and found himself on the second floor.

The workmen hadn't gotten to these rooms yet. Four solid wooden doors appeared to be the only entrances, and there were no windows. With a deep breath Rhee knocked on the first.

The papers were in his hand again when the door opened and a young woman looked out.

"I am looking for the Department of Agriculture," Rhee said.

The woman's eyes traveled to the ceiling, and she pointed up.

He mounted the next set of stairs, finding another stone hallway and wooden doors. Stopping at the first door, he took a deep breath and felt his heart flutter. Lifting his arm to knock felt as if he was hoisting a hundred-pound dumbbell. He rapped lightly. When he got no response, he moved on.

No one seemed to be behind any of the doors on the second floor, and by the time he got to the end of the hallway, he was ready to move on up the stairs. As he stopped at the final door, however, his hand poised in the air, he heard the dull drone of an electric motor behind the wood.

His stomach turned sour. Hwang had told him about the circular saw delivered to Stavropol. It took all his willpower to bring his fist down against the door.

The buzzing sound halted immediately. A voice called out in Korean. But the accent was not Korean. It was Russian, and as the door started to swing back, Rhee was certain he would vomit.

A haggard face stared out through the crack in the door. The cruel eyes, set deep in the wrinkles, told Rhee that the man must be Boris Stavropol.

The papers began to shake in his hand. He was about to say he was from the Department of Agriculture, then realized that Stavropol might well be aware that that department was the cover used to finance the expenses for the trip to Seoul. If so, the statement might give him away.

"Well," Stavropol growled, "what do you want?"

Rhee started to answer, then his eyes moved past the man at the door to the open boxes on the carpet. To one side of the boxes was the circular saw, and on the other were the remains of what had once been a coffee table.

For the second time in less than a minute, Rhee was certain he would throw up.

"I don't have all day to wait, young lady," Stavropol snapped. "What do you want?"

Gathering his wits about him, Rhee blurted out, "I am sorry. I was looking for the ladies' room."

"Down the hall to the left," Stavropol said, and slammed the door in Rhee's face.

Rhee hurried away, stopping at the stairs to catch his breath. He pressed his back against the cold stones of the wall and felt as if he would hyperventilate. Opening his purse, he shoved his face into the opening to rebreathe the air. It seemed to calm him somewhat, and he found himself regaining his balance.

He was certain the man he had just spoken to was Stavropol. But he had seen nothing that would indicate that Curtis Levi was in the room with the Russian.

Levi had to be close by. But where?

Rhee Yuk forced himself to mount the next set of stairs. He moved up and down the hall, knocking on each door but getting no response. Taking to the stairs once more, he came to the castle's top floor. The fourth story was identical to the second and third—a long hallway with closed wooden doors. He moved along, knocking and waiting.

When he reached the fourth door on his right, Rhee raised his hand. But before he could knock, he heard a faint sigh beyond the heavy wood. Pressing his ear to the door, he heard the garbled sound of singing. In *English*.

"... jingle bells, jingle bells, jingle all the way..."

Curtis Levi was beyond the door. It had to be him.

Summoning up all that remained of his dwindling courage, Rhee reached out for the doorknob. He twisted, and was horrified to find it unlocked. Slowly he eased the door open a crack.

Through the crack Rhee saw a straight-backed chair in the center of the room. Blood stained the stone around the chair. The singing came from somewhere out of his vision, and he inched the door open farther.

"... in a one-horse open sleigh ..." the pitiful voice moaned.

Rhee saw the bed against the wall and the straps that bound Curtis Levi to it. His eyes refused to focus, and his brain refused to record any more of the atrocity he saw before him.

Closing the door and shoving the papers Myung had provided back into his purse, Rhee hurried to the stairs, his breath coming in short pants. He descended back to the first floor, then paused for a moment to gather himself. He still had to get back past the guards without drawing suspicion.

Rhee Yuk walked stiffly, wondering if the guards would notice he was upset. He needn't have worried, for once again their lecherous eyes were glued to his body. Still, he felt as if he might faint as he passed them, and his head begun to pound.

But it was over. *Over*.

At least until Levi had been rescued and the mad dash for the border began. He had done his job and now he could report back to the others and let *them* go in on this suicide mission to rescue the American rocket scientist.

As for himself, Rhee Yuk planned to take a hot bath, put on his favorite nightgown and go to sleep.

CHAPTER FOURTEEN

The pain was horrible. But the times between sessions, when the monster left the room but Curtis Levi knew he would be back, were almost as bad. It was then that Levi's mind returned to some semblance of coherence, and he remembered where he was, what was happening to him and what he had done to deserve it.

It was then that he could think about an alcoholic wife and a job that didn't pay what he thought he was worth. The excuse he had used to rationalize what he'd done no longer worked. Curtis Levi knew he could have divorced Betty without deserting his country. He needn't have become a traitor.

Strapped to the chair in the center of the room again, Curtis Levi stared at Stavropol as the old Russian and two other men entered the room. The men carried a small table and several other items, but Levi couldn't see what they were. Blood from last night's session was caked over his eyes and limited his field of vision.

Stavropol wheeled his chair toward Levi as the other men left the room. The American looked around the dried blood to focus on his face. At first glance Stavropol looked like any other man serving out his twilight years. But Curtis Levi had looked beyond Boris Stavropol's facial features. Through the old man's eyes he had seen glimpses of the deranged mind that lived inside him.

And Levi knew that the face he saw there was the face of evil.

Stavropol took his seat and smiled at the American scientist. He began speaking in a soft, soothing voice, as if he were trying to regain Levi's trust or even reestablish a friendship. The American knew better. Each period of torture had begun that way, and it was obviously some psychological technique the Russian used along with the physical pain.

"As I have already told you but will tell you again," Stavropol said, smiling pleasantly, "this is your final chance to remain a whole man, Curtis. So far, I have employed only level-one interrogation. But the second phase is about to begin, and once it does, certain things will be done that simply cannot be reversed." He paused and smiled again. "Wouldn't you like to spare yourself all that, Curtis?"

Curtis Levi didn't answer. He had made his decision during the long hours of night when the pain had finally eased to the point he could think. He would *not* talk. If he had lasted through the torture of the past three nights, he could do it once more. And once more, he suspected, would be all he would have to endure. Stavropol had already described the amputation of limbs and other atrocities—acts from which he knew he would eventually bleed to death.

Well, Levi realized as he continued to meet the eyes of the demon standing over him, that was what he wanted. *Death*. Death was his goal. To hold out until death swept a soothing darkness over his soul and ended the pain once and for all. He would not talk, he would not scream and he would not sing "Mary Had a Little Lamb" or senseless American jingles in vain attempts to divert his mind from the pain.

He had performed a cowardly act during a weak moment in his life, but he would die a man. Death. He not only wanted it, but he *deserved* it. He had betrayed his country and his family. This last act—his silent death—was the only semblance of atonement available to him. He would take advantage of it, and may the God in whom he had never before believed have mercy on his soul.

Stavropol lifted one of the items from the floor, and now Levi could see it was a small power saw. He felt the blood rush from his head and a plummeting of his stomach as though he had dropped into an abyss.

"I have decided to start with your left foot," Stavropol said with the emotion of an accountant choosing black over blue ink. "When I have cleaved it at the ankle, I will bandage the wound to slow your blood loss, then place the severed foot there." He turned and pointed toward the table the other men had brought in. "You will be able to see it while I go to work on your other foot."

Stavropol paused to let it sink in, then chuckled. "Perhaps if you are able to hold out long enough, you will get to see your entire body rebuilt on the table."

The thought seemed to tickle the Russian, and he laughed uproariously.

Then he flipped the switch of the saw.

Curtis Levi heard the demonic buzz as the blade began to rotate. He closed his eyes as Stavropol's free hand reached down to his left calf. Sweat broke out on the rocket scientist's forehead, rolling down to mix with tears streaming from under his clamped eyelids.

Then a ringing suddenly sounded over the buzz of the saw. Stavropol grunted in disgust, and Levi opened his eyes.

The diabolical noise died down as Stavropol flipped the switch again and the blade slowed to a stop. Setting the instrument on the floor, he reached into his jacket and pulled out a small cellular phone.

"What is it?" he demanded, irritated.

Curtis Levi closed his eyes again, silently praying to his newly found God, giving thanks for the interruption. The reprieve might last only seconds, but to the American those seconds were seconds in which he would still have both feet.

Stavropol's conversation, however, went on for several minutes. He spoke in Korean, and Levi understood not a word. But to whoever had called, Curtis Levi gave his heart-felt thanks and undying appreciation.

When Stavropol finally disconnected, he looked down and said, "It seems that there is an effort being made to rescue you, Curtis." He smiled like someone's favorite grandfather, then said, "Would you like to hear about it before we go on?"

Levi nodded, again grateful for anything that delayed what was about to happen.

"It seems North Korea is a den of traitors." Stavropol sighed. "A certain State Department official with a penchant for wearing women's clothing drew the attention of his secretary this morning by forgetting to remove his nail polish. Like any good comrade, the woman reported this unconventional behavior." Stavropol shook his head in disgust. "Women's clothing," he said. "Can you imagine anything so sick, Curtis?"

Levi looked down at the saw on the floor. He didn't answer.

"Eventually," Stavropol went on, "word went through channels, and North Korean Intelligence was brought in. Surely you must realize that a man such as this is ripe for blackmail. So it was decided to check the random telephone recordings made of all government officials." The Russian chuckled again. "As you Americans like to say, *bingo!* They found a connection to internal transport, and learned that men from both departments had been tracing my progress since we were in Seoul." Stavropol arched his back slightly, grimaced, then frowned in thought. "There is no doubt they are in league with an old enemy of mine. The man who tried to retake you when we left the hotel. Do you remember?"

Levi could see that Stavropol was winding down. Tiring now of the explanation. "Who is this man?" Levi asked quickly, anxious to keep the talk flowing.

Stavropol shrugged as he reached down to retrieve the saw. "An American, a very special American who is known by a number of names. He is smart, he is persistent and he will not give up until he has found you or he is dead. I do not know which it will be, but I can assure you of one thing."

"What?" Levi asked excitedly as Stavropol flipped the circular saw on again. "What can you assure me of?"

The Russian grinned. "He will not find you before I have cut off your foot."

He had promised himself he would scream no more. But Curtis Levi shrieked louder than he ever had in his life as the whirling saw blade descended toward his ankle.

The gunshots sounded suddenly, drowning out the whir of the spinning blade. Levi saw Stavropol's hand stop, the saw blade an inch from his leg. The Russian jerked back to a sitting position and turned toward the closed door as more rounds exploded in the hallway.

Dropping the circular saw, Stavropol shoved himself to his feet and crossed the room. He cracked the door, peeked through the opening, then turned back to look at Levi as the firefight outside intensified.

Then, flinging the door all the way open, he hurried from the room and disappeared from Curtis Levi's sight.

Two of the large crates in the white car contained large filing cabinets, just as they had when Bolan and Hwang had procured the vehicle.

The third crate now contained the Executioner.

Bolan shifted his body slightly as Hwang turned a corner toward Koguryu Castle. Seizing the vehicle had presented no problem. The .45 ACP Norincos had persuaded the deliverymen to cooperate without a shot being fired. They were now bound and gagged in Myung's bedroom. Bolan had tied the knots loosely, and he estimated the men would eventually work themselves free.

But that would be no problem, either. Katz had found Jhoon and his family at the hotel where Bolan had dropped them off, then delivered them to Myung's before heading back to the U.S. He had already left again when Bolan returned with the van, and by the time the deliverymen reported the kidnapping, the Israeli would be halfway to Spain. Rhee Yuk, Sachiko, Jhoon and the rest of his family would be waiting in Myung's car at the south edge of Pyongyang, and, if all went reasonably well, Bolan, Hwang and Myung would be on their way to meet them, with the rescued scientist in their protection.

Or they'd all be dead. Either way, the Executioner knew that exposing Myung's house at that point would make no difference.

Arrangements had been made by Hwang with the South Korean special-forces guards stationed at the North Korean end of the tunnel through which they'd entered North Korea. The soldiers would have an FM radio tuned to the frequency of Myung's transmitter, and would be waiting to give their support—if Bolan and his charges made it that far. The South Korean special-forces men had orders not to leave the tunnel area under any conditions, and there was no time to appeal to the bureaucracy that could change those orders.

His last act before entering the crate had been to call the phone number Wonkwang had given him before the Hwarang Warrior leader had been killed coming out of the drainage pipe. A man who identified himself as Tang had answered the phone, and after a time Bolan had convinced Tang he was indeed the American the other survivors of the hotel assault had spoken of, and Tang had agreed to lend whatever assistance he could.

Bolan gave the man a rough idea of what he wanted over the phone—there was no time for a meeting or details—and he had agreed.

He glanced at the luminous hands of his wristwatch as the van slowed. It was well into evening, and he wondered how heavy Stavropol's night guard would be. There was no way to know. He had counted over two dozen special-force troops outside the castle that afternoon, and more had to be inside. For all he knew, security might double when darkness fell. He would have to wait and see, deal with whatever resistance they met as they came to it.

Myung's voice penetrated the box. "We are a block from the front entrance of the castle. It looks as if there are more guards outside than there were this afternoon."

Bolan felt the van slow, then stop. "See the front entrance yet?"

"Yes," Hwang answered. "Four men. Two are the same that we saw this afternoon."

"Good," Bolan said. "They won't recognize you and Myung, but they should remember the van and uniforms. Do your best to bluff your way through on that. But don't let them radio Stavropol again. If they try that, it'll be shooting time. Get me out as fast as you can."

He heard both cab doors open, and then the side door slid back. He felt himself lifted onto a dolly, then was being wheeled up the ramp toward the castle's front door. He remembered the area from seeing it earlier, and wondered if Tang and his men were in place.

A brief conversation in Korean ensued between Hwang and the two guards on at the entrance. The Executioner carried two of the Norinco .45s, both cocked and locked in his belt. Silently he drew one of them now and rested his thumb on the manual safety. He breathed slowly, evenly, ready to spring to his feet firing should the discussion turn ugly. But it didn't.

Thirty seconds after reaching the entrance, the crate was lifted over the threshold and wheeled inside. Neither Hwang nor Myung spoke, but Bolan heard other voices as they proceeded down a long stretch, then turned a corner. One set of footsteps pattered quietly away again, then Hwang's voice whispered softly through the box. "We are in the hall below Stavropol's office. The workers have not begun restoring this wing. Half a dozen special-forces men in the other hall. This area appears deserted." Bolan heard him take a deep breath. "Myung is checking the rest of the floor before we open the box."

Myung finally returned, and he whispered something to his partner in Korean.

A moment later Bolan was climbing out of the crate. His eyes took a second to adjust to the overhead lights, then he turned to Myung. "Any more guards?"

"They are all congregated in the main hall, but we must assume they periodically check this wing. Particularly if this is where Levi is. But I don't believe they are expecting anything special tonight."

Bolan checked the chambers of both .45s. "So let's give them a surprise," he said. "Wherever he is, Stavropol will have guards with him. Either in his office, or in Levi's room on the top floor." He glanced at Myung. "You spot the stairs?"

"One at each end of the hall. I recommend the one we have already passed. We don't know what we might find at the other one."

Bolan led the way silently to the stone staircase, then up the steps to the second floor. Like the first, it was deserted, and he followed Rhee's directions to the last door on the right.

The Norinco in his hand, he quietly twisted the doorknob. As soon as he heard the bolt open, he pushed the ancient wood forward with his shoulder and burst into the room.

The South Koreans were at his heels, with Hwang sweeping his .45 across the right half of the room while Myung covered the left. But their tactics were unnecessary. Stavropol's office was deserted.

Bolan looked down at the empty boxes on the floor. A foam-rubber packing pad, a cutout the shape of a small power saw in the middle, looked back at him. "He's already upstairs," the Executioner said. "Let's go."

With Hwang and Myung behind him, Bolan shot back out into the hallway, raced down the hall, and turned up the stairs. Taking them three at a time, he passed the third floor and then suddenly stopped, halfway to the fourth.

Voices in the fourth-floor hallway drifted down the steps. Holding a hand up behind him so the others would wait, Bolan silently crept on. At the top of the stairs, he pressed his back against the wall and peered around the corner.

Ten uniformed NK special-forces men lined the hallway—five on one side, five on the other. Another couple of men flanked the door of the last room on the right. Chatting in low voices, they appeared not to have a care in the world. But all twelve men had Type 58 assault rifles slung over their shoulders in battle-carry mode.

Bolan pulled his head back around the corner, turned toward Hwang and Myung and held up five fingers. Rolling them back into a fist, he repeated the process, then finally held up only his index and middle finger.

Bolan wished he had a Beretta 93-R with him, but along with his Desert Eagle, the quiet 9 mm machine pistol had died in the flames of the Firenza almost before the mission had begun. He wasn't likely to be shooting sound-suppressed 9 mm Berettas, or .44 Magnums for that matter, until the Stony Man armorer had worked over another pair of handguns for him.

But he would make do with what he had. He was focusing on a plan of action that had a chance of success.

The adrenaline of approaching battle coursed through the warrior's veins as he turned back down the steps and waved for Hwang and Myung to follow him. The men looked curious, unable to fathom what his next step would be. He led them both to the first floor and stopped beside the box he had used to infiltrate the castle. He already had one foot inside when he felt Hwang grip his arm.

"What are you doing?" the undercover man asked.

"Load me back up and take me upstairs. Wheel me right down the hall just like you know where you're going. Don't refasten the lid, just close it. As soon as we get there, flip it back open."

"What if it doesn't work?" Myung asked.

"Then we'll all die together," Bolan said matter-of-factly. He lowered himself down into the crate. "Now. Let's go find out which it's going to be."

The top flaps closed back over his head, and once again the crate was wheeled down the hall. At the stairs the two men stooped to lift the dolly, then struggled up the steps with their cargo.

Under the circumstances silence was impossible. The sounds of the heavy load scraping the steps and walls, and the heavy breathing the labor brought on in Hwang and Myung, seemed to echo as loud as gunshots. He estimated they were halfway up the steps to the top floor when the gruff voice called down from above.

Myung, out of breath, replied. The answer he got in return didn't sound satisfied. Both Hwang and Myung began talking as they continued to haul the crate up the steps, not setting him down until they reached the landing.

By now Bolan could hear several other voices around the box, and the exchange was growing more heated by the moment. Then Hwang suddenly switched languages. "Very well, Myung," he said in English. "They insist on inspecting the contents, we shall let them."

Bolan drew both .45s from his belt and thumbed the grip safeties down. The English had been for his benefit—to alert him that the time for combat had arrived. He also knew that while it might not give them away to the guards, the sudden change in language would alert them.

The lid was pulled up, and the Executioner burst out of the crate. The top of his head butted a soldier who was leaning over the side. Bolan heard the man's nose crunch, then the sound was drowned out by the roar of the Norinco in his right hand.

He dropped the front sights of the same .45 on the middle button of the dress tunic of a man directly in front of him. He pulled the trigger, and the big .45 ACP drove the gold button into the man's chest ahead of it. The special-forces guard opened his mouth in shock as the explosion echoed off the stone walls.

Raising the Norinco in his left hand, Bolan let the sights stop between the eyes of a guard with a wispy mustache. His second .45 exploded in another shower of blood and flesh.

More rounds erupted as Hwang and Myung drew their weapons and fired at guards on down the hall. The roaring .45-caliber reports seemed amplified in the hallway. As 7.62 mm rifle rounds joined in from the guards' rifles, the pandemonium threatened to deafen everyone within earshot. Bolan twisted his right-hand weapon toward a stocky NK sergeant and pulled the trigger.

But nothing happened.

Rounds from the sergeant's Type 58 streaked toward him as he dived from the box and rolled across the floor to the wall. He cursed silently under his breath as he came to rest in a prone position and turned the .45 in his left hand toward the man. Bolan pulled the trigger. The Norinco exploded, and the round took the sergeant high in the shoulder. Bolan lowered his aim and squeezed again.

And again he got nothing.

Dropping the left-hand Norinco, he slammed the palm of his hand up against the butt of the other .45, then grasped the slide with his hand over the ejection port. As he'd suspected, his fingers brushed away an empty casing "stovepiped" in the port.

Bolan drew the slide back, racking another round into the chamber. The "tap-rack-bang" drill had taken less than a second to complete as he lined the sights up on the sergeant's chest and pulled the trigger.

The "bang" part of the drill sent the NK back against the wall.

The firing in the narrow passageway continued, with Myung and Hwang crouched on the floor, guns blazing in both men's hands. Bolan grabbed the other .45 from the floor and cleared its jam, looking up to count five of the guards still standing. He had started to swing one of the .45s on a tall, muscular guard when he saw a flicker of movement on the floor.

Miraculously one of the men downed by Hwang a second earlier seemed to come back to life. As blood spurted from his chest like water from a fire hose, the man rolled to his side and raised his rifle.

Bolan pulled the trigger. Another .45 hardball entered the man's chest, and the miraculous recovery was over.

He turned back down the hall as a door at the end suddenly swung open. As he squeezed the trigger, fell-ing a special-forces corporal, he saw a wrinkled face take a quick look into the hall.

It was Stavropol.

Bolan was still riding the recoil of his last round as the former KGB man loped awkwardly through the door into the hall. Ducking behind two soldiers, the Russian ambled toward the door at the end of the hall.

The Executioner heard a whizzing by his head. The rifle round buffeted the wall to his side, and a chip of rock struck his cheek. He ducked under the next two rounds, then rolled away from the attack and came to a halt on his belly. Gripping the Norinco in both hands, he aimed at the fleeing Stavropol's back. The sights fell on the middle of the Russian's back. Bolan squeezed the trigger.

Again the tight new Norinco jammed.

The warrior cursed again as he executed another tap-rack-bang. The Norinco .45s themselves were not at fault—few weapons built from the time-proved Colt Government Model pattern could be relied on until a break-in period had smoothed and loosened the working parts. Lack of breaking-in time had meant he had to take the pistols as they were, but that didn't mean he would be any less dead if the gun choked at the wrong time.

By the time he had cleared the .45 and jacked another round into the firing position, Stavropol had disappeared through the door. Only one of the guards remained standing, but even as Bolan turned his newly charged weapon toward the man, Hwang and Myung both pulled triggers and sent the NK sprawling on the cold stone.

Bolan leaped to his feet and made his way down the hall to the door Stavropol had left open. His heart told him to racc on down the back stairs and overtake the former KGB man while he had the chance, but his brain said otherwise. He had a bigger goal than eliminating one man, however vile that man might be. Unless he got Curtis Levi away from the North Koreans, America and the rest of the world would face the threat of nuclear missiles.

He came to a halt at the side of the open door, took a deep breath, then swung around the corner with the Norinco leading the way. He stopped three feet inside.

Hwang and Myung followed through the door and moved up to flank him.

"Oh, my God," Hwang whispered, his face white.

Myung looked too ill to speak.

Bolan moved forward to the chair in the center of the room, reached down to the still-buzzing circular saw on the floor and flipped the switch to the off position. An eerie silence fell over the room as the small electrical motor ground to a halt.

They had finally found Curtis Levi.

CHAPTER FIFTEEN

Boris Stavropol loped down the rear steps of the castle as fast as he could. He felt a mixture of panic and mental euphoria. His body protested, but his brain felt as if he'd mainlined pure cocaine. He would again face a worthy foe!

He reached the second floor and turned down the hall toward his office. Above, the shooting had stopped, which meant either the American or all the special-forces guards on the fourth floor were dead. The Russian suspected he knew who was still standing. He had seen the way the battle was going as he made for the stairs.

Reaching the door to his office, he rushed in and locked it behind him. He knew immediately upon entering that the American had stopped here before climbing the steps to Levi's room. How he knew, he couldn't say. He just did.

Quickly he went across to his desk and slid open the bottom drawer. Withdrawing a black leather pistol rug, he placed it on top of the desk.

He collapsed behind the desk in his chair. His heart pounded like a battering ram, but instead of worrying about a heart attack, he knew it was the adrenaline rushing through his body. A rush like he had not ex-

perienced in years. Certainly not since the shadowy
world of clandestine operations had become a circus of
amateurs.

Stavropol sat still, his breathing evening out, if not
his mood. For years now his only thrill had been the
administration of levels one and two interrogation. He
had taken great satisfaction in the ability to coerce information from unwilling subjects. But interrogation
was only a third of what he was good at. There had
been a time when he was the most skilled assassin in the
Soviet Union. He had also been the one to whom the
other agents looked when a particularly intricate plan
was called for.

His assassin days were long gone, but his mind was
as sharp as ever. He had simply not had a chance to
exercise it.

He unzipped the leather pistol case and withdrew the
Nagant Model 1895. The blue had long ago worn away
from the 7.62 mm revolver, leaving it a dull, flat gray,
and the Russian's mood swung suddenly from eu-
phoric to nostalgic as he remembered his father teach-
ing him to shoot the weapon so many years ago.
Mikhail Stavropol, the hero of the revolution, had held
his arms around ten-year-old Boris to help him man-
age the recoil. They had shot two boxes of cartridges.

It had been the best day of Stavropol's life—his
fondest memory. When the shooting lesson ended, he
and his father had visited the zoo, then spent the rest of
the day at the park before returning home.

Tears filled the old Russian's eyes as he remembered that enchanted day. A week later his father had left for Moscow, and Boris saw him only once more after that. His father's death had been the first real pain he had known. That lack, that loss, caused some change in him, a major shift away from real emotion.

Now he began to load the revolver. The Model 1895 had been manufactured in a double-action version, but his father's was one of the original single actions. It had come into Stavropol's possession upon his father's death, and he had secretly sworn not to fire it until he suspected his own life was near its end. That time had come. He was old, he was tired and he was ready to die. The pain was almost over. But not until he had accomplished one last act by which to be remembered.

Before he pushed the barrel of the Nagant into his mouth and pulled the trigger as his father had done, Boris Stavropol would use it to kill his old adversary, the American.

The sudden resurgence of gunfire above him caused the Russian's eyes to jerk toward the ceiling. It could only mean that he'd been right—the American had won the first round on the fourth floor, and now guards from other parts of the castle had arrived to renew the battle.

Stavropol finished loading the revolver and listened to the gunfire. He had no intention of climbing the stairs and joining the battle. It was not his kind of fight—the odds would not be in his favor. Perhaps he would lose his chance for a last match of wits, but he thought not. Somehow he knew the special-forces men, as many as there were, were still no match for such a seasoned professional.

The Russian's eyes moved across the room to the closet. He knew where the American would have to go if he escaped the castle. When he did, he would find Stavropol already in place. And if the man died here in Pyongyang first, it would simply mean he hadn't deserved to match wits with a man of Stavropol's quality after all.

What a pity it would be if it turned out that way.

He looked down at the Nagant in his hand, then cocked the hammer. Slowly he lowered it again and watched the cylinder of the unusual revolver move forward as the chamber aligned for fire telescoped the barrel. Yes, the gun had an unusual design. But his father had been an unusual man.

And so was he.

BOLAN LOOKED DOWN at Curtis Levi and wondered what kind of man—if Boris Stavropol could be called a man—could have methodically inflicted such suffering on a fellow human being. Cuts and burns covered every square inch of the American rocket scientist's body. His head had even been shaved to expose the tender scalp area. None of the small injuries in and of themselves was serious, but each would have brought on excruciating pain—both physical and mental.

Boris Stavropol clearly knew how to take a man as close to death as possible without going over the line. What Bolan saw before him was the work of a twisted and perverse artist, with Curtis Levi's body serving as the madman's canvas.

He looked down at the near-crazed eyes sunk deep in the rocket scientist's sockets. "Levi, can you hear me?" he said.

Slowly Curtis Levi nodded.

"Then let's get you out of here and back home." Bolan turned to Hwang and Myung, who stood staring in shock. "Watch the door while I get him ready," he said.

The South Koreans jerked out of their stupor and moved toward the hallway. Bolan found Levi's clothes piled in the corner of the room and quickly helped the man into them. Levi winced in pain as the material scratched across his violated skin, but the wounds were shallow and had scabbed over. The bleeding that started up again was not serious.

"Can you walk?" Bolan asked as he helped the scientist to his feet.

Levi nodded but pitched forward into Bolan's arms when he tried.

Bolan lifted him over his left shoulder. Levi's helplessness was psychological rather than physical. Stavropol's "work" had been painful but hardly disabling. The Executioner glanced to the power saw on the floor. Disability had been coming, however. Next. But as things stood now, Curtis Levi would heal. At least his body would.

Bolan glanced again to the tortured man's eyes. He wouldn't lay bets on Levi's mind.

New gunshots exploded in the hallway, and Bolan turned toward the door. He saw that both Hwang and Myung had seized assault rifles from the guards on the floor, and were firing down the hall toward the stairs. Drawing one of the Norinco .45s, Bolan hurried out of the room.

Four more special-forces soldiers had joined the ranks of the dead as he entered the hall. With Levi babbling incoherently over his shoulder, Bolan let Hwang and Myung lead the way toward the stairs. The South Koreans stepped over the newly dead and stopped to peer around the corner.

A burst of autofire came up the steps. Jerking his head back behind the stone, Hwang swung his Type 58 back around the corner and moved his arms back and forth, blindly spraying the stairwell. A moment later he led the way cautiously down the steps.

Bolan thumbed the safety back up on his .45 and shoved it in his belt, stooping to pick up one of the rifles on the steps as he descended. The stiff new Norincos were jamming too much, and although the Type 58 would be less maneuverable with Levi in tow, at least it could be depended on to fire.

Hwang on the right and Myung to the left, the South Koreans moved carefully down both sides of the stairs. Bolan followed, taking the steps sideways to protect

Levi. They made the third floor without interference, then heard running footsteps as they neared the second. The procession froze.

Four more guards came sprinting obliviously up the stairs. The lead man looked up in surprise as Bolan fired one-handed. The 3-round burst propelled the man back into the three others behind him.

Bolan continued firing, with Hwang and Myung joining in. The men tried to recover but had no chance as the slugs led them in a gruesome death dance.

Skirting the blood spatters, they continued to the second floor and started toward the ground.

"Hold it," Bolan whispered suddenly. Below he had heard the faint sound of footsteps. More careful than the four men who had just given their lives to carelessness, the NKs on the first floor were moving quietly. But that wasn't the only difference.

His ears told him there were far more than four men congregating around the stairwell on the first floor.

They froze in place, waiting. It was impossible to tell just how many men were taking up position, but Bolan's guess was at least ten. Maybe twenty. They had heard the fighting on the floors above and would be preparing to charge up the stairs in an orderly assault. The Executioner readied his rifle, turning sideways to put his body between Levi and the attack. There was no time to retreat back up the steps. And even with the high-ground advantage the stairs afforded, he held little hope that three men would be able to hold off such overpowering odds in the narrow confines of the staircase.

Bolan's jaw tightened. That "good fight" was not quite over. If necessary, he would take as many of the North Korean special-forces men with him before their numbers finally ended his career.

Below, words were spoken in Korean. Both Hwang and Myung turned to Bolan, their faces as devoid of fear as a *sulsa* warrior's of the ancient kingdoms. Or in the case of these South Korean special-forces soldiers, Bolan realized, ancient Hwarang warriors.

"They are preparing," Hwang whispered.

Bolan nodded silently. He looked from Hwang to Myung. Good men, both of them, and if the time to die had come, he could not ask for better company.

A loud shout came from below, and suddenly the stairwell was filled with uniformed men. Boots pounded up the steps. Rifle barrels rose threateningly.

Bolan cut loose with a steady stream of fire that drew a figure eight in the air, dropping the first three in the assault on the stairs. Hwang and Myung joined the battle, each taking out their targets.

But it made no difference. Like maddened kamikazes who had no fear of death, the human wave continued. Bolan, Hwang and Myung kept their triggers back. More of the enemy fell, but still others stepped over them.

As Bolan's rifle ran dry, he heard the sound of distant gunfire. The explosions sounded as if they came from the first floor—from the direction of the front entrance.

As he dropped the Type 58 and drew the .45 from his belt, he saw special-forces men waiting to mount the steps turn down the hall. A moment later they jerked spasmodically to the floor.

Hwang and Myung ran their magazines dry and switched to the Norincos as Bolan double-tapped a special-forces man who was less than ten feet away. He turned the .45 toward another NK, who pushed his comrade's body out of the way and moved on. This man was less than four feet away when the full-metal jacket created a third eye in his forehead.

Then the .45 jammed again.

He brought the barrel of the Norinco around in an arc, smashing it into the head of a man directly in front of him. Levi moaned on his shoulder, and with no free hand to clear the malfunction, Bolan dropped the weapon and drew the other .45 from his belt. He heard Hwang and Myung popping away with their pistols as he thumbed the safety down and aimed down the steps.

But there were no targets.

The gunfire from down the hall continued, but the stairs were suddenly quiet. Bolan squinted through the smoke in the air, the smell of gunpowder thick in his nostrils. The stairs were littered with the bodies of North Korean soldiers, but none was left standing.

Below, the gunfire gradually died down until only a few sporadic shots continued. Readjusting Levi on his shoulder, the warrior descended among the bodies to the first floor. Hwang and Myung followed, picking up new rifles along the way, and Bolan was handed another Type 58 as they reached the ground floor.

Bolan turned down the main hall. Like the stairs, it was littered with fallen NK troops. Other men, dressed in civvies, walked up and down the passageway, checking bodies and occasionally kicking in doors to look for any of the enemy that might have hidden.

Then a familiar face came walking down the hall. Bolan grinned as he saw Yakov Katzenelenbogen kneel next to a body and trade his empty rifle magazines for the full ones in the dead man's battle vest.

"That was a fast trip to Spain and back," Bolan said.

Katz looked up, grinning. "Never even got on the plane. Grimaldi told me over the radio that the deal was over—hostages home, bad guys in jail." He shrugged. "What can I say? Once in a while the negotiators do their job." He stood up. "Anyway, I figured as long as I was still here..." His voice trailed off, and he glanced down the hall to where a muscular Korean wearing a gray sweatshirt was probing a prostrate body with the barrel of his rifle. "I met up with Mr. Tang outside. We hit it off, and he let me join the fun."

The man identified as Tang heard his name, looked toward them, then walked up to where Bolan and Katz stood. "You are Pollock," he said, nodding. "I am Tang." He indicated the men up and down the hall with a wave of his hand. "And these are my Hwarang Warriors."

Bolan let a smile creep across his face as he reached out to shake the Korean's hand. "Glad you could come," he said.

WITHOUT A DOUBT, the NK soldiers would have radioed for reinforcements. Confirmation came for Bolan with the roar of approaching personnel vehicles down the street as they piled into the delivery van.

Bolan deposited Levi in the back of the van and circled the vehicle to take the wheel. Hwang slid into the shotgun seat, while Katz and Myung dropped to cross-legged positions on the floor and steadied the traumatized rocket scientist. Tang closed Bolan's door for him and stuck his head in the open window. "We will hold them here as long as possible," he said. "But I fear that will not be long. Good luck." Without another word, the Hwarang Warrior turned and shouldered his rifle, firing a quick burst down the street at the approaching vehicles before sprinting back up the steps to the castle's front entrance.

Bolan pulled the van away from the curb and floored the accelerator, the tires screaming as they headed for the rendezvous with Rhee. None of the trucks bringing reinforcements to the castle followed, but that could mean either of two things.

If they had been lucky, the enemy hadn't paid attention to the van leaving the scene. That wasn't likely. What was far more probable was that they had radioed back to their base, described the van and left the vehicle to other troops while they prepared to take back the castle.

Their route took them quickly through the city and onto the road leading down the bluff. Reaching inside his shirt, Bolan pulled out the FM radio transmitter that had caused them so much trouble at the Bureau of Internal Transport and handed it over the seat to Myung.

Myung knew what to do. He flipped it on before saying, "Sachiko. We are nearing your position. Be ready."

A moment later they had turned away from the bluff onto the road paralleling the Taedong River. A full moon had risen in the night sky, casting a tranquil glow along the water. The ambience was one of peace, and didn't reflect the hard, cold fact that they had just finished a battle in which dozens of men had died a bloody death. It further gave no indication that more blood would likely be shed before they again crossed the border into South Korea and safety.

After roughly a mile along the curving route, Bolan pulled off the road and up to a grove of trees not far from the water.

"Sachiko," Myung relayed into the transmitter, "we are here."

Through the thick branches and leaves, they could barely make out the indistinct lines of a vehicle. Rhee Yuk was the first to emerge from the thicket, running quickly to the van and grabbing the sliding door.

Sachiko came next, prodding Jhoon and Kimi along in front of her. Kimi clutched the baby in her arms.

Myung jumped down from the van and helped the others up and into the cargo area, then leaped back in himself and slid the door shut again.

"Sachiko," Bolan ordered, "take charge of Levi." He turned to see that Myung's wife was already ministering to the American scientist.

The van pulled back onto the road. Katz and Myung immediately broke into the weapons taken from the police armory, allotting the rifles, extra magazines and vests, .45s and grenades.

Bolan wasted no time returning to the river road. By now he knew the word on the van would be out. Even as they raced toward the intersection with the highway, troops would be making plans for roadblocks to cut them off. That they would head for the southern border was a given—with Communist China to the north and the sea on both sides, they had no other choice.

Once they made the turn onto the highway, Bolan allowed himself a quick breath of semirelief. Their only ally was speed; their only hope was to make the drive through Kaesong to the border before the roadblocks had time to be set up. He had half feared that a barricade would already be in place before they turned onto the highway, and while they were hardly home free yet, at least the first potential obstacle had not materialized.

The highway was deserted as the van raced along under the full moon. As the crow flew, the distance between Pyongyang and the border was less than a hundred miles. But on the twisting highway that shot straight south, then bent gradually back east toward Kaesong, the distance would be a little over the century mark.

The first hour went well, without any sign of impending danger. Katz and Myung kept up a vigilant watch through the window in the van's rear door while Bolan and Hwang scanned the road ahead. Rhee, Sachiko, Jhoon and Kimi whispered in hushed voices as the vehicle ate up the white line in the middle of the highway. The baby boy slept and woke, slept and woke, crying each time he regained consciousness until Kimi fed him.

Bolan smiled. The kid would be too young to remember this night in the years to come. And there was no assurance that he would live to hear the stories his mother and father would tell him about it. But if he did—if any of the North Koreans survived the fight Bolan knew was coming—they would live the remainder of their days in freedom rather than as slaves of the failed political experiment the world called communism.

The villages of Songnim and Sariwon were asleep as the van raced through them. When they finally angled back east toward Kaesong, the road began to straighten. Clouds drifted over the moon, and the sky darkened with the deep blackness that comes just before dawn. The Executioner stared ahead at the lonely tunnel of illumination the headlights formed on the deserted highway.

They were still five miles north of Kaesong when the NK jeeps pulled out from behind the small hill.

Bolan saw them out of the corner of his eye as the van flashed past. Four in number, the jeeps fell in behind but made no attempt to overtake them. Though the silhouettes of rifle barrels stood out in bold relief against the lightening sky, not a shot was fired.

Clearly the failure to instigate hostilities could mean only one thing. The jeeps trailing them were not the core of the strategy to stop the fleeing van. They were the rear guard only—there to end the flight in case the van chose to reverse directions when they met the main assault down the road.

Which came almost immediately.

The van took a gentle curve and entered a straightaway a mile outside the Kaesong city limits. Ahead were a few flickering lights around what had to be a roadblock. Too far away to make out what vehicles comprised the barricade, Bolan raced on.

The initial gunfire erupted while the van was still a half mile away, the muzzle-flashes looking like tiny matches being struck at that distance. The jeeps behind them fell back to avoid the rounds, which flew wide of the van. Bolan twisted the wheel, jerking them through a series of zigzags to avoid the continuing fire as they drew nearer. Hwang reached forward to steady himself on the dash as the people in the back bounced back and forth against the walls of the serpentining vehicle.

A quarter mile from the roadblock, Bolan straightened their course long enough to say, "Hwang, roll down the window and stand by." Then, turning toward the rear of the van, he directed, "Katz, you and Myung get ready to cut off our tail."

Hwang whirled the window down. Behind him the Executioner heard the sound of shattering glass as a rifle barrel was thrust through the rear window. Hwang knelt in the bucket seat, strapping down his calf with the seat belt.

By the time they were just over a football field away from the roadblock, the sun was finally peeking over the horizon and casting a gray dawn over the land. Bolan squinted ahead. He could see now that the roadblock had been hurriedly put together and consisted of two jeeps parked nose to nose in the center of the highway. He smiled inwardly. Whoever had been in charge was inexperienced—the vehicles should have been staggered. As they were, if he could ram the point where the front grilles met directly in the center, the jeeps should swing back like gates.

If. A far bigger word than it looked on paper. Pulling the van out of the mad, zigzag course mandated by the onslaught of bullets, then centering the front of the vehicle perfectly between the two jeeps just might be possible. But if it wasn't, it was the next-best thing. Still, it was their only chance.

Bolan waited until they were a hundred yards away to give the order. "Okay...*now!*" he yelled.

Hwang leaned out the window and opened up with his rifle. Behind him the sound of two more Type 58s set on automatic fire erupted.

Enemy fire still blew around them, but only a few rounds struck the van and those hit nonvital areas.

Fifty yards from the roadblock, Bolan straightened the wheels and floored the accelerator. The van shot forward, bearing down on the two jeeps. Six men standing in front of the military vehicles dropped their weapons and dived to the sides. A second later the van struck the fronts of the jeeps. Sparks flew up like Fourth of July sparklers. Metal crunched metal. Steel screamed. Above it all could be heard the sound of voices howling in Korean.

The jeeps folded back on either side like opening doors, and a moment later Bolan looked up into the rearview mirror to see that they were a hundred yards past the roadblock. "Damage report!" he yelled as they hit the city limits, racing through stoplights and weaving around the thin early-morning traffic.

"Two of the followers down and out for the count!" Katz bellowed from the rear of the van. "The other two are already in pursuit, and the rest of the roadblock's mounting up to follow!"

Bolan looked to the mirror and saw the two jeeps following. Far behind was another, and beyond that a larger personnel carrier.

He raced on until they came to the junction with the border road. They were leaving the city, and Katz and Myung opened up with their rifles once more. But the jeeps had learned a lesson and now they zigzagged across the road to avoid the firing.

"Grenades!" Bolan shouted.

Several explosions blasted to their rear as Katz and Myung began dropping Chilean hand grenades in the path of the oncoming jeeps. But the drivers dropped back and evaded the charges as easily as they had the bullets. Just as before the roadblock, they made no attempt to overtake the van, and their strategy became evident. They had radioed ahead to the border, and even now the troops stationed there would be blocking the crossing big time.

"Hwang," Bolan said tersely. "Get on the transmitter and tell your friends at the tunnel where we are. Tell them to get ready."

Hwang flipped the switch of the FM device and spoke into it. With the one-way communication, they'd get no response to ensure that the South Korean special-forces men picked up the transmission. To stack the odds, Hwang kept repeating the communiqué as they neared the bean farm where the tunnel was hidden.

Bolan kept the van's pace fast as long as he could. As soon as he turned off the highway onto the road leading to the barn, he knew the men in the jeeps would snap to the fact that he didn't intend to cross the border in the conventional manner. The NKs might not know exactly what was planned, but they would cease simply tailing the van and turn aggressive.

"Hang on to something," he warned the others as the dirt road appeared ahead. He let up slightly on the accelerator. Katz and Myung took advantage of the gap that suddenly narrowed between the van and jeeps, their rifles chattering again. In the mirror Bolan saw the jeeps drop back again.

He stomped on the brake suddenly, veering sharply off the highway and onto the road. The front wheels dropped into a deep rut, and a sharp crack exploded from the right front of the vehicle.

Frustration swept over the warrior. They had found Levi, rescued him from the castle, evaded their pursuit and made it through a roadblock—all without suffering one casualty. Now they were all going to be shot because of a flat tire.

The van was limping along as the jeeps quickly closed the gap. In the side mirror he saw men stand in the backs of both vehicles and press rifle stocks to their shoulders. Katz and Myung continued to fire out the back window. But the bumpy road hindered the placement of accurate shots.

A volley of fire blew from the jeeps, and the van dropped as both rear tires blew. Then it stopped suddenly as the rims dug deep into the earth. Another volley of 7.62 mm lead chugged the engine to a halt.

Bolan grabbed his rifle as he turned to the back. "Myung, get the others out and follow Hwang! Katz, carry Levi!'' Shoving open the door, he rolled out of the van.

Round upon round of enemy fire pounded the walls of the van as he rose to one knee. Holding the trigger of his Type 58 back, he laid down a steady stream of cover fire. The surprised NK soldiers dived for cover as Katz, Hwang and Myung dragged the others through the sliding door. Hwang pushed them toward the bean field, then sprinted past to lead the way up a short ridge.

Return fire began as the NKs composed themselves. Bolan rolled back between the flattened tires as hot lead pummeled the van. The sound of other vehicles turning off the road told him the third jeep and the personnel truck had arrived. The jeep would bring with it four more of the special-forces men. The transport vehicle might well have as many as forty.

Crawling toward the rear of the van, he continued to fire from under the vehicle. His plan now was simpler. He would continue firing while Hwang led the others to the safety of the tunnel. He'd empty his rifle, then the rest of the spare 7.62 mm magazines. Then he'd fire both Norincos dry before throwing the first of his two grenades.

The second grenade he would save. Once the explosion of the first died down and no more fire came from beneath the van, the attackers would begin to wonder if he'd been hit. Eventually they'd creep forward to find out.

At that point he would pull the pin and release the handle. He would die, yes. But as many of the North Koreans as possible would go with him.

Bolan went through the rifle magazines quickly as new bullets from the recently arrived reinforcements strafed the van. The Norincos digested their .45s even faster and, for once, flawlessly. An ironical smile twisted the Executioner's lips as he realized that now that he no longer needed the weapons, both .45s were finally broken in and dependable.

Bolan jerked the first grenade from his vest, pulled the pin and rolled it out from under the van. He heard a scream of terror, and a second later the explosion rocked the sides of the van. Grabbing the last of his hand bombs, he jerked the pin free but kept the handle clamped tightly in his fingers.

And waited.

The firing continued to blast the van for a good two minutes. Then, little by little it died down as the NK soldiers realized the return fire had ceased. Finally the assault halted altogether, and whispering voices became the only sound.

He continued to play possum as he watched the first pair of shiny black boots move cautiously forward. When no ill luck met the man wearing them, others fell in behind. By the time the leader had stopped directly in front of him, at least a dozen others were within range of the grenade.

The man in the lead bent down to look under the van.

The Executioner watched him squint as his eyes tried to adjust to the darkness. Bolan released the handle on the grenade, held it up in front of the man's face and smiled.

The soldier's eyes adjusted suddenly, and his mouth dropped open in horror.

A second later a voice behind the van screamed, "Striker!" Then new volleys of fire opened up from the direction of the barn. The NKs around the van began to fall. The terrified soldier who had seen the grenade was among them.

Clamping his fingers back around the handle, Bolan rolled to the side of the van. Atop the ridge leading to the escape route, several men in farmer gear fired down at the NK troops. Others raced through the undergrowth to flank the bumpy road and take up firing position.

Bolan scrambled out from under the van and grabbed a rifle from one of the fallen NKs. He hurled the grenade toward the jeeps and followed up with a long burst of fire before turning and racing up the ridge.

The attackers began to fall back now. Bolan reached the top of the ridge and looked into the valley beyond. Hwang and Myung stood at the barn door amid more disguised soldiers. Then they ushered Rhee Yuk, Curtis Levi, Sachiko and Jhoon and his wife and child inside. Katz brought up the rear, with the scientist draped unceremoniously over his shoulder.

Bolan breathed a sigh of relief as he and the South Koreans sprinted down into the valley. No matter what happened to him now, Levi and the others were safe.

He ran on, swiveling around to return fire now that the pursuers advanced over the ridge. Just ahead of him, a South Korean took a round in the calf. Bolan reached down as he passed, hooking an arm around the wounded soldier.

Four South Koreans reached the barn door first, and dived through. As Bolan and the wounded man neared, he saw their rifle barrels reappear through the opening.

With stable positioning from which to fire now, the South Koreans opened up on the advancing troops and began dropping them to the ground. Pursuit slowed but still continued.

Bolan assisted the injured man through the door and saw that all had already disappeared into the tunnel, except for Katz, Hwang, Myung and the South Koreans who traded fire with the enemy. A pickup filled with wounded was being lowered into the tunnel, and lifting the wounded man in his arms, the Executioner deposited him into the truck bed.

Bolan turned back to the doorway as the rest of the South Koreans raced into the barn. He joined Katz and the undercover men at the windows, laying down more cover fire to slow the still-advancing North Koreans.

"Hwang!" he shouted over the clamor. "You and Myung get the rest of the men into the tunnel! We'll hold them off until you're started, then follow!"

Hwang and Myung turned and began herding the other South Koreans toward the pit. The pickup had been the last of the vehicles, and the platform had stayed at the bottom of the tunnel mouth. Bolan glanced over his shoulder to see the men jumping over the side.

When they had all dropped from sight, Bolan fired his rifle dry and yelled, "Now, Katz!"

Pulling the trigger one more time, Katz dropped his empty weapon and turned to race toward the hole. Bolan and Katz went over the side together, landing upright, then rolling to their sides to break the fall.

As he jumped back to his feet, the Executioner heard the South Koreans pounding toward the border ahead of them. He jerked Katz upright, and they paced each other, their own footsteps pounding hollowly along the narrow passage. They had run for perhaps thirty seconds when they heard the sounds of the North Koreans dropping down into the tunnel.

The Israeli shook his head as he ran. "Surely by now they have figured out this is a tunnel," he said between breaths. "Don't they know they will emerge in enemy territory?"

"They're counting on catching us—at least anybody they can—while we're still below ground." Bolan grinned at his old war partner. "And unless you get a move on, Katz, they *will*."

Katz said something in Hebrew, and they raced on.

Gunfire came from the rear, ricocheting off the walls of the tunnel. Ahead Bolan finally saw the ramp leading upward. Hwang and Myung stood on the near side of it, urging them on, and from just above them the light of a South Korean morning filtered down into the tunnel.

A hundred yards from the ramp, a gunshot sounded behind them, and Katz stumbled. Bolan caught the Israeli with one hand. "You hit?" he asked as they ran on.

Katz shook his head as they picked up speed again. "My boot," he said.

Bolan glanced down to see that one heel of Katz's black combat boots had been blown from the sole.

Then, almost before they knew it, the Executioner and Yakov Katzenelenbogen had joined Hwang and Myung and were racing up the ramp. They emerged in the barn where Bolan and Hwang had begun the mission. In South Korea. In democracy. In *freedom*.

The barn was alive with activity. Adrenaline-pumped special-forces men crowded the building. Jhoon stood off to the side next to his wife. He held the crying baby in his arms and bent over the boy, humming softly into his ear. Several vehicles Bolan had seen on the Communist side of the border were parked around the barn. Sachiko and Rhee Yuk still sat in the back of a pickup Bolan assumed had brought them over. Curtis Levi was being loaded from the back of another truck into an ambulance.

As they all caught their breath, Hwang nodded toward a sergeant who was standing by a control panel built into the barn wall. The sergeant flipped a switch, and an iron door rolled across the entrance to the tunnel to cut off the North Koreans.

A second later Hwang waved the sergeant away and walked to the control panel himself. Turning to Bolan, he said, "I suppose it goes without saying that the tunnel cannot be used anymore."

As if to emphasize the exposure of the secret crossing, the North Korean soldiers finally reached the end of the tunnel and began pounding on the iron door.

His chest still heaving, Hwang threw another switch, then pressed a series of buttons.

The explosion behind the iron door rocked the barn, yet sounded distant.

The wind blew softly against the huge picture windows that looked out on the runways. The muted sound of aircraft landing and taking off drifted in through the glass panels. In the private waiting room off the main concourses, Bolan and Katz sat facing the door, where they could also see runways and be ready to board as soon as Jack Grimaldi touched down. The pilot still had the rest of Phoenix Force in tow, and they'd all be returning to Stony Man Farm together.

Sachiko sat directly across from Bolan. The beautiful young woman beamed at him, then turned to her husband and spoke.

Myung smiled with her as he translated. "She says to tell you that when our baby is born, he will carry your name. He will be called Myung Rance."

"Myung Rance?" Bolan laughed. "You ever think it might be a girl?"

Myung translated, and Sachiko frowned as if the possibility had not crossed her mind. Then her face suddenly brightened. "Myung Kimi Rance," she said.

Now Myung, Hwang, Rhee Yuk and Jhoon and Kimi all joined in the laughter. Katz elbowed Bolan in the ribs. "Don't laugh," the Israeli whispered so only

Bolan could hear. "It beats calling the kid Myung Executioner."

As the good spirits continued, Bolan's thoughts turned to Curtis Levi. The American scientist was under heavy U.S. Army guard at a base hospital. As soon as he was well enough, he'd be flown back home. Levi had been lucky to survive. He had learned the error of his ways the hard way. But that might well have been the *easy* part.

Bolan wouldn't have wanted to be in the rocket scientist's shoes when the time to explain rolled around.

In the hall leading to the main airport, the loudspeaker announced flights in several languages. A matronly woman in the light blue uniform of an airport housekeeping worker pushed a broom past the door to the waiting room. Seated across from Bolan, Rhee Yuk twitched nervously, his head jerking spasmodically toward her.

Rhee had fallen victim to the pressures of his profession. He was no longer even sure who he was. He seemed unable to go ten seconds without glancing over his shoulder, and had watched the doorway almost constantly since they'd arrived. It was as if he feared the special-forces men in the tunnel had escaped the explosion, dug their way out and were preparing to come after him in the waiting room. The Executioner could only hope the man received help now that he was back in friendly territory.

Myung leaned over and took his wife's hand. "This has worked out beyond my wildest hopes or dreams," he said. "I owe you much, Rance Pollock."

Bolan smiled. "You owe me nothing," he said. "But you owe your wife and the child she's carrying. Give them a good life, Myung. They deserve it." He paused. "And so do you."

Although Bolan had been prepared to keep his word and fly Myung and Sachiko back to the U.S. with him, Myung had finally decided against it. He had chosen instead to stay in South Korea and face the music. Hwang had sworn to stand by him before the board of inquiry he would have to face.

Hwang sat on Myung's other side. Bolan glanced to the man who had been with him every step of the way in Curtis Levi's rescue, almost bleeding to death in the process. Bolan had met few men as skilled in the art of subterfuge as Hwang Su, and he wouldn't be surprised if the creative little South Korean not only got Myung off the hook but got his special-forces commission back for him, as well. Brognola had been right when he called Hwang Su a worker. They had been back in South Korea for less than four hours, and Hwang already had Jhoon and Kimi's citizenship papers being processed and had lined up employment for Jhoon.

"You look unhappy," Katz said. "Smile. Things have turned out well."

Bolan realized he'd been frowning. "I was thinking about Stavropol," he said. "My only regret is we didn't get him. That ghoul's going to raise his ugly head again someday."

Katz shrugged. "When he does, you will shoot it off then."

More flights were called out over the loudspeaker, and the housekeeping woman passed the door with her broom again. Rhee Yuk shot another nervous glance that way.

Jhoon said something in Korean, and Hwang turned to Bolan. "He wants you to know that although Hung has already been named, he and Kimi will be eternally grateful to you."

Kimi spoke now, and Hwang laughed. "She says perhaps they will change the baby's name."

Bolan smiled. "That won't be necessary," he said. "One Korean named Rance should be plenty."

The phone attached to the wall rang suddenly, and Myung stood up to answer it. He spoke briefly, then hung up and said, "That was the control tower. Your pilot is descending."

Bolan nodded. It would still be a few more minutes before Grimaldi arrived on the private runway, and he and Katz had no luggage to gather.

The housekeeper pushed a large trash container through the door and began circling the room, dumping ashtrays. Rhee watched her like a hawk. Finally his face turning white, he turned to Bolan. "Pollock," he whispered in a near-hysterical voice. "That woman. She is *not* a woman."

Hwang Su rolled his eyes and patted Rhee on the shoulder. "Relax, Rhee," he said in a gentle voice. "It's okay now."

Bolan glanced across the room to where the woman was wiping an ashtray with a rag. He frowned. There was something familiar about her. Something—

"Pollock!" Rhee suddenly screamed, no longer able to control himself. "Believe me!"

As Bolan turned back toward the woman, his mind returned to the beginning of the mission—when Stavropol had whisked Levi away from the hotel. The Russian had infiltrated the hotel dressed as a woman.

"Pollock, *please!*" Rhee yelled, tears running down his eyes. "Who would know better than *me!*"

Bolan's hand dropped to the Norinco .45 in his belt a second before the woman turned from the trash can to face him. In the blink of an eye he saw through the makeup to the hooded eyes beneath. He recognized the eyes from the files of Stony Man Farm. And in them, he saw madness.

The Norinco didn't jam. Instead, it sent a double-tap of .45s into Stavropol's chest as he tried to set the sights of an ancient Nagant revolver on the Executioner. As he pulled the trigger to send a third hardball through the bridge of the torturer's nose, Bolan wondered briefly why a trained assassin would choose such an obsolete weapon.

The Russian dropped to the floor. Bolan walked forward, stooped over and jerked the wig from the bloodied head.

Behind him, from the runway he heard the sound of the engines as Jack Grimaldi touched down. The mission was over.

**Exiles from the future in the
aftermath of the apocalypse**

JAMES AXLER

DEATH
LANDS ®

Stoneface

In 2001, the face of the earth changed forever in a nuclear
firestorm. Generations after the apocalypse, Ryan Cawdor leads
the courageous struggle for survival in a brutal world, striving to
make a difference in the battle raging between good and evil.

In the Deathlands, the war is over...but the fight has just begun.